Alberto Moravia was born in Rome in 1907. He [illegible] his first novel in 1925, and then became [illegible] correspondent in London, Paris and elsewhere for *La Stampa* and *Gazzetta del Popolo* of Turin. In the later years of Fascism his books were banned and he had to write articles under a pseudonym. During the German occupation of Italy he went into hiding in the mountains, being liberated by the Americans in May 1944. He died in Rome in 1990.

Also by Alberto Moravia in Abacus:

EROTIC TALES
THE VOYEUR

JOURNEY TO ROME

Alberto Moravia

A NOVEL

Translated from the Italian by
TIM PARKS

An *Abacus* Book

First published in Italy as *Il Viaggio a Roma*
First published in Great Britain by Martin Secker & Warburg Limited 1990
This edition published by Abacus 1993

A CIP catalogue record for this book is available from the British Library.

ISBN 0 349 10273 2

Printed in England by Clays Ltd, St Ives plc

Abacus
A Division of
Little, Brown and Company (UK) Limited
165 Great Dover Street
London SE1 4YA

ONE

The Journey to Rome

During the flight I opened at random my collection of poems by Guillaume Apollinaire. My eyes fell on the line: 'Here you are in Rome, sitting under a Japanese loquat tree,' and I began to let my mind wander: why a Japanese loquat? What did this Asian tree have to do with Rome? And, given that Apollinaire was my model and mentor, what role would the Japanese loquat tree play in my life once I'd arrived in Rome?

My mind wandered and wandered, then grew drowsy, until at last I slept, slept deeply. Recently, in Paris, I'd been suffering from insomnia. I would wake with a start in the night and immediately find myself thinking of my journey to Rome. I felt it was an absurd journey whose apparent purpose – that of seeing my father again – merely hid another, more real and authentic, which, however, escaped me. True enough, over the phone, the man who claimed to be my father had welcomed the news of my arrival with, to put it mildly, enthusiasm. But it was precisely this unexpected, surprising welcome that had left me with a feeling of distrust, irritation almost. Why call me, 'My dear, dear son,' after a total silence of going on fifteen years? And what could the line, 'Your family is waiting for you,' mean when spoken by someone who knew perfectly well that by now my real family was that of the uncle who, on my mother's death, had generously taken me into his Paris home and raised me as his son alongside his own two children, Paolo and Silvia? Finally, why had this mysterious and complete stranger gone so far as to saddle himself with the cost of my trip by immediately sending me a pre-paid air ticket?

So I slept, or rather fell into a doze, during which I was confusedly aware of doing something I'd never have done if I was awake. I sensed a female presence sitting beside me, a presence at once gentle and amenable, and I was pressing my arm against her full, soft breast. Indeed I had managed to locate the nipple with my elbow and was now stroking it with an insistence I vainly hoped might seem accidental. I realized that the woman I was caressing like this was a complete stranger, yet all the same I went on consciously and voluntarily doing what must have started as something unconscious and involuntary. The idea of a holiday affair didn't even cross my mind. On the contrary, I knew perfectly well that as soon as I woke up I'd pretend both to the woman and to myself that I had only dreamt what in fact had belonged equally to dream and reality.

And, yes, as soon as I woke up, there I was quickly drawing back and apologizing. At first I was dazzled by the intense sunlight on an Alpine landscape of snow and crags beneath us. Then, after a moment to adjust, I looked at my neighbour. I saw a prim, lean face with something hawk-like about the dark, close-set eyes and hooked nose, the thin, curving lips. I lowered my eyes. Her jacket was open. Through the transparency of a white blouse, I recognized the exuberant mounds of those breasts I'd been stroking so urgently while asleep.

On the seat to the other side of the woman sat a long, loose-limbed girl with brown hair brushed out in a doll-like fan on both sides of a perfectly oval face. While still half asleep I'd heard her urging my neighbour, who must have been her mother, but whom she called Jeanne, to get me off her once and for all, with a hefty shove if necessary. She had spoken in an ill-mannered, childish voice and her tone was far from benevolent. Her mother had answered, indulgently and reasonably, that she didn't have the heart to wake me: I was sleeping so soundly.

But by now I was wide awake. I apologized again, and thus began one of those leisurely, casual conversations between fellow travellers, complete with the usual exchanges of information. This didn't last long, however, for all at once Jeanne asked quite bluntly what I was going to Rome for.

I felt that the question was premature and indiscreet, though justified by the passivity, not to say complicity, she had shown a short while back when I had been caressing her in my sleep. At the same time I sensed, I don't know why, an irresistible impulse to confide in her. I answered frankly, 'You won't believe it, but I'm going to Rome to find my father.'

'Why shouldn't I believe it? It's a very natural and right thing to do.'

'I hardly know him. I was five when I last saw him.'

She looked at me hard now, smiling a little, perhaps ironically. It occurred to me that while I was asleep my hair had maybe got rumpled and I ran a hand across my head. She went on, 'And does your father know you are coming to find him?'

'Yes, he does. I spoke to him on the phone.'

'And was he pleased?'

'Very.'

I fell silent a moment, then added, 'I don't know why.'

'What do you mean, you don't know why?'

'He didn't bother to get in touch for fifteen years. I just can't understand his enthusiasm now.'

'How did he show he was enthusiastic?'

'Financially as much as anything else: he sent me a pre-paid air ticket. Otherwise I'd have gone on the train.'

'See what a good father he is!'

'Yes, but he only sent me a ticket for the journey down.'

'Maybe he's hoping you'll stay in Rome for good.'

'On the phone he said: I'll be rediscovering a son, and you a father.'

'What a nice thing to say! You see, he really is a good father! What's your name?'

'Mario.'

'Mario what?'

'Mario De Sio.'

'You're Italian, but you speak French like a Frenchman.'

'I'm more or less bilingual.'

'And apart from your father, what will you be doing in Rome?'

'What do you mean, what will I be doing?'

'I mean, what do you normally do? What are you? A student?'

To which I should have replied that, yes, I was indeed a student. But instead, unexpectedly and ridiculously, I went and blurted out something I'd never told anyone before, something which, into the bargain, as we shall see, wasn't even true: 'I'm a poet.'

I was expecting – hoping – to make her smile that indulgent smile again, albeit tinged with irony. Instead she said primly, 'A poet? How can one *be* a poet? And then why proclaim the fact? A poet writes poems, but he doesn't go around saying he *is* a poet.'

I felt my cheeks turning red and quickly corrected myself. 'To be honest, I don't write poems. So far I haven't written a single one.'

'Then why do you say you're a poet?'

I realized that in asking this question she was aiming at what I considered the secret and never-confessed justification of my life. But once again the impulse to confide got the better of me. 'I don't write poems, but I think of myself as a poet because I identify with someone who wrote all the poems I would like to have written and, what's more, wrote them infinitely better than I ever could.'

'And who is this poet?'

This time I was aware that the impulse to confide was fading, and fading for reasons I felt were insuperable. The poet I identified with was Guillaume Apollinaire, but I didn't want to admit this because, as well as having written the poems I would like to have written, Apollinaire had something else in common with me: he too had practically never known his father. Now I hadn't hesitated to tell Jeanne that I was going to Rome to find my father; but on the other hand I was ashamed to admit that at the origin of my quest was not so much the nostalgia of the orphan as my would-be poet's identification with the author of *Alcools*. This seemed to me to be a kind of snobbery through imitation, as if I considered myself a poet not just because Apollinaire had written the poems I would have liked to have written, but also because he, like me, had never known his father. I said quickly, 'It doesn't matter who.'

I saw her glance at the book I had in my hands. 'I bet it's Guillaume Apollinaire.'

'How did you know? This is just any old book.'

'No, it's a poetry book. One has to have a good reason for reading poetry on a plane.' She was silent a moment, then explained, 'As it happens you've run into someone who knows Apollinaire well. Before moving to Italy I used to teach literature in France.'

Trying to make a joke of the conversation, I said, 'Well then, seeing as you're a teacher, maybe you can tell me why Apollinaire wrote: "Here you are in Rome sitting under a Japanese loquat tree." Why a loquat? The sort of trees you find in Rome are pines, oaks and cypresses, aren't they?'

She looked at me, at a loss. But her daughter, who seemed to be following our conversation impatiently, interrupted, 'But Jeanne, the gardens in our street are full of loquat trees.'

Still looking prim, her mother quickly agreed, 'Right, true. But that's not the point. I'm sorry, but why do you identify with Apollinaire? What do you mean, he wrote the poems you would like to have written yourself? And then Apollinaire lived in a completely different period from the one you're growing up in; physically he was the opposite of you, fat and burly, whereas you're thin and lanky. Why the identification? The fact is, you want to boast that you're a poet even though you've never written any poetry. That's the real reason for your identification.'

Her tone was aggressive, but teacherly. I sensed the severity of the schoolmistress telling off a lazy pupil. Desperately I cast about for another reason for identifying with Apollinaire. I thought of his character as it came across in his work. 'I do have at least one thing in common with Apollinaire.'

'What's that?'

'Openness. Reading Apollinaire I was struck by his openness, I mean his readiness to accept any experience life offered him.'

'So?'

Under her enquiring gaze I suddenly felt confused. All the same I opened my copy of Apollinaire and read aloud: 'Well, here's what he writes in this poem: "You drink this alcohol fiery as your life – your life that you drink like an aquavit." That's what I call openness.'

'Fair enough, but I still don't see what this openness of Apollinaire's has to do with you.'

'Just a second, I'm getting there. My main character trait, not to say defect, is precisely my openness. What do you think persuaded me to come to Rome? You really think I felt the need to get to know my father? Not at all. It was my openness, unhealthy openness if you like, which made me come. I said to myself, I have a father, I've never been to Rome, so I'll go and check out my father and Rome and then we'll see. And I set off.'

I'd got excited talking about openness. My neighbour

remarked a shade mischievously, 'In any event you like talking about yourself a lot.'

I felt myself blushing again. 'It was you who made me talk about myself. Though I can't imagine why.'

With benevolent, flattering warmth, she protested, 'He can't imagine why! What modesty! Don't you realize it's not every day one meets someone on a plane who says he's off in search of his father and that he's a poet but has never written any poetry!'

Her daughter remarked slyly, 'And who doesn't know that there are plenty of Japanese loquat trees in Rome!'

Suddenly the impersonal voice of a hostess began with the usual pre-landing rigmarole: fasten your seat-belts, put your seats in the upright position, refrain from smoking, etc., etc. Watching her mother and myself with the steady, enquiring gaze, half hungry, half sleepy, of her big, dark eyes, the daughter added, 'Jeanne, isn't it time to give Mario our address and telephone number? That way you can get together again and carry on this interesting conversation at your leisure.'

Her mother didn't take offence at the crude irony behind this suggestion. On the contrary she seemed, though jokingly, almost grateful for the timely advice. 'Yes, of course, good idea. We'll make the most of your openness. Here, I'll give you our address and number.' Prompt and precise, she took notebook and pen from her handbag, wrote, and handed me a piece of paper. 'My daughter and I are open sorts of people too. At least within certain limits.'

By now the plane was losing height with jolts and starts and instead of the hitherto empty blue sky of high above, a mass of white cloud could be seen slithering in shreds along the wings. A deep silence had replaced the roar of the engines. The daughter went on watching me with her steady, oppressive stare. Then she said, 'Jeanne didn't introduce me, though I do have a name. I'm Alda.'

I made a slight bow with my head. She warned me, 'You

mustn't think we don't care whether we see you or not. On the contrary, we care a great deal.'

Through my window I could see the brooding green of the country stretching away in the low light of sunset, white ribbons of road crossing it in every direction. Along these ribbons, with that feeling of nausea almost that the sight of an ants' nest inspires, I could follow the incessant comings and goings of the cars. I was embarrassed by Alda's stare and by her sudden intimacy. Undaunted she went on, 'One reason why we care is because we hardly ever see anyone.'

Calmly Jeanne corrected her. 'We see our friends. We don't have a busy social life, that's all.'

The plane was now racing along the runway beside luminous marker posts, but still hadn't touched down. Then the wheels hit the ground with a thud and the plane slowed. After a moment or two Alda got to her feet. 'Don't be defensive, Jeanne. We'll soon see how open he really is.' So saying, she turned away and pulled down two big bags, her own and her mother's, from the open doors of the baggage locker.

I looked away for a moment at the black profile of the airport terminal against the sunset-red sky. When I turned the two women had already gone, heading for the exit along with the other passengers. But the daughter looked back and waved goodbye, then made a gesture as if dialling a phone number.

Later, in the taxi which took me to my father's, I thought over my meeting with the two women in the plane and as a result didn't really look at the streets we were going through. But then they weren't particularly interesting. In the night air, seeing black modern blocks silhouetted against a green sky with the brash multi-coloured neon of shop signs glaring beneath, I felt, not without a sense of disappointment, that I might be in any city, it was no different from so many others. All the more reason then, for thinking about Jeanne and Alda, who at least had the merit of being fresh and new.

Why had I, right from the start, felt such a spontaneous, irresistible impulse to confide in a stranger like Jeanne? And why had she in turn been so interested in me? Finally, why had Alda been so insistent about my telephoning and staying in touch? I couldn't find convincing answers to these questions, but, to tell the truth, I wasn't particularly interested in doing so. I was happy enough just formulating them and daydreaming over them, my mind seemingly drunk with the insomnia of the past week and the fatigue of the journey. Thus the time taken to cross Rome slipped by without my having turned my thoughts for so much as a moment to my father and to the city where I would be living with him from now on.

When the taxi drew to a halt and I realized we'd arrived, I started with a sudden sense of unease mixed with repugnance and what was almost dismay. I pulled my wallet from my pocket and saw, as I handed a banknote to the driver, that my hand was trembling. I got out, took my suitcase and made to cross the road. But I had to wait. The door was on the far side of a wide road where a row of tall residential buildings looked down on the parapet of the Tiber behind me. A traffic light was shining green through the branches of the plane trees and dozens of cars streaked by furiously chasing after each other. I took advantage of the delay to look over the building where my father lived. I was struck by the considerable number of niches, cornices, balconies, columns and statues decorating the façade. The people who lived here must be rich. And I told myself that, amid all the uncertainties, at least one thing was clear: my father, about whom I knew next to nothing, save for the fact that he ran an estate agency, was not poor, his business was going well. I wasn't sure if I was pleased about this or not; in any event it was my first concrete piece of information about someone who had so far been an almost imaginary figure.

The traffic light switched to red. The cars were suddenly still in line after shuddering line. I picked up my case, crossed the road and went to press the bell beside the door. I must confess that seeing my own name, De Sio, on a plate above the bell had a strange effect on me. So my father did exist! Moments passed, an age it seemed, then the intercom crackled and a voice which gave me the impression of being affectedly low and reticent, and certainly very different from the high-pitched enthusiasm that had greeted me when I'd phoned from Paris, asked me who I was. I said, 'It's Mario.' Immediately the voice exclaimed, 'Mario? Well done Mario, you're here, are you? Come in. Come in, it's on the third floor.' Now the voice was different both from that of the phone call from Paris and that of a few seconds ago, more intimate than the former, less wary than the latter. It crossed my mind that my father was some kind of actor, capable of assuming a different voice for every situation.

There was an electric buzz. I pushed the door, went in, walked to the end of the hall and found the lift. But my continuing sense of disorientation made me press the button for the second floor instead of the third. With the result that I came out with my suitcase onto the landing, only to hear a voice calling from above, 'You've got the wrong floor, you'll have to come up one more.'

What to do? Go back in the lift? Or use the stairs? I chose the stairs, picked up my suitcase and set off. And so, bit by bit as I climbed, I got my first sight of my father as he stood waiting for me on the third-floor landing. First I saw his shoes, large with a pattern of perforations, English-style, made from an almost red leather and highly polished; then there were grey flannel trousers; then a blue double-breasted jacket with gold buttons; all rather shapeless and shabby. Finally, above a cream-coloured collar from which sprouted a thin regimental tie, I saw his face.

I had never even tried to imagine the face of the man I had spoken to from Paris. All the same, on seeing my father for the first time I couldn't help feeling a sense of disappointment, as if I had indeed pictured him as different and better. Was it possible that this broad, red-mottled face with its huge bleak forehead, its bushy eyebrows arched over eyes wide open as if in perpetual dismay, its long sad nose and crooked mouth – the face, in short, of an ageing clown – belonged to the man I must think of as my father? I had such a strong sensation of alienation and rejection that all I could manage was a curt, 'How do you do, I'm Mario.'

This was, for me, the most natural and logical way to behave with a complete stranger. But he, naturally inclined to dramatics as he obviously was, immediately made it clear that the part of the father reunited with his son after a long separation was one that suited him down to the ground. I climbed up to the landing. No sooner had I put down my suitcase than he was impetuously kissing and embracing me. I noticed, as if the fact were obscurely significant, that his kisses were – how can I put it – wet, I mean running with saliva. And I felt that this dampness of the lips was somehow connected with that of his visibly tearful eyes. My father kissed me and wept. Kisses and tears bore witness in theatrical fashion to the fact that I had a father, and a decidedly paternal father at that. After this embrace, he did exactly what I was expecting he would do; he stepped back, his hands clasping my shoulders, looked me up and down, and exclaimed, 'But let me look at you, you're a man now and you're my Mario! You really are my son, and there I was, heaven knows why, still thinking of you as a little boy.'

'Yes, I'm Mario,' I said with ill-concealed irony, 'and, if appearances are anything to go by, I'm a man.'

He made a hurried gesture of approval. 'But of course, of course. Don't pay any attention to what an emotional, happy father might say. Yes, Mario, yes, that's just how I feel, emotional and happy! Don't pay any attention, you're a man and you're proud to be a man. Good, excellent! But come on, I'll show you the house. It's been so long, but nothing has changed, not in the house, nor here, in my heart,' and he pointed a finger at his heart. Then he quickly took possession of my suitcase and went on ahead into the hall. He put the suitcase in a corner and threw open a door. 'This is the lounge.'

TWO

I Don't Know

I hesitated at the door and looked for a long time before deciding to go in. Why did I hesitate? At first, faced with this big deep room with its clusters of enormous dark armchairs and sofas, its rectangular table surrounded by too many chairs, I experienced the same sense of alienation and rejection that my father's face had provoked a short while ago. Then I saw that at the other end of the room, where, beyond the table and beyond the group of armchairs and sofas, light seeped weakly through the white curtains of two large windows, the décor was different, with less imposing, lighter, more intimate furniture: a small English writing desk with its Viennese chair, a small, floral-patterned sofa, a television, a record-player on top of a cabinet together with a record-holder, a long low shelf lined with books, a big green plant in a pot. And immediately I sensed that, unlike the, let's say, social part of the lounge, this other more private area, 'had to do with me.' Why did it have to do with me? Unexpectedly, rising as if from a still obscure and unconscious memory, came the answer: 'Something happened to me over there.' So that now it was no longer a sense of alienation that kept me hesitating by the door. Quite the contrary. It was a definite sense of *déjà vu*, of something already seen, already experienced – perhaps, who knows, already suffered. But what was it that I'd already seen, already experienced, already suffered?

My puzzled reflections could go no further, as though

the threshold on which I was actually standing were also the impassable threshold of the memory.

I looked, and my vain attempt to resurrect the forgotten ghosts this room was hinting at had me seeing double, the objects superimposing themselves one over another. At the same time my hearing seemed suspended in an empty limbo through which remote sounds arrived as though from some incalculable distance. Then, the way black tree branches will sometimes leap out of a thick white fog, so, sharp and sudden through the droning dazed silence, came my father's voice. 'Over there's the part of the room your poor mother used to like. She was always in here. She used to say that a lounge wasn't just for eating and entertaining in, it was for living in too. And certainly she lived in here, oh yes, she lived in here and no mistake.'

I picked up a sarcasm in his voice that I couldn't quite place. I asked quietly, 'What do you mean, she lived in here?'

'I mean your poor mother used to do everything here.'

'Everything?'

'Sure, reading, music, television, phone calls, letter-writing, naps, conversation and the rest.'

'The rest?'

'That's right, lovemaking too.'

For a moment I had the unsettling impression that my father, barely two minutes after my arrival, was alluding to my mother's betrayals, betrayals which, as I knew, had led in the end to their separation. I sent him a look of amazement. Immediately, like an actor who has mistaken his lines, he corrected himself in an almost jokey tone, 'With me of course.' Then he went on, with a nostalgia that was perhaps sincere but at the same time studied and artificial, 'It's as if I could still see her, over there, in her favourite spot – like I said, she used to live in here – yes, in her pyjamas, or shorts, or a dressing-gown, or maybe half naked, stretched out on the carpet, busy listening to music, or reading, or phoning.'

'Why on the carpet?'

'Because she lived, so to speak, on the ground, on the floor. Yes, Mario, I can see her there now, stretched out on her stomach, her legs in the air, a biro in her hand; or on her back, legs in the air just the same, the telephone glued to her ear.'

'Did she write a lot of letters?'

'She certainly did, she wrote a lot of letters, made a lot of phone calls. She had to keep what I used to call her parallel life going.'

'Her parallel life?'

'That's right, the life she lived by herself alongside the one she lived with me.'

'But what did this parallel life involve?'

'It involved, quite simply, seeing the men who wanted to go to bed with her.'

So now my father really was doing what a moment before I had feared he might. I had hardly arrived and he was already talking my mother down. I obeyed an instinctive impulse: 'I didn't come to Rome to hear you insult my mother.'

He immediately approved, and noisily, 'Of course, of course. You're her son, whereas I'm her husband. A son defends his mother, of course. But Mario . . .' Here he stopped and looked at me solemnly, 'You are also, no, you are above all, a man, and I want to talk to you not as father to son, but as man to man. Understand, as man to man.'

He embarrassed me with his wide open eyes. I tried to change the subject, 'And where was I?'

'What do you mean, where were you?'

'Mother read, wrote, phoned, but where was I while she was doing all that?'

'Oh, oh, of course, you were with your governess. In your room. Or at Villa Balestra or at Villa Borghese. Not here, your poor mother didn't want you here . . .'

The words just slipped out. 'Don't keep saying "your poor mother".'

He immediately jumped at this pretext for a theatrical speech. 'But I'm not saying poor the way people normally do of the dead, but because she died so young. At twenty-nine. See what I mean? Only twenty-nine, at the height of her grace and beauty! And I loved her, Mario, I loved her. So much so that I can't walk into this room without seeing her there. Yes, there she is, in flesh and blood, stretched out on the floor, telephoning.'

He was shouting and staring at me, his eyes wide open but curiously inexpressive – perhaps, one might say, precisely because of their excess of expression. Then, reverting to a normal, informative tone, he said, 'Your mother was a good mother, in her own way. But she didn't want you in the living-room, because she didn't think of herself as a mother.'

'So what did she think of herself as?'

'She didn't think of herself as a mother, and even less as a wife. She thought of herself as a girl, without a husband and without children, and she wanted to live as though she were alone, with the habits and adventures of her parallel life. In short, as if you and I didn't exist at all.'

As we spoke we had moved inside the lounge and were now in the part my mother had preferred. To one side was the television and opposite it the sofa with floral upholstery. Between them lay a cream and blue Chinese carpet, undoubtedly the very one on which my mother used to lie on her back or stomach while reading or telephoning. All of a sudden the sensation that 'something' had happened to me here came back, sharper and more threatening now, like a warning sound or smell which, once picked up, will disappear, only to return later louder or stronger than before. I had the clear impression that whatever it was must have been something extraordinary, and as such connected to a detail likewise extraordinary in this so very ordinary, bourgeois lounge. I looked again, attention and consciousness heightened now, at the television, the carpet, the sofa . . .

Then my eyes went beyond the sofa to what was behind it. And it was behind the sofa that I suddenly picked up the unusual detail I was after: a door painted ivory white with an old-fashioned brass handle. One couldn't, however, come into the lounge through this door since the back of the sofa had been placed almost right up against it, blocking the way. This unusual, ridiculous arrangement of the sofa struck me at once, and, even more to the point, I was struck by the fact that it had struck me. I asked, 'How come that sofa's pushed up against the door? It makes the door pointless.'

'There are two other doors, the one we came in through and that one there which goes to the kitchen.'

'Yes, but this door, where does that go?'

'Into the passage.'

'And what's in the passage?'

'The bedrooms. Yours, your mother's and mine, the one the governess slept in and the guest room.'

'So anyone leaving those rooms and wanting to go to the lounge has to walk all round the apartment and come in through the hall, or the kitchen?'

'Precisely.'

'Why, though?'

'Why what?'

'Why this ridiculous arrangement?'

'Your mother,' my father answered with a dejected look, 'always your mother. Everything you see in this apartment is as your mother wanted it.'

'It was she who chose to put the sofa against the door?'

'Yes, the sofa had to be there so we could watch the television. You would have thought we could have moved the sofa and the television so as to leave the door free, but no, not at all, your mother was unshakeable. Television and sofa had to stay where they were for reasons known only to herself. And so they have.'

'Didn't she at least tell you why she wanted the sofa to block the door?'

'No, but I guessed anyway.'

'And?'

'The reason was that *I* thought, logically enough, that the door should be free. And that was enough to prompt her to apply her own logic and decide that it shouldn't be.'

'What logic?'

'The logic of contradiction. If I said white, she said black, and vice versa.'

I looked at the door again, which, after his explanation, had become more enigmatic than ever. Between the door and the back of the sofa there was a narrow space, just enough to allow a very thin person, or a child, to slip sideways into the room. My father resumed, as though following a train of memories, 'The only person who wouldn't put up with this whim of your mother's in fact was you.'

I was surprised by this unexpected evocation of my own presence in that room, a room which, as my father had already told me, my mother didn't want me to go into. 'Me, why?'

'Yes, you, it was you. You rebelled against your mother's logic of contradiction with your child's logic. You know the way children are so determined to play at any cost, they'll even play with obstacles? Oh yes, everybody has their logic!'

'And my logic was playing?'

'Yes, Mario, playing. You took advantage of the blocked door to play a game that was tricky and all the more fun for being so. You see how there's a very narrow space between the back of the sofa and the door? You invented a game which involved opening the door without making a noise, slipping in through the crack and giving your mother a surprise.'

'Which was?'

'Putting your hands over her eyes and shouting, "Guess who?"'

'But you told me Mother didn't want me in the living-room.'

'She wanted you and she didn't want you. Your mother

was very erratic. The fact that she accepted your game but wouldn't agree to having the door free is an indication of how erratic she was.'

'But when did I play this game?'

'Not during the day, since the governess would have stopped you then. But in the evening the governess went off to bed and you'd be alone in your room. Then you took advantage of the situation. If you knew we were in, you'd wait until we'd finished eating and had sat down on the sofa to watch television and then you'd play your game. You'd get up, tip-toe to the door, open it a crack, sneak in behind the back of the sofa and put your hands over your mother's eyes. The fact is,' my father concluded unexpectedly, 'you were a very affectionate child and this game was just another way of reminding your mother that she still hadn't come to your room to give you your goodnight kiss.'

'But didn't she always come at the same time?'

'Your mother was lazy as well as erratic. So she'd always come to kiss you at different times, depending on how lazy she felt. She was even capable of forgetting altogether. Then you'd come and play your game to remind her.'

'But did Mother love me?'

'If she hadn't loved you, she would have locked the door, and in fact that's just what she started doing when she realized that her love for you couldn't be reconciled with her love for herself.'

'I don't understand.'

'She was very selfish. She couldn't do something that pleased somebody else if it didn't please her as well. Let's say that for a while your game with the door was fun not only for you but for her too. Then it wasn't any more. And so she locked the door.'

I was looking uncertainly at the dead grey screen of the television and at the sofa upholstered in floral-patterned cretonne which faced it. Something had happened, of that I was sure now. It had happened when, as my father put it, my mother had realized that the pleasure she was giving me could not be reconciled with a pleasure she wanted for herself. In a trance-like voice I asked, 'And did you often sit here in the evening watching TV?'

'Yes, often. Her parallel life, as I called it, the part she kept distinct from my life, took place during the day, between two in the afternoon and nine in the evening. In the morning I'd go to the office and she'd spend the time here, reading and writing and phoning. But as a rule we spent the evenings together. Your mother would put on an evening dress and we'd eat together and then watch TV. That was when you used to play your game sometimes.'

I had a detective-story idea. Quite deliberately I suggested, 'If it doesn't bother you, why don't we imagine that this is a regular evening of fifteen years ago. You sit down on the sofa and watch the television, the way you used to with Mother, and I'll go round to the bedrooms, open the door a crack, squeeze in behind the sofa and come back into the lounge.'

An expression of concern and displeasure crossed his face. 'But what for? I was showing you the apartment. If we're going to reconstruct everything we used to do –'

'Oh go on, please, for me.'

'But really, what do you want?'

'Just sit on the sofa and watch TV. That's all.'

Unhappy and at the same time suspicious and disturbed, as if what I was asking didn't really have to do with my mother but with him, he finally gave in. 'Oh all right, if you like. But do you know how to get to this door from the other side? You have to go back to the hall and from there to the corridor.'

'Don't worry, I've got it. Look, you turn on the TV and sit down. I'll be right back.'

Strangely excited, I went back through the lounge and out into the hall. I found the door to the passage, went through and looked for and found the lightswitch on the wall. The light I turned on was low and soft, a typical passage light, illuminating a line of doors with wall cupboards in between and a brick-red floor. One door had a Liberty design of red, blue and green glass and, thanks perhaps to some unconscious memory, or to intuition, I was immediately sure that this was the door to my own old room. I thought, 'That's the door I came from. Let's see if I'm right.' I went to the door, opened it and immediately saw I'd guessed right. In the dim light of a Japanese globe of opaque white paper, I saw quite a large, irregularly shaped room with a round table in the middle and, in one corner, a twin bunk bed with two places, one above the other, and a ladder to get to the top, like the beds on sleeper trains. The room was entirely furnished in natural-finish wood with bedspreads, pillows and curtains made from cretonne with a floral design. Seated on the table with outspread arms was a big teddy bear with tawny fur, and in a corner, on the lowest of a series of shelves, was an enormous ball with blue and red spots: two toys which, because of their size no doubt, my mother had decided not to take away with her when she'd left with me for Paris. The room looked empty, but not neglected. I noticed that the beds were made up with pillows and blankets and that the wood floor had been waxed and polished. What did I feel on finding this room? Nothing, aside from the sharp and rational curiosity of the investigator attempting to reconstruct an elusive but fundamental event. But what event? I thought, almost said out loud, 'That's where I slept, in the bunk bed, the one on top obviously, since it's more fun for a little boy to climb a ladder to go to bed. So then, I would climb down the ladder, go out into the passage . . .'

And saying this to myself I went out of the room and headed straight for the door to the lounge. I reached for the brass handle, but before pushing it down looked back one last time at the passage and went over the situation again in my mind: 'Here I am, a boy of five years old, in my pyjamas, barefoot. On the other side of this door is my mother, who I love and who, at least sometimes, shows that she loves me. One of those sometimes is when she comes to give me a goodnight kiss. I've waited for her quite a while, but now I've made up my mind. I'm going to have my kiss not in the bedroom but in the sitting-room. Why don't I just wait for the kiss in the bedroom though? Obvious. Because in this game of surprising her, apart from the actual surprise of my popping up there, there is also the idea of 'surprising' my mother in the sense of impressing her with an unexpected demonstration of my feeling for her. So, 'a double surprise.'

I pushed the handle down slowly, slowly released the door, and slipped, very slowly, through the gap. My father had done as I said. He was sitting on the sofa, his head only just sticking up above the back. Opposite him the television was on. It was showing a game of football. On a large green field the small figures of the players were running about following the ball.

It's hard, perhaps impossible, to say whether, in the precise moment when one remembers something, the memory springs to mind first as an idea and then as an image, or immediately and exclusively as an image. Probably the idea does come first, then the image, but so quickly one after the other that they cannot be separated.

In any event, as I slipped in between door and sofa, I already had an idea, or rather a suspicion, that I would see the image of my mother. And indeed no sooner was I through the door than there she was. In the dim light of the living-room I saw her face suspended in the air in front of me, then her whole body. She was facing me, kneeling astride a man sitting on the sofa whose blond curly head could only just be seen above the back. My mother seemed absorbed in settling herself on the blond man's knees and at the same time, body bent forward and head leant to one side, I sensed she was busy doing something I couldn't then understand. Now, seeing her ghostly image again, I understood. With her hands, which I couldn't see, but whose movements I could imagine, she was helping the man to penetrate her. As I'd watched her that night, still not understanding, she'd raised her head, and it was then, and only then, that she saw me. At which, both in that real situation of fifteen years ago and again now in this visionary flashback, something unbelievable happened. My mother saw me, or rather was actually looking at me, but didn't consider this sufficient reason for breaking off the backward and forward movement of her thighs begun immediately after penetration. On the contrary, the urgent, eager rhythm seemed to speed up. And as she moved she stared into my eyes with a look at once anxious and imperious. Yes, there could be no doubt about it, this commanding look on my mother's face was ordering me not to move, not to go away, to stay put till she'd finished her lovemaking. Only when she and the man with the blond hair had reached their orgasms, only then would I be allowed to leave the threshold and go back to my room.

And so it was. For what seemed to me a very long time, my mother went back and forth, energetically, methodically, never taking her eyes off mine. Then, suddenly, her face which so far had been tense and concentrated, broke up in a grimace of obscure pain. Her eyes grew large, as if from terror, her mouth opened wide in a silent howl. She stayed like that, eyes huge, mouth open, for a long moment, then collapsed on the blond man's shoulder, kissing his ear and neck with unbridled gratitude. Upon which, as if with this collapse of hers she'd given me permission to go, I escaped from the doorway and ran back to the refuge of my room.

As I said, I both remembered and saw at the same time and my vision was precise and full of vivid details. During their lovemaking, for example, my mother's dress, perhaps too wide at the neck, had slid down to one side, revealing a shoulder and breast. Then as her thighs went back and forth, she'd pushed back some hair that had fallen down over her eyes in exactly the way people do when they're breathlessly concentrating on what they're doing. The blond-haired man had remained immobile throughout except for one violent gesture; he had pulled the top of her dress right down so that her naked breast slid out, low and swinging.

During this ghostly evocation, with the lightning speed thoughts acquire in moments of extreme excitement, I even had the time to sketch out two possible interpretations of that incredible and imperious look with which, fifteen years before, my mother had ordered me not to move, but to witness her pleasure right to the end. The first was that my mother had wanted to add to the entirely natural pleasure of her lovemaking the perverse pleasure of the profanation of my innocence. According to the second interpretation, however, the innocent party was not only myself, but also and above all her. Innocently, with the same anxious gaze of the bitch as she allows the dog to mount her, my mother was asking me not to disturb her, not to interrupt her, to let her make love in peace, through to the end.

But behind both these different interpretations lay, I sensed, just the one logical question that would not go away: why had my mother done this? Or rather, why had she made me suffer like this? The answer, or answers, I knew very well, in the sense that only a moment ago I'd explained it to myself in two different ways. And yet I couldn't help asking a question that went beyond my individual experience and implied the fundamental question: why does suffering exist? It was a philosophical question, albeit an anguished one, and as such it required no answer. But the pain which had prompted it was real enough.

All this lasted no more than a moment. Then I tried to hide the shock of my discovery with a parody which, I was perfectly aware, was in dubious taste. I put my hands over my father's eyes and exclaimed, 'Guess who!'

'My dear, dear son Mario, just arrived from Paris,' my father cried promptly, jumping at the chance to show off once again his histrionic paternal love. 'My beloved son Mario come from Paris to live in Rome with his father.'

I pretended not to hear, stretched out my hand and snapped a switch, turning off the main light in the living-room. Now there was only the flickering, restricted glow of the television screen. I felt awkward and ashamed and didn't want my father to see it on my face. In the dark light I sank down on the cushions next to him and asked, 'You said that in the end Mother decided to put a stop to my game and locked the door. Why did she do that?'

My father didn't answer at once. In his shadow next to me I sensed all the weight of an insoluble quandary. Finally he offered, 'There was a reason and I've always known what it was.'

'So?'

'I could tell you a great deal, Mario, but first let's get things straight: not as father to son, but as man to man. Yes, Mario, this is very thorny territory and we can only talk about it as man to man.'

I didn't answer. My father insisted, 'You did right to turn the light off, Mario. Really, to talk about some things one needs the dark of the confessional box. Because, in a manner of speaking, I'm confessing myself, Mario.'

'Do you want me to turn the television off too?'

'Yes, Mario, why not? It's easier to talk in the dark, Mario, easier to confess.'

'There.'

There was a remote control on the arm of the sofa. I pressed a button and the screen went dead. From the darkness came the sound of my father's voice. 'Your mother, perhaps they told you this, was not a faithful wife. On the contrary, she betrayed me – we may as well get it out in the open – with every halfway passable man who showed any sign of wanting to go to bed with her. Don't be angry with me for telling you that. It's the truth and the truth never offended anyone. Anyway, she never hid it from me. Right from the start she warned me, "If you want to stay with me, you'll have to promise not to be jealous." "Why?" "Because I can't help having other men." I remember I jokingly asked, "How many?" And she said grimly, "As many as one a day, maybe." I thought she was boasting, but I soon realized she had told me the truth. To put it bluntly, as far as love was concerned, your mother wasn't a woman, but a man. She was twenty, and what does a man do at twenty? He goes after women and the more he has the more he wants. At least that's what I was like at twenty and your mother behaved in exactly the same way. She wanted affairs and if she didn't have them she was unhappy. So in order to have as many as possible, she didn't wait for the man to make a move. She took the initiative herself, without beating about the bush either: the way she looked at them, the way she moved; she wouldn't hesitate to make an exhibition of herself or even start feeling them up. Oh yes, your mother was a female Don Juan, a Casanova, nothing less. And I'll tell you something, Mario. I'd been the same when I was younger, so I could understand her perfectly. Like her I'd been through a time when life seemed unbearable if I wasn't having an affair. If I was having an affair, or about to start one, great. I'd be happy, light-hearted, carefree. But if I wasn't having one, the world would fall down around my ears, and everything was mud, fog, chaos. The same thing used to happen to her, Mario. I knew perfectly well when your mother was cheating on me, because she'd be kind and affectionate. But if she didn't have an affair lined up, she'd be catty and even hostile, so that I might actually find myself wishing she did.'

My father paused and lit a cigarette. In the dark I saw the flame of the lighter approaching the invisible cigarette, flaring up for a moment, disappearing. At which my father said, 'I don't like smoking in the dark, though. The visual aspect is important too. So, where was I? Yes, your mother had to be having an affair and didn't think twice about getting her men in the fastest way possible. Once, for example, I saw her with my own eyes pull the top of her dress down to one side so that the man sitting opposite her could see her breast. Later I pointed out that we'd been in a café and that everybody had seen. She said, "What do I care if the others saw? All I cared about was that *he* saw." But let's get on with the story, Mario. You may be amazed to hear me say this, but in the end these affairs weren't the worst part. I understood her, I understood that she couldn't do without them, that for her they were like a drug for an addict. If she didn't have them she was unhappy, she craved for them. No, the worst thing for me was what I called her parallel life.'

I was struck at this point by the rational, moderate tone my father had adopted now he was talking in the dark. It was as if his histrionics, like any spectacle, needed light and spectators. I remarked hurriedly, 'Yes, you mentioned it before, but I don't really understand. Why parallel?'

'Simple. What is the main property of two parallel lines? Obvious: they never meet. And this was what your mother did with me. She had created a second life of her own (or rather I should call it her first life, since her parallel life was far more important to her than the life she lived with me) and made it into a watertight sealed compartment where I could never enter under any circumstances. You see, at a push I could have handled it if when she went out right after lunch she had told me straightforwardly, "I'm off to see my lover." Yes, I could have handled that, Mario, because I would have had a real reason for being jealous. But what I couldn't tolerate was that instead of being frank, she'd say, "I'm off out, see you this evening." Yes, Mario, it wasn't so much her unfaithfulness that upset me, as the way, if we can put it like this, she organized it all. Take the phone, for example. Whenever she spoke on the phone, it didn't matter who was on the other end of the line, she would always lower her voice to a barely audible whisper. That way she achieved two things at once: first, gave me the often mistaken impression that the person she was speaking to was, invariably, a lover. Sometimes my nerves got the better of me and I'd ask who she'd been speaking to. You'll never believe what she answered: "I don't know." Understand? "I don't know!" Or, here's another example of this hermetically sealed life. Like I told you she generally stayed in here in the morning, but after lunch, barely half an hour after we'd got up from table, there she was dressed to the nines with her regular, "Okay, I'm off, I'll see you this evening." Sometimes I'd find myself asking her, quite naturally, the way one does, "Where are you going?" And under protest she'd say: "I don't know." "How can you not know?" "I don't know, it depends." "Depends on whom?" "On the person I'm seeing." "But who is it? What's his name? Mario, Paolo, Giovanni?" "Ask him yourself." Understand? "Ask him yourself!" But the day she broke all records was when, at lunch, I noticed the red mark of what I suppose you'd have to call a ravenous kiss on her neck. So I asked, "Who did that?" She glanced at herself in the mirror in her bag, then said, "I don't know." Understand? I don't know! So I said to her, "Was it Dracula, eh, last night while you were asleep?"'

'And what did she say?'

'She didn't say anything. Silence was her way of closing the door of that sealed compartment in my face, for ever. And what I couldn't stand was exactly this sealed door. I didn't feel betrayed so much as excluded. In fact what made me jealous was not so much your mother's affairs as the simple fact that she existed without me. Of course, what lay behind this behaviour was her pathological need to have affairs. Only by completely excluding me from her life, from two till nine o'clock every day, could she find time to hunt out the next man on her list. But this exclusion hurt me just the same. Perhaps because I realized that without the exclusion there wouldn't have been any betrayal.'

'What's the difference? Every betrayal is an exclusion of the betrayed in favour of someone else.'

'Not at all. In your mother's case at least, the exclusion was an end in itself. I got proof of than when I had her followed by a private investigation agency. It was then that I really discovered that she was excluding me from her life not just to have her adventures, but also for the sole and obsessive need to exclude me.'

'You had Mother followed?'

'Naturally. I was her husband. If it wasn't a duty I at least had a right to do it. I had her followed for a fortnight. Not long enough, maybe.'

'Why not long enough?'

'Because I found out all about the exclusion side but not enough about the betrayals, which, as I saw it, lay behind that exclusion. Yes, for example, a typical week would go like this: "Monday: your wife went to the cinema on her own. Tuesday: your wife walked down from Via Veneto as far as Piazza del Popolo, then right along the Corso as far as Piazza Venezia and from there all the way back to Via Veneto again where she caught the bus home. Wednesday: she crossed Villa Borghese, walked as far as Piazza Fiume, then from Piazza Fiume to Via Veneto where she went into a building and stayed there for two hours, though it proved impossible to ascertain who she had visited. The building is full of beauty parlours, dressmakers, massage services and the like. Thursday: your wife took a long walk as far as the Gianicolo, then she got into a foreign car driven by a blond man. The car drew up in front of a small block on Via Aurelia. There were a lot of cars, a reception. Your wife and the blond man got out and went into the garden. It proved impossible to ascertain whether they went to the reception, which was on the ground floor, or up to the second floor where there is a private apartment. Two hours later they came out again and the blond man drove your wife home. Friday: your wife went on her own to the amusement park in EUR, stayed there four hours and came back home alone. Saturday: your wife met a dark-skinned man, perhaps an Indian, in Piazza Risorgimento. The man was driving a green car and they went together to the Vatican museums, then to a hotel in Via Veneto where they stayed in the bar. In the end the Indian drove her home. Sunday: your wife walked the length of Via Flaminia as far as Ponte Milvio. In Viale Tiziano she went into the block where her doctor lives and stayed there two hours. Finally she walked back home along the river." As you see, it was a somewhat disappointing report.'

'Why disappointing?'

'Because, to all intents and purposes, she went to a party with the blond man, stayed in a bar with the Indian and went to see her doctor on Sunday. There was no proof of her unfaithfulness. All I got was proof of my exclusion. But this, in turn, had its origins in her unfaithfulness.'

Suddenly I felt irritated. 'But what are you complaining about, for God's sake? Perhaps Mother was faithful to you, she just wanted a bit of freedom. And then, what do you think she should have done? That's what I'd like to know!'

'Just stayed with me.'

'Doing what?'

'Oh, I don't know, spending time with the people I spent time with, keeping me company, I mean just being a real wife, not a stranger who lives in your house as if it were a hotel.'

I still felt irritated, and I knew why. In my heart I knew my father was right. What he called exclusion had been nothing other than a cover for unfaithfulness. But secretly hoping I was wrong, I exclaimed, 'In short, you were jealous and she was faithful. That's what comes out of your story.'

'Slowly does it. Later on I discovered that the blond man, the Indian and the doctor had been your mother's lovers, and, what's more, all three at the same time. True, I found that out myself in another way, but that merely shows that private investigation agencies are useless, not that your mother was faithful.'

'How did you find out?'

'Well, because in the end, directly or indirectly, she would always tell me herself. For example, when I was making a scene once, being jealous, she shouted in my face, "Okay then yes, I've been to bed with my doctor, I've been going to bed with him for two months or more." Or on other occasions I understood without her telling me anything, from the way she was behaving.'

'And how was she behaving?'

'Some days, instead of coming home at nine, she'd be back around, say five. She went straight to the bedroom, lay on the bed and stayed there until the following morning, without coming to dinner and without offering any explanation. That was all. She went to bed and lay there quite still, the bedclothes pulled up to her nose, on her back, her eyes open, her hair spread on the pillow. Well, Mario, what this meant was – excuse me if I put it crudely but we are talking as man to man, aren't we? – what this meant was that she'd started a new affair that very afternoon and had had a particularly violent fuck. It was all so obvious that sometimes I couldn't resist sitting down by the bed and asking her almost affectionately, "What's the matter?" As usual she'd answer in a ghost of a voice, "I don't know." "Who reduced you to this sad state?" "I don't know." "But you've been making love, right, haven't you?" "I don't know." "With your doctor?" "I don't know." Just once, instead of answering, "I don't know," she made what you could call a definitive statement: "Every time you suspect someone, you can be sure you're right." She couldn't have got much clearer than that!'

My father fell silent for a moment, then went on, 'Mario, someone who's in love can't help being jealous, and I was madly in love with your mother, so I was madly jealous. But my jealousy, we can say, went through two successive and different phases. At first I was jealous after the traditional fashion, the fashion of Othello: I'd maybe think of killing her, her lover and myself. Then, very slowly, the idea that

I was jealous not so much of her unfaithfulness but because of the way she excluded me gradually took hold. And from then on I was no longer jealous after the fashion of Othello, but after the fashion of Riccardo De Sio. Yes, Mario, my own fashion!'

I suddenly said, 'Can you give me a light,' and immediately understood why I'd said it. There'd been a sort of surge of pride in my father's voice and I'd had a premonition that I was about to hear what he had called his confession. And this confession, I sensed, would be obscurely connected to the vision I'd had just a few minutes before of my mother making love on this very sofa to the man with the curly blond hair.

I heard my father move, rummage in his pockets. Then the flame of his lighter lit his face for a moment before coming towards me. With more insight than I'd expected of him, he said sarcastically, 'You want to see what Riccardo De Sio's like, whether he's really any different from the Othello of a moment before? Look at me, go on, look at me. Yes, he is different, very different – fortunately for him.'

I couldn't help accepting his invitation and I shot him a glance. And saw that he was right. There was something different, not in his features perhaps, but in his expression. So far I'd had the impression of a ham playing the part of the father. Now this same ham was playing the part of the husband, of the particular kind of husband he had been with my mother. The flame of the lighter went out and he resumed, 'So now I'll tell you the difference between Othello and Riccardo De Sio. The difference is that Othello is an idiot, whereas Riccardo De Sio on the other hand is a very, but *very* intelligent man. Let's say, Mario, that Riccardo De Sio, as well as still being Othello – because there's no way round it, either you're jealous by nature, or you're not, and I am – was also another Shakespearian character: Iago. In Shakespeare's play, Iago prepares the traps and Othello falls into them. In my play, though, Othello and Iago work together, they are the same person and with loving care they get together to prepare the traps that Desdemona falls into.'

'Who would Desdemona be?'

'Your mother, my dear boy, your mother of course, the woman who always said, "I don't know." And you know when Othello realized he'd have to call Iago to his aid? Well, one day, your mother appears, dressed to the nines as usual, barely half an hour after we've got up from lunch and announces, as on all the other days, "I'm off out, see you this evening." Heaven knows why, but it just comes to me to offer, "If you want, I'll give you a lift." She looks at me a moment, and then, whether because the lift really was useful, or because I'd taken her by surprise, she says, "Okay. Just drop me at the beginning of Via Bertolini." Now there are no shops in Via Bertolini, nor, as far as I was aware, did anybody we knew live there. So I realized at once that she was going there for reasons that had to do with her parallel life, probably to see a man. Then, while I was driving, and brooding over my old, painful feeling that I was being excluded, I suddenly thought: But if you'd set up and arranged this appointment of hers, about which you know nothing and never will know anything, if, instead of just accepting her "I don't know" like an idiot, you in fact knew everything, absolutely everything, precisely because it had been you who had pushed her into the arms of her lover, don't you think perhaps you'd be able to replace this feeling of exclusion with that of, well, inclusion? And, what's more, with the pleasant sensation of omnipotence the puppeteer has when he pulls the strings of his puppets?'

'The puppet being my mother?'

'Yes. And the man I selected to play the part of the lover.'

I don't know why but the deep darkness we were sitting in allowed me to express myself with vengeful vulgarity. 'In other words, you wanted to make a cuckold of yourself, on purpose, so as not to feel left out.'

'You're cruel, Mario, you're ruthless, but you're absolutely right. In short, let's say that I was obliged, as they say, to make a virtue of necessity.'

'Sorry, maybe I'm tired from the trip – and then I find it impossible to speak of Mother completely objectively. Okay, you talk about inclusion. But what do you mean by inclusion?'

'I mean the end of her sealed compartment, my own participation in her parallel life. As Othello, I hadn't been able to take part in that life. As Iago, I could – or rather as Othello plus Iago I could, that is, as Riccardo De Sio.'

'But how?'

'How would Riccardo De Sio, alias Othello plus Iago, pull the strings of the puppets in his life? Easy: by applying his intelligence. And you know what intelligence means for a puppeteer? It means knowing your puppet through and through, it means having observed her, analysed her, studied her, mastered her, anatomized her.'

'And you had anatomized Mother?'

'Yes, the way a surgeon anatomizes a lifeless corpse. Jealousy doesn't always mean blindness; it may mean observation. Meticulous, maniacal observation. I lived with your mother for nine years. She was eighteen when we married, twenty-seven when we split up. I had all the time in the world to study her in depth. Obviously, in the early days my observations were infatuated, contemplative. I loved her and I loved watching her. Soon though, very soon, when I realized that the apple had a worm in it, that she wasn't faithful, my watching was no longer an end in itself, it became practical. I watched her to find out how, when and with whom she was betraying me. It was then that Othello made an alliance with Iago. But Mario, you mustn't think that I watched her with hatred. With detachment, yes, but always lovingly. I simply wanted to love her as she was and not as it would have suited me for her to have been. With her faults as well as her qualities, or rather with her faults above all. But while I wanted to know everything about her, I didn't want her to know that I knew. You see what a puppeteer's like? A puppeteer is someone who knows everything about his puppet, but the puppet knows nothing of the puppeteer, and above all doesn't know that the puppeteer knows that they don't know.'

Another pause. My father lit a second cigarette with the stub of the first. In the dark I saw the two lighted cigarettes touching each other, then one of the two was stubbed out in the ashtray anchored to the arm of the sofa with a stretch of braid. My father resumed, 'We were talking about the way I anatomized your mother's behaviour. As I said, your mother, although she was a female Don Juan, was not a worldly woman: she led the life of someone who has no time to lose in social gatherings; she had, as it were, cut herself off, deliberately. To make up for that, she would exploit every single occasion that her casual, aimless days offered her. For example, imagine there was a tennis tournament; she would go, pick out one of the players, chat him up, make love, then go on to another and then yet another. Or maybe it was the turn of the fashion designers. She would get herself fitted out by one dressmaker, then by another, then by yet another, and every time she went to bed with them. Or she'd start hanging around people in TV, maybe starting with someone from that crowd who'd stopped her on the street. And so on and so forth. To put it bluntly, anyone was fine so long as the affair got going fast and finished soon. Even intellectuals.'

'Why do you say *even* intellectuals?'

'Because your mother wasn't educated and she felt uneasy with intellectuals. But it doesn't matter. The fact was there was one circle she still hadn't done the rounds of and that was my office. Perhaps out of a sense of insecurity which my presence aroused, perhaps merely because it had never occurred to her, I don't know. Then, all of a sudden, all that changed.'

My father paused for a moment, as if to stress the importance of this change. If only to fill up the silence I said, 'What happened?'

'Who knows? Perhaps she couldn't think of any new hunting grounds right then. Perhaps she liked to think that she could set up her parallel life inside my own life. In any event, I realized that she'd got her eye on my office.'

'How did you realize?'

'In the past she never, and I mean never, turned up at the agency. Then suddenly there she was dropping in with one excuse or another more or less every day. The agency was much busier then than it is now and there were five of us working there: an older man who was very experienced in the field; a new recruit, very young, a handsome boy, smart, well-bred, socialized a lot; the accountant, a middle-aged man; my partner, and, of course, myself. It goes without saying that your mother's excuse for visiting the agency was myself. It goes without saying that I immediately excluded the possibility that she was really coming to see me. Which left the other four. I could rule out the older man, who knew his job well: he was too old and what's more too attached to his wife and family. I also ruled out the accountant, a shallow, mean character. Which left the smart, handsome boy and my partner. Something told me that your mother wasn't coming for the youngster. You know why? Because he was going after her. You'll say, so much the better, no? And I have to answer you, no, so much the worse. Because your mother, with her usual capriciousness, or spirit of independence if you like, would not make love to a man who went after her. "I make the moves," she used to say, "it's me who decides." And so it turned out: the young lad flirted with her, but she cold-shouldered him and went after my partner.'

I don't know why, but at this unexpected conclusion, I had for a split second before my eyes the apparition of a short while ago, my mother that is, watching me as she straddled a man sitting on the sofa, a man with broad shoulders and a thick head of blond curly hair. I couldn't help but cry out, 'Was your partner a tall man with broad shoulders and blond hair?'

'How do you know?'

'I was five when Mother took me to Paris. Children remember things. I remember him perfectly.'

'Yes, Mario, my partner – Terenzi his name was – was tall with broad shoulders and blond hair. But I should tell you something at this point, Mario: when your mother decided to throw her cap at my partner, I was no longer Othello, but then I wasn't yet Riccardo De Sio, or rather Othello plus Iago either. I had, it's true, thought of bringing together Othello and Iago, but I hadn't as yet got beyond the theory to the practice. Oh, it's a tough business changing one's character! As a result, when your mother started flirting with Terenzi it was the perfect opportunity for me to put my theory into practice, and I jumped at it.'

'But how did you realize that Mother was, as you say, throwing her cap at Terenzi?'

'I realized one day after she'd turned up three or four times for no good reason. Your mother arrives, we talk for a moment about things of no importance, and then, for some reason or other, she slips through the door into the next room which was, of course, Terenzi's. I had things to do, and stayed in my seat, but the door was open and I heard.'

'What did you hear?'

'Nothing special as far as the conversation was concerned. Your mother talked about a friend of hers who was looking for a place to live and asked Terenzi if the agency had anything available. What was special, though, was the way she laughed during this business conversation.'

'And how did she laugh?'

'The way some birds do during the mating season. Her laugh was a mating call. Your mother had a most beautiful voice and when involved in one of her adventures she sounded like a nightingale in summer, she trilled. I never understood how she managed these trilling laughs, as I called them. They might be little laughs, or long ones, husky, throaty, barely hinted at, or positively raucous, and they were always slipped in without any apparent reason between the phrases of a conversation that was nothing out of the ordinary nor had anything especially funny about it. All I know is that this trill meant an affair. Or rather, to be exact, it indicated with extreme accuracy the beginning of an affair. So, hearing these trills, I hastily decided to act in line with the new personality I was creating for myself, that is, an Othello who was also Iago, or, if you like, a Iago who was also an Othello.'

'And what did you do?'

'I got up from my desk and followed her into Terenzi's room. Your mother was sitting on one side of the table, Terenzi on the other: perfectly normal behaviour in any office. But your mother was roaring with laughter, and Terenzi was watching her, flustered. "Listen, Terenzi," I said with the relaxed but precise manner of the businessman, "I overheard what Dina's been telling you; why don't you show her the apartment on Via Archimede? It's just what her friend's after. Then maybe she can go and see it for herself. For the moment it would be better if Dina sees it for her right away. We've already got some offers, I wouldn't want her to miss the chance." Your mother watched me as I spoke, with eyes which gradually seemed to pass from an expression of puzzlement to one of joy. She said hurriedly, "Riccardo's right. We should go straight away, this morning if possible." As for Terenzi, either he hadn't realized that he was attracted to your mother, or he'd realized that he was attracted more than was good for him, and he seemed frightened by me. Reluctantly he remarked that unfortunately he didn't have his car. It had broken down, it was at the garage. I said at once, "Oh but take mine, take mine, both of you, and go. Hang on, I'll give you the keys."

'Ever seen anyone making a run for it? That was your mother: she was out of her seat and heading for the door, then she stopped for a moment, looking impatiently at Terenzi and myself while I told her what to do and gave him the keys to the car and the apartment. Finally, as he caught up with her, she grabbed him by the arm and literally, indecently, dragged him away. She wasn't trilling any more now, she was raring to go, she couldn't wait to get to the apartment in Via Archimede and throw herself into Terenzi's arms. As they were leaving I shouted after them, "Make sure you get through with it quickly and bring me back the keys before one," and quite lucidly I reflected that with that, "get through with it quickly," what I'd really meant was, "get through your lovemaking quickly." My consolation, however, lay in telling myself, "There, in about ten minutes at the most she'll be doing with Terenzi what she's already done with so many other men. But this time she'll be doing it because I wanted her to do it."'

'And you felt good, thinking that?'

'I don't know if I felt good, but certainly it was something new in my relationship with her. After all, I was no longer excluded from her life, I was involved in it, deeply involved, in fact I was directly responsible for what she was doing.'

'It didn't occur to you that you were involved in her life in a way that was, let's say, hardly flattering?'

There was a long pause, as if of reflection. Then my father said calmly, 'You mean as my wife's pimp? Of course it occurred to me, but, Mario, better her pimp than nothing, nothing at all.'

I realized now that my father's so-called confession had become an interrogation of my father by myself; and that likewise this interrogation was focusing more and more not so much on his relationship with my mother, as on what the apparition of a short while ago had allowed me to glimpse about my mother's relationship with myself. All the same I couldn't resist satisfying a curiosity which I sensed was at the same time both indiscreet and painful, and I asked, 'So then, did they make love that day?'

'Of course they did. And so violently that, as soon as she got home, around two, your mother skipped lunch and went straight to bed to snuggle under the covers. I ate alone, then went to her bedroom and sat down next to her. She was lying quite still, on her back, her legs tight together, like a mummy in its sarcophagus. I didn't talk this time, just watched her. You may find it strange, but right then I felt I was loving her more than ever, truly loving her for the first time since we'd married. I had got into her life, albeit by the back door, into that parallel life she'd so far always excluded me from. I was in there, I was part of it. And she, having fooled me so often, had been fooled herself this time. She must have suspected something, because when I couldn't bring myself to speak she said, "What's up? Why are you looking at me like that?" Moved and sincere, I answered, "I'm looking at you because I love you." It was the truth: I loved her partly because I felt I had somehow made love to her through Terenzi, who would never have done it if I hadn't decided he should.'

I asked impatiently, 'But what's all this got to do with my game with the door?'

'I'm getting there, I'm getting there. After that morning in the apartment in Via Archimede, your mother and Terenzi had a very intense relationship; it was as though they were in love, or at least their feelings were so intense they thought they were in love. They went wild if they couldn't see each other. She came to the office every morning. He was visibly impatient waiting for her to arrive. But there was the problem of finding a place to be together. They couldn't go to Via Archimede now, he had his wife and children at home and he didn't have a second house. Which left either a hotel, or the car, or her place, that is, my place. And so' – at this point my father's voice took on a triumphant tone – 'and so, Mario, I arranged things so that they could make love, at least once, at home.'

'Here, at home?'

'Right, at home. It was summer. Terenzi's wife had taken the children to Forte dei Marmi, but there was a maid in the house who might have found them out. I knew all this and in the end, one evening, I invited Terenzi to dinner.'

'And then?'

'And then I put my plan into operation. What was my plan? Well, once Terenzi had got here, shortly before the meal, I would leave them alone with the excuse of going out to pick up some ice-cream in the café down the street. I calculated that I'd have to be out long enough to allow them a furtive quickie, that is the ten or fifteen minutes it usually took your mother to reach orgasm. Then I'd get back with my ice-cream and have the satisfaction of seeing on both their faces that they hadn't wasted their time.'

'On their faces?'

'That's right! There are some things you can't hide!'

'I'm sorry, but what kind of satisfaction was it for you to see on their faces that they'd made love while you were away?'

'I told you, the satisfaction of the puppeteer who controls the movement of his puppets! Now we get to the game with the door. I tell your mother I've decided to invite Terenzi to dinner. I tell her the day and the time. She agrees, she changes the subject for a while, then she comes back to it and says: "By the way, your inviting Terenzi reminds me I must lock that door in the lounge." With a pretence of innocence, I ask, "Why?" "Because Mario's game of coming into the lounge in the evening when I'm least expecting it can't go on. I can put up with it when we're on our own. But when we've got someone to dinner, like Terenzi, it really won't do for Mario to be playing his game. A little boy bursting into the lounge for his goodnight kiss smacks rather too much of the *petit bourgeois*."

'Understand? She was already thinking that somehow or other she'd be able to have some time alone with Terenzi. She was already getting ready for five or ten minutes of furious, no-nonsense sex. You'll say, but how could she have known I'd be going out to buy some ice-cream? Mario, you won't believe this, but there was a sort of complicity. I wanted to lay a trap for her and she asked for nothing better than to fall into it.'

'What do you mean?'

'I mean that we had exactly the same idea at exactly the same moment. And in fact that's how it turned out. Came the evening I'd invited Terenzi. He arrives, we eat an excellent dinner, but then at the end, what's this? For some reason or other there's nothing for dessert. The maid brings a simple bowl of fruit with whatever was in season. You should have seen your mother. As if struck by a sudden brainwave, she cries, "Riccardo, what we need in this weather is ice-cream. Why don't you go and pick some up at the café down in the street?"'

I remarked pedantically, 'But then it wasn't you who was pulling the strings, but her. You were the puppet and she was the puppeteer.'

'Wait a minute. We'd had the same idea, but I could still choose what to do, whereas she couldn't. I mean I could still be or not be the puppeteer. Instead of staying out fifteen minutes I could perfectly well come back after only a couple and catch them in the act. I could, and that was enough for me.'

'Enough in what sense?'

'Enough to have the impression that I was the puppeteer, that I was controlling their moves.'

'But wouldn't it have been better to have caught them in the act?'

'Very smart! Then I'd have found myself excluded again, cut out of your mother's parallel life. And to make matters worse, she'd never have trusted me again.' My father fell silent a moment, then asked casually, 'But why on earth are you so determined to have me tell you what happened about your game with the door?'

I answered hurriedly, 'No particular reason. I'm curious, that's all. I'm interested in anything that has to do with my mother.'

'So obviously you'll be interested in knowing how our relationship broke up.'

'Obviously, of course. For the moment though we were talking about my game with the door.'

'You're right, each to his own, you're thinking about the door, me about my marriage. In any event, they both finished together, your game, my marriage. So, your mother asks me to go and pick up the ice-cream and I think to myself, "There, she's had the same idea, she's caught me off balance," but I don't say anything. I announce that I'll go at once, even ask what flavours they'd like, then hurry out and down to the street. There is a café right below our apartment actually, but as I said I had to stay out for at least ten, fifteen minutes. So I invent for myself the excuse that the café is closed and that I have to get the car and go and find another further down the street. I go into the café, order an ice-cream, then, seeing that they've got a TV, sit down on a stool and pretend to be interested in the game. I like football and a game on TV always gets me excited. But that evening I had other things on my mind! I said to myself, "Now they're embracing, now they're kissing, now embracing again, now kissing again. Now he's lying on the sofa, now she's letting herself be pulled down after him. Now they've got themselves in a bit of a mess, their clothes are in the way, they're in too much of a hurry. Then, right, they've sorted themselves out to make love now, him underneath, her on top. There, she's spread her legs, easy enough with the miniskirt she's wearing, and he's in; now the real sex starts in earnest. How long can it last, how long will it last?" Well, I waited, glancing alternately from the TV to the clock, for about nine minutes. I couldn't hang on for ten. I take my pack of ice-cream, pay slowly, counting out the notes, looking for change, and go slowly back into the block. I close the lift door behind me slowly and, once back to the right floor, slowly open the front door. I'd got my calculations right. As I came into the living-room I immediately saw that they'd done what I wanted them to and were waiting for me, all calm and satisfied.'

'How did you know they'd done anything?'

'From the way they were behaving, Mario. He immediately pretended to be too interested in the football, shouted too loudly that I'd missed a great bit. Your mother, on the other hand – she was more intelligent – couldn't conceal her suspicion and asked me how come I'd taken so long to go and get the ice-cream. I answered innocently that the café was closed and I'd taken the car to go and get ice-cream elsewhere. And that was the end of it.'

'It hardly seems convincing proof – that he was interested in the game and mother was surprised that you'd taken so long.'

'There was another proof. When I'd gone out there'd been an ashtray on the arm of the armchair. I'd stubbed out a cigarette in it myself only shortly before leaving. It was full of stubs. While I was away someone had knocked it over and the stubs were scattered over the carpet. It was clear that with all their flurry to make love they'd knocked it over and hadn't realized. The ashtray and cigarette-ends were there, on the floor, telling their story.'

'But you said they would have made love lying on the sofa. So how could they have knocked over the ashtray?'

'Easy does it. I said that because it was the most obvious position. But there are all kinds of ways of making love on a sofa.'

I hesitated, overcame my repugnance, then forced myself to ask, 'For example?'

'Oh, all kinds of ways. For example, Terenzi sits down near the arm. With his elbow he could perfectly well knock over the ashtray.'

'But why? Why would he have moved his elbow?'

'Imagine that she was sitting on his knee and he moved his arms to pull her closer to him. Or maybe she knocked the ashtray over.'

'With her elbow again?'

'Right, with her elbow. But Mario, what matters is not this evidence, what matters is that later a number of things happened to confirm in every detail that the puppeteer had pulled his strings as he intended to that evening. Unfortunately, however, he didn't stop in time, he overdid it, and everything went wrong.'

'What's that supposed to mean?'

'What does a puppeteer do after he's amused himself pulling on his puppets' strings? He gets bored and puts the puppets back in their box. And that's what I wanted to do, Mario, put your mother and Terenzi back in their boxes, that is break off their affair. And here I made a mistake. Because at this point the puppets realized, as it were, that they had strings, and they rebelled.'

'I'm afraid this puppet metaphor is confusing me. What actually happened?'

'What actually happened was very simple. By now they were lovers, they went on loving each other on their own, so escaping my control. Regaining control would mean, inevitably, breaking off their affair. And anyway the time was ripe. I realized from all kinds of signs that your mother was tired of Terenzi: she was promiscuous, she liked adventures, not relationships. So what does the puppeteer do? I'm sorry but I'm forced to used the metaphor again, it's indispensable. I knew that one of the people who would gladly have taken Terenzi's place in your mother's affections was a South American client of ours, very rich, fortyish. He wanted to settle down in Rome and he was looking for a place to buy. One day around then I asked your mother to take him to see an apartment. Since she'd started visiting the agency I'd occasionally asked her to show people things. I'd already seen that it might prove a good ruse for ending her affair with Terenzi. Your mother accepts, of course, and sets off with the South American to visit the apartment. Now, I'd been careful to keep Terenzi in the dark about all this, so at this point I tell him that he should go to such-and-such an apartment in such-and-such a street at such-and-such a time, where he will find the South American client. I tell him I've already given the client a key, and I give one to Terenzi too. I was sure that as soon as the South American was alone with your mother, he would jump on her. The way I'd calculated it, Terenzi ought to arrive precisely at that moment. And in fact everything went according to plan. Terenzi arrives, goes up to the apartment, opens the door with his key and finds her and the client, for want of a bed, making love on the floor. At which everything I had planned should happen, happens, except, unfortunately, that something else happens too; the two men start a scuffle, your mother runs off, but not before having found out from Terenzi that it had been me who had sent him there to catch them. At the time, neither she nor the two men told me anything. But the South American didn't show up again, Terenzi found an excuse for breaking off our business relationship, and within a month your mother had herself invited to her brother's in Paris. Your mother's excuse was yourself, that is that she wanted her brother to see you. I took you both to the airport, thinking you'd soon be back. And instead it was the last time I saw either her or you. What still upsets me, though, is that we parted badly, after the fight between Terenzi and the South American and an argument between herself and me. I had hoped to put things right, to explain myself. I loved her. I was no longer Othello and Iago fused together, I was no longer the puppeteer, just a poor man in love with his wife and afraid of losing her. But she wrote to me immediately after her arrival in Paris to tell me that everything was over between us and to forbid me to write to her or to get in touch in any way. Perhaps despite her telling me not to I would have gone to see her in Paris anyway after a while, as soon as tempers had cooled, but sadly she died barely eighteen months after leaving. It was destiny from first to last.'

We were both silent for a while, but whereas he had said what he had to say, I still hadn't found out what I wanted to find out. Suddenly, I don't know why, with that naturalness typical of every urgent but unconscious preoccupation, it occurred to me to ask, 'You say you parted badly and that you'd had an argument. But what had you argued about?'

To my surprise, my father asked, 'Did I say that?'

'Yes, you did. That it upset you that you'd split up after an argument with her.'

'Oh, yes, that's right,' my father's voice was suddenly uncertain and reticent, as if he wished he hadn't spoken. 'Yes, we argued over something, well, futile.'

'But what?'

'You want to know everything, don't you? Something futile and that's that.'

'Why futile?'

'Because it wasn't a real reason to argue.'

'That is, you don't want to tell me.'

'Oh for heaven's sake, I'll tell you right away. Your mother started getting on at me for something I'd said in a moment of anger. I'd said that I wasn't at all sure that you were my son. Of course it was just one of those things people do say when they're angry; even while you're saying it you know it's not true. Stupid.'

We said nothing for a moment. My father's explanation made no impression on me. What struck me, if anything, was precisely the fact that it hadn't made an impression. On the contrary, I realized I was hoping his accusation might be correct, that I really wasn't his son. One thing was sure, my journey to Italy in search of my father was revealing itself for what I had always suspected it to be right from the beginning: one of the many bright ideas generated by my heedless and voracious openness to experience. Except that, as soon as there was a chance that my father was not my father, then everything that had to do with my mother took on an obscure and fatal importance. Yes, I thought with irony, I was like Columbus who had wanted to land in Asia and instead had discovered America. I'd left Paris to find my father in Rome, and instead I'd found my mother. I asked point-blank, 'Let's get this straight, am I or aren't I your son?'

'Of course you're my son. I said you weren't in a moment of anger. No, there can't be any doubt about that.'

'Why not? Mother had other men, one of them could be the father.'

'No, Mario, I'm reasonably sure you are my son.'

'Reasonably?'

'Let's say eighty per cent sure.'

'And if I belonged to the other twenty per cent?'

'Eighty per cent is good enough for me, Mario, I don't ask for more.'

'It hasn't been good enough for you for fifteen years. If it had been, you would have got in touch with me.'

'The past is past, Mario. Let's look to the future.'

At which point I felt inclined to go back to the reason for their argument. 'So, you and Mother had a row. You told her I wasn't your son. And what did Mother do?'

'She took it very badly, though as I say it was just something that slipped out in a moment of anger. It was the same night I'd invited Terenzi to dinner. She suddenly shouted, "I don't want to sleep with you any more. I'll go and sleep in Mario's room." And so saying, she got out of bed, in just her nightdress, banged out in a rage and went to sleep in your room. Now, I'll show you your room in a moment; I've kept it exactly as it was and you'll see right away that it wasn't the kind of place where she could sleep. There's only a bunk bed with two places, one above the other, like the couchettes in a sleeper train, kids' beds really! I imagined it was just a gesture, I thought she'd come back that night, but she didn't! Naturally the following day I did everything I could to get her to change her mind, but she was immovable. She kept on saying: "I've been neglecting Mario for quite a while. From now on I'm going to spend my time with him." And from that night on she slept in the bunk under yours.'

I listened to this with a vague but growing unease. Then suddenly I understood. My mother felt a sense of remorse for having forced me, with the incredibly commanding way she had looked at me, to watch her making love to Terenzi through to the end. The decision to sleep in my room was meant to be a way of making amends.

But having settled the question of the change of beds, another question immediately arose. My mother's remorse made it clear that I really had played my game with the door that night. Yet just a few days before, my mother had foreseen, no, planned, to be alone with her lover. With this in mind she had even told my father that she wanted to lock the lounge door. So why then was the door not locked that evening of all evenings? Why? Out of my mother's negligence? And even if it was feasible that my mother, distracted by her passion, had forgotten to lock the door, how could my father, who said he loved me and at the same time had set up this trap with such meticulous lucidity, how could he not have taken this precaution? Trying to use the calm voice of disinterested curiosity, I asked, 'Okay, you set a trap for my mother and she fell for it. But, to go back to the game again, tell me something, the night of the trap, did you lock the door I used to use to surprise Mother?'

'I don't understand, what do you mean?'

'I mean, before dinner, did you go and check the door and lock it? Didn't it occur to you that I might see Mother and Terenzi making love?'

I said to myself: There, got him. Either he forgot, which is bad, or he went and checked, found that my mother had forgotten, and did nothing about it, which is worse. I waited a long time for his reply, waited with a keen, lucid expectancy. Finally, in the dark that hid him from my eyes, I heard him say, 'It may seem strange, Mario, but however hard I try I just can't remember that particular detail. After all, fifteen years are fifteen years in the end.'

'What? You don't remember whether you locked the door or not? But you knew very well that I used to play that trick on Mother!'

'I can't remember, Mario. I'm sorry but I can't.'

'But it was important to have it locked. How can you not remember something so important!'

'Mario, I don't know what to say. It's as if there were a gap in my memory here.'

I wanted to scream at him: You forgot and I saw what I saw, and the proof that I saw is that Mother felt so bad about it that she wanted to make up by coming to sleep in my room. But I was held back from such an outburst by precisely the inquisitorial obsession which had taken me over now and seemed even stronger than my pain. I took my lighter from my pocket, flicked up the flame in front of my father's face, and, holding it firmly so that I could look at him while I spoke, said, 'You and Mother had the same plan for that evening. According to this plan, at least if what you say is true, she and Terenzi were to be alone for ten or fifteen minutes. But there was the danger that I might play my game with the door and see them. How could you both have forgotten about me?'

In the glimmer of the flame I saw my father's eyes open even wider that usual, and he shook his head. 'Mario, perhaps we did both forget you, each for our different reasons.'

I shut off the lighter and for a moment almost admired the symmetry of life. The result, by which I mean the wrong done, was the same in both cases, just that their reasons for doing it were different. My mother had forgotten because distracted by desire perhaps; my father by jealousy. But there was also the possibility that both of them had forgotten 'on purpose', she out of perversity and sadism and he to take revenge for her betrayal on the son he didn't believe was his. Finally there was a third explanation that would do for both of them: indifference. They had remembered and despite remembering had done nothing. This explanation seemed the most likely and in fact, as I formulated it, I felt the most acute and reasoned sense of disappointment: my father and mother were not two monsters deliberately involving their little boy in their marital games. They were just two strangers.

Perhaps my father realized I was thinking over his reply. He started speaking again, less hesitant now, as if seizing on an irrefutable argument. 'But Mario, why think about the past; let's look to the future instead. I'm looking to the future. When you phoned me from Paris I was happy, so very happy. And you know why? Because I saw before me, in the future, the chance – no, the certainty that I could build a family again, as if those fifteen years had never been.'

'But Mother's dead.'

'Your mother's dead, yes, but she lives in our memory. Your mother lives, Mario, she's here with us, and she's telling us that you and I are father and son and that from now on we must live together.'

Having made this declaration, pronounced in the dark with emphasis and conviction, my father got up from the sofa and went to turn on the main overhead light. We looked at each other for a moment, dazzled. 'The confession is over, Mario, let's move. Come on, I'll show you the rest of the apartment.'

THREE

The Repetition

I had left Paris as though for a joke, to have an adventure, one of the many adventures I like to embark on in my perpetual state of openness to experience. But already that first evening, after my father's so-called confession, I realized that this was no adventure. It was merely the life of fifteen years ago, which had never really changed nor been interrupted, resuming its old course. I had, as the psychoanalytic jargon goes, repressed my memory of the scene I'd witnessed. For fifteen years this repression had turned my life into a dream. Now I had woken up to reality and I came to realize, without regret, but without satisfaction either, that at least as far as my mother was concerned, this awakening was irreversible. One might have questioned whether waking up and knowing the truth were really necessary. Perhaps they weren't, but the fact was that I had woken up, I did know.

The sensation that I had been dreaming for fifteen years was reinforced by a detail from that evening of so long ago. Having gone back to bed, after witnessing the scene in the lounge, I'd nevertheless waited a long time for my mother to come and give me my goodnight kiss, until in the end I fell asleep. While I slept, my father, my mother and Terenzi had finished eating, Terenzi had left and then my mother, evidently feeling bad about having made me stay and watch her lovemaking, had reminded my father that it was time they went to say goodnight to me in my room, as on every other evening. My father had agreed and so they both came to my room and my mother woke me to give me a kiss while my father watched, standing behind her. Now, in the confusion of the trauma I'd experienced and of being woken up, I was amazed not to see Terenzi behind my mother, since I had such a clear image of him sitting beside her on the sofa in the lounge just a short while ago. Why had Terenzi disappeared? Why had my father taken his place, seeing that he hadn't been in the lounge when I had looked in? Perhaps the scene I had reluctantly witnessed before falling asleep had been all a dream – a nightmare rather – whereas in reality there had been no interruption to the normal pattern of family life.

But now, as I said, I had woken up to reality and knew that while I might indeed have been dreaming for fifteen years, I certainly hadn't been dreaming that night. This discovery gave rise to a weary, inert mood of depression. Yes, life had resumed its course after a break of fifteen years, but what exactly, in my case, was this life? I started thinking about it, or rather, trying to think about it, since as a subject it was obscure and muddled, and then with this kind of apathetic sadness I was suffering from I found it difficult to concentrate. All the same it did seem that life, as far as I was concerned, amounted to a sensation of the irreparable. I realized now that in that instant when I'd seen my mother and Terenzi in the lounge, I had suffered a great loss, or, if you like, had received an incurable wound, though I couldn't say exactly what it was I'd lost nor what kind of wound had been inflicted.

But this life of mine was also made up of the mysterious symmetry of the different behaviours of my mother and father. They had behaved like two strangers; but why were they strangers? Perhaps because the indifference typical of the stranger is part of life, or even is life itself? Or because their strangeness was the wrong done to me, something, that is, absolutely negative, which I could neither forget nor forgive, and which came out in my impotent question, 'Why did they do it?' Or even, 'Why does suffering exist?'

As I said, I was overtaken by a profound depression mixed with apathy and inertia, a mood at the opposite extreme to the irresponsible self-confidence and openness with which I had left Paris. And with depression came solitude.

That same evening, having seen the rest of the apartment, my father took me out to a good restaurant in town and there, after an excellent meal, explained his plans for me. So: I was to help him in his estate agency, taking and making phone-calls, driving clients in his Mercedes to inspect property. He would give me a salary for doing this, and he told me how much. It was more than I could have hoped, and I couldn't help but sense in this generosity of his the same obscure desire to make amends that I had suspected throughout in his ostentatious manifestations of paternal love. He noticed my surprise and made a point of telling me that he would have given me the money anyway. For him, he declared with the inevitable melodrama, what counted most was the family. He wanted to build up a family again, for the moment he was beginning with me. Then he would sort out the rest.

Over the following days I waited in vain to meet this 'rest', to meet, that is, the woman who, in my father's plans for re-establishing a family, was to take the place of my mother. I suspected, or rather I knew pretty well for certain, that such a woman did exist; her place in my father's life was evident from the fact that he neither dined nor spent the evenings with me. On the contrary, he made no mystery of the fact that every evening he saw a woman who he referred to generically as his 'friend'. Why he didn't introduce me to her I couldn't understand. Perhaps, as I finally came to think, because he wanted to put me to the test in my role of prodigal son returned to the paternal home. But in our case, shouldn't the gospel story have been turned on its head? Wasn't he rather the prodigal father who after fifteen years of bachelor freedom was returning to the idea of having a son and establishing a family?

While waiting to meet my father's 'friend' – though I wasn't by any means impatient, since, as I said, I had plunged to the very bottom of a kind of depressive lethargy – I began a life whose funereal regularity was the direct result of my state of mind. In the morning I had coffee with my father, then he went off to work and we met at the agency at ten. I worked there until one, we came home together and ate together. In the afternoon my father took his siesta in the traditional manner, that is, he got undressed, went to bed and slept for an hour or two, after which he'd get up and dress in his smartest clothes. Then after spending a little time with me he went out and I wouldn't see him again until the following morning. I wasn't expected to go to the agency in the afternoon, and the very few times I did go I didn't find my father there. So my loneliness, which grew out of depression, would begin, not surprisingly, in the afternoon.

It was a loneliness made up of rejection and daydreaming. The rejection had to do with the place where I was and, in general, with my life outside the house and away from the office. I was aware that I was living in a city famous for its beauty, a city I didn't know at all and might usefully have spent my time exploring. I was also aware that it wouldn't be too difficult to meet people. After all, my father had frequently offered to introduce me to relatives and friends. But both the monuments of Rome and my father's relatives and friends inspired an insuperable feeling of loathing. Why not admit it? My state of mind was that of someone who has been left by a lover, at once unable to put the experience behind them and at the same time finding everything that might help to forget it repugnant.

Given this spiritual state, it wasn't long before daydreaming took the place of active, positive thinking. And then I'm prone to daydreaming by nature. In Paris I would often spend whole hours lying on the sofa without reading or writing or doing anything at all, suspending thought completely and just wandering in my imagination from one thing to the next. Now, however, as I almost immediately became aware, I was daydreaming about just one thing: my mother.

During those long spring afternoons, I would usually go to the lounge, to the part where I knew my mother, as my father had put it, used to 'live', sit on the sofa in front of the TV and think of her. I would think of her in two ways, either repeating to myself that vain, and I knew unanswerable question, 'Why did you do it?' or evoking with invincible obstinacy the image, or rather apparition, of her in the act of straddling Terenzi's knees. The fact that my mother was dead added to both question and image an atmosphere of funereal impossibility. Yes, I might go on repeating that question and evoking that image for years, but nothing would happen: the question would remain unanswered, the image unexplained, though both would go on confirming that, undeniably, 'something had happened.'

It was an obsession, and like all obsessions, especially when for some unconscious reason we let ourselves become their accomplices, not entirely unpleasant. The question, 'Why did you do it?' was pathetic, and, as a result, consoling. The image had an inescapable erotic content, though this didn't only have to do with Terenzi and my mother, but with me too. And I knew the reason. Logically, I should have wiped out the image, destroyed it, pretended that what it represented had never happened. Yet, following some obscure and instinctive law of retaliation, I could see no other way of wiping out the sense of outrage that the image provoked than by repeating the same outrage myself; that is, to put it bluntly, by putting myself in Terenzi's place and imagining a relationship with my mother in every way similar to his, and thus incestuous. Another thing that led me to this conclusion was an analogous experience I'd recently had in Paris. Basically, I was jealous of Terenzi; well, in Paris I had overcome a similar jealousy by doing myself the thing that had made me jealous.

A few months before coming to Rome I had had an affair

with a girl called Monique who went to the same classes as I did at the university. In the end it was nothing more than a very superficial adventure, but the day when, for the first time, Monique didn't turn up for our date, I couldn't help reproaching her with inexplicable violence. 'You didn't come because you were with someone else, making love, tell me the truth.' I expected, perhaps hoped, she would deny it. Instead I heard her answer in a calm, fearless voice, 'You're right, I was with Paul and we made love.'

At which I threw myself on Monique, pushed her on the bed, tore off her panties, penetrated her and ejaculated almost at once, all in just a few seconds and without a word. Afterwards we lay one on top of the other, one inside the other, immobile and utterly exhausted by the suddenness and violence of our embrace. And I had the very sharp impression that this sort of rape I had committed had cancelled out Paul's body from Monique's and that my sperm had washed away the sperm that Paul had poured into her womb. Still lying on the young girl's body, my eyes closed as if falling asleep, I had tried to analyse and define this strange sensation of obliteration and purification. Why did I no longer feel any of the furious jealousy that had prompted me to re-enact exactly what my rival had done? The betrayal was still a reality and, in a sentimental sense, was irreparable. At this point, without meaning to, Monique had confirmed my own impression. With the same crude, blunt sincerity with which a few moments ago she'd announced her betrayal, she said, 'I'm not Paul's any more now, I'm yours.' So that, thinking back to what Monique had said and referring it to my mother, I told myself that there could be no doubt Mother had betrayed me and that I should cancel out her betrayal the same way I had cancelled out Monique's.

Except that my mother was dead. And the comparison with Monique, much as I might desire it even to the point of incest, took on a macabre air of utter impossibility. I couldn't take Terenzi's place in any real way at all. The road to incest was blocked by the grave. But, as I was immediately aware, I might be able to substitute Terenzi in my imagination by altering the scene I had witnessed fifteen years before, that is by putting myself in the position of Terenzi and another woman in the place of my mother. As in homeopathic medicine, then, I would try to recover from the wrong done to me with a representation of the wrong itself.

In any event, this resorting to a representation was also suggested by my constant imagining of the scene which I hoped would free me. For I had realized by now that, as time went by, if I didn't substitute my mother with a double and exorcize that original scene by acting it out myself, I would go on thinking more and more about her with immediate and deplorable results in terms of my longing for incest. In those lonely afternoons in my father's house, remembering my mother had become easier and easier, something ritualistic and dangerous. And instead of the question, 'Why did you do it?' I had gradually begun to ask myself the question, 'Why don't I do it?' But how could I?

I sat for hours on the sofa in front of the television. I turned the screen on, switched off all the other lights and thought over and over this temptation without getting anywhere at all. Having dragged it up from the darkest depths of my memory where it had lain ignored for so many years, I found myself recalling the long-repressed scene between Mother and Terenzi more and more often, so that it seemed to take on an indomitable and at the same time incomprehensible vitality. There, in the dark, was my mother. She appears, climbs and straddles over her lover's knees. Now she's leaning to one side, pushing back the hair that falls across her face, moving urgently to help him penetrate. There she is, working back and forth with her thighs. And now she sees me, commands me not to leave, to stay right to the end of their lovemaking. Then the orgasm; her mouth opens wide as if to scream, and, there, she suddenly collapses, her face on the man's shoulders, grateful and distractedly licking his ear, his neck.

What was I hoping to achieve by evoking these traumatic images over and over again? Basically, to put myself in Terenzi's place, to do what Terenzi had done. But at the same time, and it was a curious contradiction, to re-establish, through an albeit imaginary incest, my old chaste and affectionate relationship with my mother.

One afternoon, after the usual evocations, I fell into a deep sleep, partly as a result of the warm, rainy sirocco which had been blowing on the city for some days, partly due to the tiredness which these obstinate, macabre fantasies induced. I fell asleep and had a dream more real than reality itself. My mother had just straddled Terenzi's knees when suddenly she climbed off and came towards me. I watched her approach and make as if to pull up her miniskirt so as to be able to climb on me. To do so she bent forward and placed a hand on my shoulder. But her hand leaned down on me too hard, began to shake me in fact, and all at once I woke up.

A woman was shaking me, her hand on my shoulder, and at the same time bending over me and calling my name. But it wasn't my mother; it was my father's maid, Oringia.

Oringia was Slavonic, from Trieste, fairly young with a horsy face, small, very deep-set blue eyes, a protruding, peevish nose and chin. Immediately I understood why she was shaking me. Every afternoon, towards five, she brought me a cup of tea. She had brought me some today but I was sleeping, so she had tried to wake me up. Immediately, with lightning inspiration, I said to myself, 'Here's the woman I can repeat the scene with; I'll get Oringia to act out the part of my mother.' Thinking this, I looked her over more carefully than before and saw that despite her witch-like head she did have a fairly attractive body: well built, with wide hips, ample bust and backside, solid calves and thighs. It was a plebeian figure, very different from my mother's, but what did that matter? What I was about to ask her went beyond any limits set by resemblance, rose indeed from a desire for analogy that knew no limits at all, physical or otherwise. Naturally

Oringia sensed she was being looked at and asked attentively, 'Would you like your tea? You asked me to bring you some, otherwise I'd have let you sleep.'

I was still flustered from my dream, and I realized that my confusion hadn't escaped her. I muttered something about tiredness brought on by this sirocco here in Rome. And while I spoke I sat up on the sofa.

'You want me to pour it for you? Sugar? With milk or lemon?'

She asked me these questions in a soft voice made softer still by the softness of her regional accent. Making an effort, I told her, 'Thanks, Oringia, I'll look after myself.'

'You don't want me to serve you?'

'No, it's not that: I don't understand why I fell asleep. It really must have been the sirocco.'

She'd put two cubes of sugar in the tea; now she was stirring it with a slightly swollen red hand, leaning towards me so that her nose was almost brushing my forehead. Then straightening, she said, 'You're alone too much, Mr De Sio. That's why you fell asleep. Perhaps you should have a little fun.'

Abruptly and ambiguously I replied, 'I have fun watching TV.'

She wasn't at all put off by my coldness. Like a pointer snuffling in a bush where it knows the prey is hidden, she had scented sex and she wasn't going to forgo a now legitimate familiarity. 'I watch TV too. But sometimes I go out, I see friends, I go dancing. Haven't you got a girlfriend, Mr De Sio?'

I thought of Monique. 'Yes, I have, but in Paris.' And then, immediately afterwards, remembering that my mother's grave was also in Paris, I added cruelly, 'In fact right when you came in I was dreaming of her.'

'And what was she doing?'

'She was doing something I'd rather not tell you.'

'Anything special?'

'If you want to put it like that.'
'Was she making love, Mr De Sio?'
It was this tone of hers, respectful and servile, bold and alluring that decided me. 'Oringia, can you do me a small favour?'
'Ask away, Mr De Sio.'
'Well, I'd like you to do something that might perhaps seem strange to you, even ridiculous.'
'Why ridiculous, Mr De Sio?'
'Don't ask so many questions. Will you or won't you?'
'Why are you getting angry? Why not tell me what I'm supposed to do?'
'Well, I'd like you to climb on my knees for a moment with your back to the television and look at the door behind the sofa; then tell me what you can see.'
She stood so long without answering that I began to fear I'd offended her. I added hastily, 'It's just a kind of game. I'm not asking anything else. Don't worry.'
'Would it be the same game you were playing in your dream with your girlfriend in Paris?'
'And what if it was?'
'Nothing, but we all know how these kinds of games tend to finish.'
'Not with me.'
'You're an odd one, you know.' Her voice was less sure of itself.
'You think so?'
'Yes, very odd.'
'So?'
'You've reminded me of a game now too. I used to play it with my father when I was a little girl. First he made me bounce up and down on his knees, then he opened his legs and I fell on the floor. Are you going to make me fall on the floor too?'
'Don't worry, I won't make you fall on the floor.'
'You know, you're an odd one.' But despite these protests,

she lifted her skirt now, opened her thick, heavy thighs and arranged herself as best she could on my knees. At which I suddenly realized that my homeopathic cure had failed even before it had begun. Yes, I could have repeated the scene, could have pushed up against the bulging, prominent crotch I could just see at the end of her legs, tucked away in bright pink panties. But the very moment I began to feel the inevitable excitement, I'd realize that it was her I wanted, my father's Slavonic maid, not the ghost I'd seen just a few minutes before in my dream. And so it turned out. Oringia's thighs pushed toward me. Our two crotches were forced against each other; I felt an unmistakable urge, and then immediately drew back and asked her, 'Now tell me what you can see.'

'I can't see anything, what am I supposed to see?'

'What can you see behind the sofa?'

'A door.'

I was about to say, 'Can't you see a boy of five, barefoot, in his pyjamas,' but I held back, murmuring, 'Thank you, Oringia, okay, that's all,' and I pushed her gently away.

She climbed off my knees in a hurry and began to smooth out her skirt with both hands. 'I can't understand what you wanted me to do. Something nasty maybe.'

I sighed. 'Nothing nasty. If anything, something impossible.'

Incredulous, she repeated, 'Impossible?' And then with sudden, abrupt decision, 'Well then, if you don't mind, I'll go back to the kitchen.'

'Thanks, Oringia.'

As soon as she'd gone I began to think it over. I realized now that I must, as they say, 'do something'. My mind was extraordinarily lucid, as happens precisely at these moments when one is about to act. When Oringia had said, 'You're alone too much, Mr De Sio,' I had immediately sensed that I must at all costs break the perverse downward spiral of loneliness and fantasy into which I'd allowed myself to be drawn ever since I'd arrived in Rome. I mustn't be alone any more, as the good Oringia had advised me; and, if possible, I mustn't think about my mother. All at once I remembered my meeting with the two women on the plane, mother and daughter. They'd given me their phone number. I hadn't called them because I was depressed. But now I felt eager to see them. It wasn't just the benevolence the mother had shown me which drew me, it was the impulse to confide in her that that benevolence had inspired. Without delay I got up from the sofa, went to the corridor where the telephone stood on a shelf, looked through my notebook and dialled the number.

The phone rang quite a few times. Finally a low, reluctant, drawling voice pronounced a thoroughly impatient and bad-tempered, 'Hello.' Although I had recognized the daughter's voice I insisted on asking who it was. She answered, as if not wanting to, 'Alda.' At which, with the delight of the shipwrecked mariner who sees a ship appear on the horizon, I exclaimed, 'Alda, it's Mario.'

'Mario who?'

'Mario, the person you met a month ago on the plane coming from Paris. Don't you remember?'

'No.'

'I was sitting next to your mother, I was asleep. Then I woke up and we talked. Your mother's called Jeanne, right?'

I kept filling in the details, but I had the impression she knew perfectly well who I was.

'She's called Jeanne, yes, and so?'

I went on, 'I remember you were annoyed because while I was asleep I was leaning against your mother.'

'I don't remember anything.'

'Of course you do. I'm tall, thin, very thin, my hair's all ruffled up on top of my head and I've got a pointed, upturned nose.'

I suddenly heard her laugh, 'Like Pinocchio!', and I exclaimed, 'You're making fun of me!'

'No, why? You do have a nose that looks like Pinocchio's, don't you?'

'Tell me the truth, you're still angry.'

She answered with a sudden, awkward sweetness, 'No, if anything Jeanne and I are angry because you haven't been in touch.'

I experienced a sense of surprise. It seemed impossible that a person as lonely and desperate as myself could be of interest to anybody else. I pretended, however, to accept her ticking off and apologize. 'I've had a lot to do. And then, I wasn't really sure if you'd be happy to hear from me.'

'Why, do you want me to tell you again? Yes, we would have been happy.'

'I'm sorry, but why should you have been happy?'

'Oh come on, if I tell you yes, then it's yes! We talked about you so much. We said: I wonder if he remembers us; I wonder how many people he knows; he won't have time; he must have forgotten us. Hang on and I'll put Jeanne on the line. She's here making signs across the room. She can't wait for me to hand you over. Here's Jeanne.'

I had the bizarre feeling of somebody who gets mistaken for somebody else, as in the classic comedies based on twins. After the agony of a month spent in funereal solitude, I couldn't see myself in this image of the fashionable socialite the two women had built up around me. Yet at the same time I sensed something intentional behind Alda's flattering interest, some kind of plan almost, as if they knew perfectly well that I was lonely and friendless but for some reason all their own had decided to pretend otherwise. Suddenly Jeanne's voice with its high-pitched, cheerful Parisian lilt came shrilly down the line: 'Mario, what a nice suprise. Well done, why didn't you phone sooner?'

'I couldn't.'

'Oh come on, of course you could. If one wants to do something one can. You just forgot us.'

With the same impulse to confide in her I'd had before, I immediately blurted out the truth. 'No, I really couldn't. Otherwise I would have. I don't know why, but you make me feel I can really trust you. In half an hour on the plane I told you everything about myself. You must have thought I was blabbering. Please believe me when I say it's the first time this has ever happened to me, I never talk to people like that.'

'Don't worry, you told us all kinds of interesting things, but that's why we were upset when you didn't phone, we wanted to hear the sequel, like in those serial stories. So then, how are you, Mario, how are things?'

I answered that I was well and hoped she was too. For her part she said, 'Right at the moment I'm well because I'm happy to be speaking to you. So, let's get to the next part of the serial: did you find your father?'

Her voice, through the earpiece of the receiver, was not ironic but cheerful and affectionate. I said, 'You're making fun of me.'

'Not at all. Someone who goes and tells you on the plane that he's on the way to find his father can hardly fail to stir up some interest! Like Telemachus! Like the orphans in nineteenth-century novels! So, did you find him?'

'Yes.'

'And is he as you imagined?'

I hesitated, then realized that, as in the plane, this woman I'd seen only once and didn't know, really did inspire me with an irresistible sense of trust and confidence. 'Not exactly,' I said.

'I bet you thought he'd be handsome, aristocratic, charming, one of those grizzle-haired virile Italian men who look better at fifty than they did at twenty. Right?'

'No, I didn't have any image of him at all, to be honest. But I was disappointed just the same.'

'Why, is he very ugly?'

Overcome by some strange mimetic need to outdo her in cheerfulness, I replied gaily, 'Can you believe he's got flat feet!'

'Flat feet, how awful!'

Hearing her laughing I laid it on thicker, 'Yes, flat feet like Charlie Chaplin, an actor I detest, one pointing this way, the other that. Then he's small, but with shoulders like a porter and a coarse face that makes you think of those servants in Molière, Sganarelle, Mascarille and Covielle, who take the place of their masters and end up getting a good beating.'

I was showing off my schoolboy knowledge of French literature and she, with a laugh and a comment – 'You really know your classics' – showed that, like the good ex-teacher she was, she appreciated my allusions. I went on, 'He always dresses like some old ship's captain, blue jacket with gold buttons and grey flannel trousers. The only thing missing is a cap with a golden anchor on the peak!'

'Oh, aren't we wicked! But at least he's a good father, is he?'

'Yes, he is. He wants to get the family back together again. For starters he's even giving me a salary!'

With a sudden change of tone she asked, 'Where are you phoning from?'

'From home – I mean, from my father's place.'

'Don't you think it would be better if you didn't talk about him like this when you're in his house? It's hardly proper, don't you think?'

I felt myself going red again and thought: The hell with what's proper. I protested: 'It was you who made me talk about him.'

'It doesn't matter. Why don't we get together rather than talk on the phone?'

'Where?' I said sulkily.

I expected she'd invite me to lunch: after all, she had shown me a friendliness that was as exceptional as it was inexplicable; instead she answered after a moment's thought: 'Do you know a place called Villa Balestra?'

Now, as chance would have it, I might not yet have seen St Peter's and the Colosseum, but I did know Villa Balestra. It was a public park situated in the same part of town as the Parioli, where most of the houses my father sent me to show his clients were. I went to the park every now and then to sit on a bench and read a book or a French newspaper which I picked up in a stationer's in the same neighbourhood. I answered enthusiastically, 'Yes, I know it well, there's even a bar.'

'So, let's meet there, but not at the bar, it's always crowded. I'll wait for you on a bench tomorrow at four. Okay? See you tomorrow then.'

FOUR

The Pleated Skirt

So the following day I set off for Villa Balestra in the Parioli district. Being impatient I arrived early. For a while I tried to pass the time walking from one street to the next along railings overflowing with dusty old ivies. I even stopped in front of the local cinema, another regular haunt of mine, to look at the stills of the day's film. Finally, having picked up some French newspapers, I hung around looking at books in the stationer's. I was happy to be early and to mooch about. I had that exquisite sense of anticipated, deferred happiness one gets when one knows an adventure will be a success.

In the end I saw I was almost late for our meeting and hurried back to Villa Balestra. As I went in through the gate the large rectangular lawn which makes up the park seemed deserted. It was early and hot, people wouldn't be around until after sunset.

I looked up at the sky: the round shapes of the foliage topping the very tall, slender pines stark against the immense drift of sirocco-blown cirrus, were not waving and shifting in the wind as on other days; instead they seemed dull and immobile; the dark, straight cypresses stood still as sentinels at the four corners of the park. Beyond the parapet, the roofs and terraces of Rome stretched away, lightless and veiled in haze, as far as the tiny, distant dome of St Peter's.

Then I saw Jeanne, a female figure sitting all alone with a book in her hand on a bench beside the park wall. I recognized her generously cut, pleated skirt; she'd worn a similar skirt on the plane, and I remembered having made the realistic reflection that the large number of pleats doubtless served to cover up her unusually broad hips. But as I walked toward her, slowly and casually, it occurred to me that this was precisely why she intrigued me. The contrast between the masculine leanness of her face and the heavy femininity of her body attracted me; somehow it seemed to have a special significance that in some obscure way had to do with me. Then suddenly I understood and told myself, 'Yes, forget your wild promiscuous mother with her parallel life full of men! This is the kind of woman you should be thinking of, you should be loving, with her wise face and maternal body!'

These reflections reminded me of that mysterious impulse to confide that Jeanne had inspired on the plane. Seeing her some distance away on her bench I felt the same urge again and my spirit lifted with a surge of happiness. I would talk about myself without holding back. She would listen with interest. With that feeling of grateful joy one has when, in pleasing yourself you imagine you are pleasing someone else too, I went up to her and said in a rush, my voice trembling, 'Good afternoon, it's Mario, sorry, have you been waiting long?'

She looked up. 'Ten minutes, but it doesn't matter. Sit down here now and tell me everything.'

I sat down. 'Everything about what?'

'About yourself.'

'You already know everything. I'm such a blabbermouth.'

'Don't be so modest. Then if you're a blabbermouth, I'm curious, so we're quits, we can get on together.'

'Are you really interested in me?'

'As well as being a blabbermouth you're also vain! Of course I am, otherwise we wouldn't be sitting here together on this bench.'

With my usual involuntary elation, I proposed, 'Why don't we use the *tu* form?'

'Why should we? We're hardly old schoolfriends, are we?'

I felt myself going red and said humbly, 'If you don't want to, then please go on calling me *Lei*.'

'Now look at him blushing like a young lady! You think too much of yourself, really!'

But saying that, she had in fact switched to the *tu* form, and the casual, affectionate way she did this cheered me up. I couldn't help saying, 'The truth is that with you I feel this irresistible need to confess. I don't know why, I can't control it.'

I was sincere, yet at the same time I wasn't, partly because I sensed that, curiously, this sincerity of mine didn't take me an inch closer to Jeanne. She must have felt the same, because I sensed something forced in her approval. 'You see, and I for my part feel a great need to find out more about you.'

I said, 'I was born in Rome, if that's what you want to know. I'm twenty, my father is a businessman, rich, he has an estate agency, but that's not his only income, he also has the rent from the apartments he owns, here in Parioli . . . '

She stared at me with an expression between the indulgent and the ironic. It was embarrassing. I went on, 'I lived in Rome till I was five. Then my father and mother separated. My mother took me to Paris to live in her brother's house. She was twenty-seven when they separated and she died two years later.'

'What did she die of?'

'Peritonitis.'

'And what did you do?'

'What did they do with me, you mean? I was seven, my uncle made me stay on in his house.'

'Didn't your uncle have his own children?'

'Yes, two, a boy and a girl.'

'What does your uncle do?'

'He imports Italian wines.'

We looked at each other, embarrassed. Then she shrugged

her shoulders impatiently. 'Who cares about all this! I asked you to talk about yourself. Who cares if your father has apartments and your uncle imports Italian wines?'

'You asked me to tell you everything about myself. I'm telling you everything.'

'So Italian wine imports and apartments in Parioli are everything then?'

'Tell me what you want to know.'

'The really important things. For example, you say you are a poet but you've never written any poems. What does that mean?'

'Well, what's so strange about it? I think I'm a poet, it's a fairly common conviction and hardly original.'

'But I think it's original.' After that moment of impatience she had become affectionate again. 'And it's one of the reasons I'm interested in you. How can you believe you're a poet without ever having written a single poem? At least tell me what kind of poet you might be!'

'A poet who hasn't written any poetry, of course.'

'But wasn't your idea that someone else had already written your poems. Isn't that bizarre?'

I was happy now she was talking about poetry, even though I sensed that for both of us poetry was merely a cover for something else. 'I haven't written any poems, because Apollinaire has already written all my poetry.'

'And why not Mallarmé, or Rimbaud, or Baudelaire?'

Feeling entirely at ease with this exclusively literary, or rather high-school, sort of questioning, I answered confidently. 'Because Mallarmé is too abstract and refined, Rimbaud too egocentric and disgusted, Baudelaire too moralistic and desperate. I've got nothing in common with those three poets.'

'Yet they are all greater than Apollinaire.'

'I know, you're right, Apollinaire's not as good as the others, he's sentimental, sensual, superficial, it's bric-à-brac. Someone called him *le brocanteur*. But he's very like me, or rather, I'm very like him. For example, he didn't know his father either, and like me he had the fault of being too open to experience.'

'Yes, of course, openness, you talked about it on the plane. But why shouldn't you be open? Isn't it nice to be open?'

Without thinking I answered, 'Because my openness makes me do really stupid things, like baring my heart on a plane to somebody I've never met before.'

'Thanks.'

I blushed, then corrected myself. 'In any event, it makes me do things I wish I hadn't. For instance, what I said about my trip to Rome wasn't really the truth. In the end I didn't come to Rome to see my father, but out of a sheer spirit of openness. Having or not having a father means nothing to me.'

'Do you regret having come to Rome?'

'I regret having come when there was no need to come. The last thing I needed was a father.'

She looked at me, smiling and indulgent. 'So what's this father of yours like then?'

'I was trying to describe him on the phone yesterday, but you told me it wasn't right, criticizing him in his own house.'

'Okay, but now we're here you can. Come on, what kind of man is he?'

'He's an actor.'

'An actor? A couple of minutes ago you said he was a businessman!'

'Sorry, I mean he's an actor by nature, not by profession.'

'I see. And does he act well, at least?'

'He acts the part of the father. And no, he doesn't act well. He almost always hams. Sometimes he seems sincere, but that's even worse.'

'Why is it worse?'

'Because with a completely false ham you can enjoy

the show, but a sincere ham makes you feel embarrassed.'

'What's sincere about your father's hamming?'

I thought about this seriously before answering. I realized that, as if by instinct, Jeanne's questions were prodding at what I considered the secret of my life. Because of course if I had spoken about the sincere side to my father's hamming I could hardly have helped talking about my mother; and I immediately realized that however strong it had been at the beginning, my impulse to confide didn't go this far, it was like a ship whose keel, in the depths of the sea, unexpectedly strikes a mysterious and insurmountable obstacle. I said rather vaguely, 'My father is sincere when he talks about the family. He's very nostalgic and he'd like to set up another family.'

'Who with?'

'Me, to start with.'

'And the woman who's supposed to take the place of your mother?'

'He hasn't told me. I know he's got a girlfriend, he sees her every evening. Perhaps it's her. In any event, when he talks about the family he's sincere, but at the same time he hams even more than usual. That's what bothers me.'

'But would you like to live in a family with your father and this woman?'

I pretended to hesitate, whereas in fact I was thinking of something else. For now, perhaps in order to evade her not disinterested questioning, I was asking myself if I fancied Jeanne and looking at her for the first time with the eye of the seducer. True, I did realize that once again I was giving way to the temptation to be entirely open to experience; but I justified myself by reflecting that any man in my position – confronted, that is with such determined friendliness – would behave likewise.

So, Jeanne; she was sitting up straight, erect even, her short jacket, made from the same coarse linen as her skirt, open at the front, thus letting me see her white blouse and, faintly pinkish inside it, her magnificent, youthful breasts, so surprising in a woman nearer forty than thirty. My gaze slid down below her waist to her hips whose outline could just be seen beneath the pleats of her skirt. And it was then that I noticed something odd. For a moment I thought I'd made a mistake and I looked more carefully. But no, no mistake; at the same time as she'd been asking me questions with that teacherly severity of hers, she'd also quite surreptitiously been managing to move up closer to me, and now, under all the accordion pleats of her skirt, her knee was almost imperceptibly sneaking towards mine. In fact it was the pleats that gave her away, since as her leg inched towards me they gradually opened up. I raised my eyes: Jeanne's face betrayed embarrassment, her eyes were questioning, imploring. As if waiting for an answer to an unspoken question.

But the answer I needed to find was the answer to my own question, not hers. Did I like Jeanne? I immediately thought that, perhaps, off the cuff, I didn't actually in principle dislike her; but then I certainly didn't feel any particular desire for her either. That intense feeling of hope which had so moved me a short while ago now revealed itself for what it was: the deceptive product of my loneliness. But somehow or other I would have to answer her question. I said with sincerity, 'No, I wouldn't like to. I can't see myself living together as a family with my father and his girlfriend.'

My words must have seemed encouraging, for no sooner had I spoken than her knee made a definite, though minimal move in my direction, promptly confirmed by a minimal opening of the pleats in her skirt. 'If that's how you feel, why stay with your father?'

I shrugged my shoulders. 'I don't know, I haven't met his girlfriend yet, I'll wait and see.'

'Wait and see what?'

'What happens. I think for the moment I'll hang on in Rome and work in my father's agency. Then I'll see.'

There was nothing minimal about the movement of her

leg this time, it was brutal, almost a shove. She cried vehemently, 'What do you mean, you'll see? You want to stay in the same house as someone who, okay, may be your father, but who you consider a ham, a buffoon? What kind of man are you?'

Wanting to escape from the strong, insistent pressure of her knee, I tried to change position on the bench. But obviously I didn't know how to go about it, since all of a sudden I found my whole thigh squashed against hers. With an urgency doubtless intended to hide her own confusion, she exclaimed, 'Didn't you hear what I said? What are you thinking about?'

'About you.'

She asked hopefully, 'Why about me?'

I corrected myself. 'I meant I was thinking about what you just said. Yes, for the moment I really do think I'll stay with my father. It's an experience like any other. I'll do it, then when the interest wears off, I'll decide.'

'An experience like any other! An experience, having yourself kept by a complete stranger! This is your eternal openness again, isn't it, telling you to do this?'

I sighed. 'Maybe you're right, but there's no need to remind me.'

'Don't you realize that anyone else in your position would pack his bags and get out?'

'Yes, I realize that.'

'So?'

This time I made a big effort and, with no attempt to hide it, shifted along the bench to get my thigh away from hers. I said firmly, 'I'm not anyone else.'

'What do you mean?'

'I mean that although I may have problems, the question of whether I stay with my father or not is not one of them.'

I saw her glance down at the bench, as if to measure the distance I'd put between us. Then she said boldly, 'So what is your problem?'

I supposed that we were talking about the same thing: that is whether or not I was going to accept the invitation she was sending me via knee and thigh. I said to myself: Why not accept in the end? and so I answered, 'My problem is my openness.'

'That again! Why don't you let yourself go a bit more!'

'That's exactly what I don't want to do.'

'Why not?'

'Outside circumstances are continually putting me under obligations to do things I don't feel like doing, when what I would like to do is obey my inner impulses, if you see what I mean.'

'Give me an example.'

Her pedantry exasperated me, this teacher-with-a-difficult-pupil manner she had. I said brutally, 'For example, if you were to make it clear that you fancied me, I would immediately feel open, available, even if I didn't really care about you at all.'

Her immediate reaction was confusion, then she hardened. 'But I don't want you to think anything of the kind.'

What I would have liked to say now was: So why were you giving my knee such a hard time just a few minutes ago?, but I held back and said, somewhat exasperated, 'So let's imagine that your daughter was being very friendly. Well, I'd immediately feel drawn to make love to her, just like that, without feeling anything, simply to be open to experience.'

She exclaimed with a laugh, 'But she's a little girl, she's barely thirteen. What are you thinking of, or do little girls turn you on?'

I answered fearlessly, 'Little girls? And why not?'

'I don't think that your making love to myself or Alda would be such a big demonstration of openness. All men are more or less open in that sense.'

She fell silent for a moment, then added carelessly and with an unexpected change of tone, 'I hadn't actually thought about that; in the end I've got nothing against it. Okay, so start being open with me.'

I thought I must be hearing things. But no, no mistake, the pathetic, uncertain, imprudent expression which now replaced her normal look of wise rationality confirmed it. I looked away. 'You deserve better.'

'I don't deserve anything.'

'And then,' I lied, 'the fact is there's another woman in my life.'

'You didn't tell me.'

'You didn't ask.'

'No doubt another woman attracted by your openness, am I right?'

I had lied without thinking of anything in particular. Then I remembered my attempt to repeat with Oringia what Terenzi had done with my mother, and I understood: what I'd thought was a lie was actually the truth. It was my mother, or rather the memory of my mother, that prevented me from desiring Jeanne. And suddenly I felt afraid of this obsession which was insinuating itself into my relationship with a woman who I might otherwise have desired. I said hurriedly, with the impression that this time I wasn't lying, 'Yes, but it's something that can't last, it'll have to end soon.'

I saw her lower her eyes, humiliated. 'So to have a place in your life I'll have to wait for this mysterious woman to bow out?'

'In a certain sense, yes.'

'But is she in Rome, or Paris?'

'Paris.'

'And are you very attached to her?'

'Unfortunately I am.'

'Which leaves us no other alternative than to improve our friendship. Let's be friends, are you happy now?'

It was my turn to feel frustrated. Having refused her, I was suddenly afraid of losing Jeanne. 'Why, are you disappointed with me?'

'No, on the contrary. But there's the other woman, the one in Paris.'

I experienced a feeling of horror almost: something which so far had only existed in my imagination was now imposing itself as reality in actual life. I remembered our excitement, Jeanne's and my own, a short while ago when I arrived, and I had no doubt at all that what had killed off the desire that should have gone hand-in-hand with our mutual attraction was none other than the cruel and enigmatic vision that had come to me on being shown round my father's apartment. I protested sincerely enough, 'But I told you, that relationship is almost over!'

This time she didn't speak, just gazed at me as if from far away, gently shaking her head. At which I made a move, as surprising to me as to her: I bent down to the side, put my head on her knees and repeated in confusion, 'Honestly, I swear, it's almost over.'

She didn't say anything, but she didn't push me away either. I felt her hand lightly touching my hair. How long did I stay in that position? Perhaps only a few seconds, though it seemed an age. Then a female voice, at once rude and childishly mocking, made me start. 'Good afternoon, Mr Mario De Sio. Sorry to disturb you, but it would hardly be polite not to say hello.'

FIVE

La Vie lente et l'espérance violente

I got up quickly, confused and dazzled. Standing very erect in front of us, Jeanne's daughter, Alda, was watching with malicious impatience. Her long thin legs and short narrow bust made her look more than ever like a newborn foal which hasn't yet learnt to walk but is trying all the same. 'You know I've been standing here a good hour and you were so busy with each other you didn't notice?'

Jeanne was unruffled; she must have been used to her daughter's crudeness. 'What are you talking about?'

'Him with his head on your knees and you stroking his hair. You think I didn't see? The whole of Villa Balestra saw.'

Her tone was odd, somewhere between satisfaction, albeit ironic, and, strange though it may seem, jealousy. Jeanne asked carelessly, 'But where did you get to?'

'I went right to the bottom of the park, the other side of the bar, and for at least an hour, one whole hour, I've been playing with the dog. All so that you two could be alone. Go on, go fetch.' These last words were addressed to a small white woolly dog quivering with excitement by her feet, its head lifted towards her, a stone in its mouth. She grabbed the stone from its teeth and threw it; the dog ran off, rolling over once or twice as it ran. She finished, sarcastically, 'Congratulations! You were really cute!'

Jeanne looked at her vaguely, as if thinking of something

else. Then she got up from the bench. 'I'm off. Mario, if you want to see us you can find us here at Villa Balestra at more or less the same time every day. We live in that house over there.' She turned and pointed to the upper floors of a white apartment block which rose above the wall around the park. 'Villa Balestra is our garden, in a way. See you soon, then. What are you doing, Alda? Coming with me?'

'No, I'll stay here. But take the dog with you. I'll have to go to Emilia's for my lesson soon.'

Jeanne called the dog and set off toward the park gates. I glanced at her as she walked away, perhaps to confirm that impression of maternity I somehow got from the combination of thin face with broad thighs and generous breasts. Alda, who had now sat down on the bench, followed my eyes and asked, sardonic as ever and addressing me in the familiar *tu* form, 'You fancy Jeanne, don't you?'

I was taken aback; I hadn't expected her to say anything like that. 'Why do you ask?'

'Why did you turn to look at her?'

So we were already up to our eyes in a quarrel, intimate to the point of embarrassment! When so far we had exchanged no more than a few words over the phone! I tried to change the subject and could think of nothing better to talk about than her eyes. I'd already noticed them on the plane, the way they conveyed an expression at once languid and hungry, and now this expression struck me again in a way I couldn't understand. I said brusquely, 'Talking about looking, why do you have that look in your eyes?'

'What look?'

I tried to decide exactly what impression it was that Alda's eyes had on me. And suddenly I realized: that same impression of *déjà vu*, of already having experienced something, suffered something, that I'd had when I first saw my father's apartment. But again I found myself unable to cross the dark threshold of memory. Faking the meticulousness of the optician, I leant forward to examine her eyes and pronounced with playful pedantry, 'Drooping eyelid cuts pupil in half giving impression of drowsiness, typical in subject unable to stay awake. At the same time, expression of eyes could be one of desire rather than lassitude. Thus we might reasonably say that eyes have expression somewhere between torpor and desire.'

'Desire for what?'

'How do I know? Everything, most likely.'

'Everything, eh? Come on, tell me straight? Are they pretty or not?'

'Being pretty is not what's important.'

'So what is important?'

'I don't know.'

'But I want to know: do you think they're pretty?'

'Yes.'

'And what about my face?'

'You've got a face like a doll.'

'So, finally, I've got eyes like a doll. By which you mean dumb, I suppose. Thanks a lot. But I don't come into this and it's no good your pretending you're interested in me when it's obvious that the person you're really interested in is Jeanne.'

'Why do you call her Jeanne and not Mother? Aren't you her daughter?'

'I've always called her Jeanne. Perhaps because we're so different. And you still haven't answered my question: do you fancy Jeanne?'

I couldn't help wondering, what kind of answer did Alda want to hear? That I did fancy Jeanne or that I didn't? Then it occurred to me that in any event the best thing to do was to say yes, and with a reasonable amount of sincerity I said, 'It would be strange if I didn't like her. She's attractive and she's very friendly to me.'

She gave me a sidelong, ambiguous look. 'Watch out.'

'Watch out for what?'

'If I were you I wouldn't expect too much. She always does this. First she flirts, then she plays hard to get, and that's the end of it.'

'The end of what?'

'It. I mean the end of what she spends all day and night thinking about.'

'Which is?'

'This.'

'What are you talking about?'

'I told you: this.'

She threw me another one of her sidelong glances, half drowsy, half hungry, then lowered her eyes. I followed her gaze and saw she had her hands together on her lap: she'd made a ring with the thumb and index finger of her left hand while the index finger of her right hand pushed in and out. Obviously it was an allusion to sexual penetration, yet made without the vulgarity that usually inspires and accompanies such gestures, as if, not knowing the right words, she had been obliged to resort to this. She added, 'But don't worry, maybe it's real this time. If you knew how much she talks about you, how disappointed she was when you didn't phone! You take it easy, I'll help you. You can count on me.'

Now of all the new experiences that my openness had prompted me to take on board, this business of the young daughter acting as pimp for her mother was one of the few which, if it didn't actually stop me, did at least amaze me. In fact I was so amazed that I thought I'd misunderstood. 'You say you'll help me: but to do what?'

She looked meaningfully down at her hands again, still linked in the same gesture, then said impatiently, 'Oh come on, you know better than I do.' She fell silent for a moment, then resumed in a tone of complicity, 'Jeanne likes having a few drinks, champagne particularly. One day soon she'll invite you over to lunch, you'll see. So you bring along a bottle of champagne.

Between the two of us we get her tipsy and then she'll make love.'

All at once I felt I couldn't believe what I was hearing. I looked in her eyes and caught a glint of complete innocence. 'You do know what making love means?'

She looked down at her hands and retorted with annoyance, 'It means doing this, doesn't it?'

'And what is "this"?'

'It means making love. And don't ask me so many questions.'

'Who taught you to do that?'

'A girl at school.'

'But how old are you?'

'I'll be fourteen in five months time.'

'So you're thirteen.'

'And a half.'

'And how old is this friend of yours?'

'Fourteen, but she does it, she makes love.'

'Who with?'

'With a boy. They've been doing it for a year already.'

'And you?'

'And what about me?'

'Do you make love?'

'I'm not interested, and then I'm too young.'

'But has your friend at least explained to you what making love means?'

'Oh come on, no, she hasn't explained anything, and I haven't asked her. As it happens, I don't care.'

'But you do care whether I do it with Jeanne or not, right? Why?

'Because.'

'What do you mean, "because"? Don't be so childish.'

'But I *am* a child, aren't I?'

'Look, who do you take me for? You want me to make love with Jeanne, but you don't know what making love means. A bit much, isn't it?'

'A bit much of what?'

'It's as if you told me to jump out of the window, but when I ask you why, you tell me, "Because."'

'Jump out of the window! Is that what making love means for you?'

'In this case, yes.'

'You should do it because you fancy Jeanne, that's all.'

'But who said I fancied her?'

She rounded on me with enigmatic boldness. 'So why were you feeling her up with your knee before?'

So, she'd even noticed the almost imperceptible movement of Jeanne's leg under the pleats of her skirt. I couldn't help exclaiming with childish indignation, 'It was she who felt *me* up.'

'You or her, what's it matter! The important thing is you felt each other up. Feelies!'

This epithet invented on the spur of the moment struck me as unpleasant. Just as the verb 'to feel up', at once crude and innocent, smacked of classrooms and schoolgirl chatter. 'Okay, so we felt each other. So what? What's it matter to you?'

As though at some incredible ingenuousness on my part, she said, amazed, 'Oh, that's nice, because it matters to Jeanne to have a husband and me to have a father.'

'But what are you on about? A father? Me, your father, with only six years between us!'

'Seven.'

'Okay, seven then. What kind of father would I be?'

'Okay come on, what's a husband? A man who lives with a woman, right? And if this woman has a daughter, as is the case with Jeanne, then the man's not just a husband to the woman, but a father to the daughter as well. I mean, you have a family: father, mother, daughter.'

'A family, eh?'

'Right, a family.'

'But why are you so eager to have a family?'

'Because I haven't got one.'

At which I was reminded of my father: he too wanted a family because he didn't have one. Alda added after a moment's thought, 'I really can't handle living with Jeanne any more.'

'Why not?'

Again she thought about it carefully. 'If Jeanne had a husband, I wouldn't have to stay up at night, till dawn sometimes, talking to her. I have to go to school early in the morning and I'm always half asleep and the result is I can't do my work properly and the nuns shout at me.'

'Till dawn! Talking about what?'

'About love.'

'Love between whom? The way I understood it, Jeanne hasn't got a boyfriend.'

'Right, she hasn't, and that's precisely why she talks about love. If there was a man in the house, you or somebody else, she could get it off her chest with him and leave me in peace to get some sleep.'

'That's all it amounts to? You'd like a father so as to be able to get some sleep?'

'Isn't that reason enough?'

'It's one reason, but hardly reason enough.'

'For me it's enough.'

'But what does Jeanne want?'

'Only she knows that. I suspect: to make love and not to make it, to have a man, and not to have one.' Suddenly she jumped up from the bench. 'What about taking a walk round the villa?'

She set off towards the bottom of the park, walking ahead of me. I was left a little way behind because I had to go back to get my French papers which I'd forgotten on the bench, and then, as with Jeanne a short while ago, I wanted to take a look at her. She was tall, taller than me perhaps, with long, perfect legs, though they didn't have the classic female shape as yet; they were thin and seemed to go right up to her waist and at every step she took they gave the impression of moving of their own accord, gangling and uncertain. Clinging to her thighs and extremely tight, hanging a good hand's breadth above her ankles, her jeans accentuated her wobbly gait. It was almost as if her body could barely support the weight of her thick hair, brushed out fan-like above her shoulders. She realized I was looking at her and half turning said, 'Why are you looking at me?'

How different from her still adolescent body were those dark, drowsy, hungry eyes! 'I'm looking at you because you're in front of me.'

'No you're not. You're looking at me the way you looked at Jeanne before.'

But what's come over me now? Hardly stopping to think I tell her, 'True, but with this difference: I don't fancy Jeanne, but I do fancy you.'

'Why me and not Jeanne?'

By now I was already headed blindly into the unknown. 'Because I don't feel anything for her. Whereas I do feel something for you.'

She'd picked up a stalk of grass and was chewing it with a reflex movement of the lips whose sulky sensuality I now noticed for the first time. 'What do you mean you don't feel anything for Jeanne?'

'I mean she doesn't rouse anything in me.'

'You're saying you couldn't love her?'

'No, I mean I don't get any physical feeling. I don't desire her.'

'What difference is there between loving someone and desiring them?'

For a moment I thought this was a trick question. But a quick glance at her rather worried face was enough to tell me that all she had in mind was that unusual, impudent complicity with the mother. 'There's an enormous difference, a man feels it immediately.'

'Oh yes, feels what?'

Again, what's come over me? Out of nowhere a sudden excitement has my cheeks flushed and hot. 'He feels he'd like to make love.'

She said pedantically, 'Does that mean you'd like to make love with me?'

I finally realized where that sense of excitement had come from. It was the look Alda had given me a few moments ago when she turned and asked me why I was watching her. Not just because the eyes, in contrast to her young body, were those of an adult, but because, once again, I had the impression of having seen the same expression in another woman's eyes. But whose? I was aware of hesitating at the dark door of memory. I made an effort to go through it and suddenly felt I'd succeeded. Yes, of course, now I knew, no doubt about it: it was the same hungry, torpid expression my mother's eyes had had so many years ago when she took them from the object of her desire, her lover's sex, and lifted them to look at me. It took no more than a split second: I registered the similarity between these two women's eyes and then wrote it off as mere coincidence. Not at all surprised by what in the end amounted to a declaration of love, Alda insisted, 'You wouldn't like to make love with Jeanne, but you would with me. How do you know, though?'

'A man always knows when he desires a woman.' I hesitated, then concluded, 'It's something you can feel.' And I couldn't help adding a second conclusion to the first. 'And see too.'

'See in their eyes?'

'Not just in their eyes.'

She was quiet a moment, then asked carelessly, 'Really! Where can you see it? Now for example, where should I look for it?'

I didn't answer; she announced, disappointed and suggestive, 'If you don't want to say, you don't have to. But I can't see anything.'

'Of course you can't. You'd see if I was naked.'

'But why can't I see when you've got your clothes on?'

'Because I've made sure to hide it.'

'How?'

Exasperated, I decided to combine a didactic tone with maximum crudity. 'Because I've put my hand in my pocket, grabbed hold of it and pointed it upward.' Alda took in this information with no sign of excitement. Talking, as I had, about my penis without actually naming it, she asked, 'What if it wasn't pointing up, would I be able to see it?'

'Of course.'

'A lot?'

'It depends on the person. With some men a lot, with some less so.'

'So let go of it and let's walk along beside the parapet. I don't believe you want to make love to me. Now we'll see if it's true.'

I said nothing: I was struck by the difference between my arousal and her near-scientific objectivity. I took my hand out of my pocket and started walking along beside her, trying not to look at the bulge my penis was making in my pants. Fortunately the park was still deserted. From where we were all the way to where the grass ended, no one was to be seen, just empty benches, pines and cypresses. Alda skipped a little way in front to get a better view. Finally, impressed, she said, 'You're right, you can see it. But what's it like?'

'It's . . . hard.'

'Hard?'

'Yes.'

'Does it hurt?'

'No, but I'm embarrassed.'

'How long does it last?'

'As long as the desire. Once the desire's satisfied it goes back to normal and you can't see it any more.'

Carefully, looking around and stretching out her arm, she lightly brushed the bulge with the tips of her fingers. 'It's so amazing.'

'How?'

'I don't know, it seems strange.'

'In what way?'

'First you couldn't see it, then you could. And you didn't do anything to make it go hard.'

'That's enough for now, I'll put it back up.'

'No, wait. You said it didn't turn hard with Jeanne?'

'No.'

'So you don't desire her.'

'It seems not.'

'Whereas you do desire me.'

'It seems so.'

We had now reached the far end of the parapet. I felt ridiculous with the bulge in my pants. Partly because Alda, frowning and thoughtful, now seemed to be thinking of something else. And in fact she turned to face me and said brusquely, 'Forget all of this.'

I was amazed. 'What am I supposed to forget? Nothing has happened!'

'All I ask is one thing.'

'What though? What do you want?'

'Don't be so angry.' She suddenly threw her arms round my neck, so tightly I thought I was going to suffocate. Fighting her off, I said, 'What's got into you? Leave off!'

'No, I won't let go until you promise me one thing.'

'What?'

'That you'll make love to Jeanne.'

'But I told you, I don't feel anything for her.'

She stood still a moment, as if thinking, though without loosening her grip. 'But you do feel something for me, don't you?'

'Yes.'

'Okay then, if you won't do it for her, do it for me. Make love to Jeanne. And I'll love you the way a daughter loves a father; and we'll all three of us be happy, you, me and Jeanne.'

'Let go. Okay, I'll do it, but let go!'

'You swear?'

'Yes, I swear, now let me go.'

She let go and rushed off, running in an odd, clumsy way, skipping a couple of paces, then running normally for a stretch. I walked slowly across the big lawn and went out through the gate, but when I reached Via Ammannati and the white building that Jeanne had pointed to as the place where they lived, I stopped and looked up at the façade for a moment. I thought of Alda's longing, so similar to my father's, for the family she didn't have and would like to have. What kind of family would it be, I asked myself, with mother and daughter operating as unconscious rivals? Still, even as I asked that doubting, ironic question, I realized that the idea of domestic happiness was something that tempted me too. Yes, a family, even if contradictory and divided, was preferable to being on one's own. At which, quite suddenly, out of nowhere, I was struck by an unexpected wave of emotion. I looked at the façade of the house, thinking that perhaps, up there, behind those windows, already predestined and decided, lay my future. I said to myself: Life, life, you haven't betrayed me after all, but almost immediately I felt ashamed of these emotive, emphatic words. I remembered Apollinaire: how he had said the same thing so much better, toning down the sentimentality of the line with a perhaps ironic assonance: '*Comme la vie est lente/Et comme l'espérance est violente.*' Yes, my life was slow, too slow for my impatience to be living; and my hope was violent, too violent for my capacity to wait. Oh, but in the end, what a lot of fuss over two women, even if they were mother and daughter, and accomplices, and rivals into the bargain!

SIX

The Resemblance

After that first meeting at Villa Balestra, my relationship with Jeanne and Alda rather unexpectedly took on a relaxed atmosphere, without any particular intimacy, as though between holidaymakers who find themselves staying in the same seaside resort and, without actually arranging anything, meet every day in the same café and exchange the same banal chat.

I'd go to Villa Balestra with the French papers, or maybe with a book, in the early afternoon when the day was still hot and the park deserted. I'd sit on my own at the bar or on a bench, reading or looking around without a thought in my head at the pines, the cypresses, the clouds, the sky; finally Jeanne and Alda would turn up, or at least one of them would. We'd talk or, as I said before, chat, happy and relaxed; and so, as if by magic, it would be evening. I enjoyed the bland, rather dull pleasure one gets from friendly conversation free from any sentimental overtones. Jeanne still didn't attract me physically, while Alda and I never went beyond the limits of a playful ambiguity. At most Alda might try to be faithful to her extravagant promise to help me seduce her mother and would find ways of leaving us alone as often as possible, giving all kinds of excuses for having to be elsewhere. Finally she would come back and then, as soon as there was a chance of speaking to me without Jeanne hearing, she'd ask, 'So, what did you get up to? Did you feel her up?' It wasn't very clear what she meant exactly by the expression, though what she was after obviously was irrefutable proof of the fact that Jeanne, as she had once put it, 'thought of nothing else'. I would shrug my shoulders and answer that I'd neither 'felt her up' nor been 'felt up' by her. Clearly she was disappointed, but didn't press the point. She'd change the subject or run off somewhere. In fact my feelings for Jeanne lay somewhere between the affectionate and the respectful – were almost those of a son for a mother, really; and I considered this sort of seduction conspiracy that Alda had proposed as nothing more nor less than a childish game of no consequence.

Sometimes I'd find myself thinking that this was the sort of family life my father talked about with so much nostalgia and which Alda aspired to with so much determination: being together, never saying anything important, communicating almost the way animals do, through glances, postures, tones of voice. Of course, we were in a public park, in view of anybody taking a stroll in Villa Balestra. But I told myself that even within the four walls of a house, the relationship between us would hardly have been different. And then, it was nice to think that after a rash and hasty beginning my life in Rome was finally settling down.

But I was wrong. One afternoon, when Alda had as so often left us alone, Jeanne and I started talking once again about Apollinaire and my conviction that he had already written the poems that I would have liked to write myself. I don't know how the subject came up, but she was once again being affectionately critical of my identification with the poet of *Alcools*: 'You're just immature, that's why you think the way you do. It shows you're still a boy, an adolescent. One day you'll overcome this fixation and realize how different you are from Apollinaire, and then if you really are a poet, you'll write your own poems, which will be exclusively yours and no one else's.'

I liked listening to her, especially, I have to admit, when she was talking about me. I answered with the same old story: that I identified with Apollinaire not just because of what he said and how he said it, but also because he'd never known his father, and above all because of his openness to experience.

As if she'd been waiting a long time for just this opportunity, she answered promptly, 'You're not actually as open as you like to think. For example, you're faithful to this mysterious woman you claim to have in Paris.'

I don't know what came over me. Perhaps all those afternoons spent in casual chat, that pseudo-family-holiday life, had dulled my defensive reflexes. I exclaimed, 'It's not true that I'm faithful, and here's the proof.'

And before she could stop me, or I could hold myself back, I'd reached out a hand and put it on her breast.

I didn't try to kiss her, which would have been the most natural thing, partly because I could scarcely have done so without being seen by the people in the park, but mainly because it had been with my caressing her breast in the plane, albeit involuntarily, that our relationship had begun. I left my hand there quite still for a moment, the palm touching her breast, the fingers spread, then I closed my fingers on the thin material of her blouse to squeeze her bulging, elusive breast. And as I did so I looked into her eyes, as if searching there for something that would provoke the arousal I still couldn't manage to feel. She said nothing, but didn't push me off. She sat still and very erect, her eyes staring into mine, but I felt her breast throb as though in spite of herself under my fingers and saw her thin, curving lips part and remain half open, trembling as if from some powerful emotion.

Then she said in a languid voice, 'Enough,' and I immediately withdrew my hand. She added quickly, as though to pick up the conversation I'd interrupted, 'We were talking about Apollinaire. Quote me a line or two of his.'

'Something I like, or that you might like?'

'That I might like.'

'Okay: "Yes, I want to love you, but love you just a little / And my suffering is delicious."'

'And now something you like.'

'"You drink this alcohol fiery as your life – your life that you drink like an aquavit."'

Trying to recover our relaxed holiday-chat atmosphere, she said, 'They're lines made to measure for almost any adolescent. Anyway you quoted them before, on the plane. Don't you remember?'

'Well, here are some lines that aren't for adolescents: "Nothing is dead except that which doesn't yet exist. / Compared with the radiant past / Tomorrow is colourless, / Shapeless too set against what is perfect, / What contains at once the endeavour and its outcome."'

'Too philosophical!'

'Perhaps you'll prefer this: "Open this door where I knock weeping."'

'Too sentimental.'

'Which leaves me no alternative but to quote you these five lines: "I know people of every kind / Not suited to their destinies / Indecisive as dead leaves / Their eyes are half-extinguished fires / Their hearts move like their doors."'

'Nasty, eh? Like that is it? I'm supposed to be indecisive as dead leaves with eyes like half-extinguished fires, and, worst of all, my heart moves like my door. Is that it?'

'Yes, but it's a door where I've knocked weeping.'

'You're very quick and sharp.' She was quiet a moment looking at me. 'It's strange but one would think you really might have written Apollinaire's poems. While you were reciting those lines, your eyes shone in a strange way.'

'What do you mean, strange?'

'Normally they're sad. But while you were reciting those lines they weren't sad any more. They were alive, sparkling.' She fell silent a moment. 'Beautiful.'

I lowered my eyes, embarrassed; I was happy to be praised, but didn't know how to respond. I felt her hand touch my cheek in a light caress. 'In any event, if one day, as I hope, you come and have dinner with us, I'll be careful to make sure all the doors are shut.'

I don't know why but I answered rather boorishly, 'No need for you to feel you have to take precautions like that.'

'Why not?'

I suddenly realized now that my boorishness had, albeit unconsciously, been calculated: without realizing it I was acting along the lines of the seduction plot Alda had imposed on me. 'Because you've already taken them. We've been seeing each other every day for nearly a month and I still haven't set foot in your house.'

'You're right, but you could have made the point a little less brutally, couldn't you? Knocking on the door is fine, crying is fine, but don't start kicking it down.'

'Forgive me.'

'In any event, the door to my apartment, that door at least is open to you. Come and have dinner with us: today is Thursday, we might go to the sea for the weekend, come on Monday or Tuesday.'

'Let's say Wednesday,' I said, instinctively trying to postpone the day of the invitation.

'Why Wednesday?'

'My father,' I lied, 'is going to visit some friends and I have to go with him.'

'Okay, Wednesday then. Now give me a last line of Apollinaire, something to go with this invitation.'

So she was using the poetry as a game, just like the literature teacher she was; but it was a game I enjoyed precisely for its old-fashioned, provincial flavour. I thought a moment, then quoted: 'I walked along the Seine / An old book under my arm / The river is like my suffering / It flows and never stops / But when will the week be over?'

She exclaimed cheerfully, 'The Tiber isn't the Seine. Your suffering is just like the water in the Tiber, not much. And it's not a week till next Wednesday, only five days.'

At which point a voice I was all too familiar with, Alda's coarse, childish sing-song, exclaimed from behind us, 'Wednesday, what's happening on Wednesday?'

'On Wednesday,' Jeanne said calmly, 'Mario is coming to dinner.'

'Oh good, about time, you've made up your mind at last. But Mario, remember to be polite and bring something along with you, bring a bottle of champagne, it's the gift we like best.'

'That *you* like best,' Jeanne said curtly. 'One glass and she's drunk.'

'You can't imagine how important this invitation is, Mario,' Alda said, skipping around the bench. 'Our house is sacred in a way. When Jeanne invites someone she's like a priest letting you into a chapel that's usually forbidden to strangers.'

'Alda, don't talk rubbish!'

'But it's true, Jeanne, that's how it is. You're a priest and our house is a chapel.'

'Mario, I'll see you here tomorrow, in Villa Balestra, then on Wednesday in the evening. Alda, come along home with me, come on, you've got to help me.'

'To do what?'

'To put away our winter clothes so the moths don't get them.'

Instead of obeying, Alda came straight over to me and sat down next to me. 'You do it, I'm going to stay here with Mario.'

The two women looked at each other, Alda with an expression of challenge, Jeanne of puzzlement. 'Okay,' Jeanne finally said, though reluctantly, 'I'll do it on my own.' And without waiting for a reply she walked off.

I immediately asked Alda, 'Sorry, but why did you say to your mother that your house is sacred like a chapel and that she's the priest of the chapel, and so on? She looked pretty annoyed.'

'I know, no one likes hearing a real home truth.'

'But what is the truth?'

'What I said.'

'That is?'

'Our house is sacred and just like a chapel, or rather, one of the rooms is sacred.'

'Which room?'

'Their bedroom.'

'Whose?'

'Jeanne's and my father's.'

She gave me one of those sleepy, hungry looks which I now knew made her resemble my mother; and once again I was struck by this resemblance, and disturbed. 'What's so strange about that? It's only right that the room should be sacred for her. Your mother loved your father and remembers him with love.'

'Yes, but is it right for her not to sleep there and to preserve the place exactly as it was the day Father died, with her nightdress and his pyjamas all nicely laid out on the bed? To deck it out with flowers every two or three days? To spend hours and hours there doing heaven knows what, sitting on the edge of the bed?'

Genuinely amazed, I said, 'I didn't know anything about that. She must have loved him a great deal.'

'Whereas she says she hated him and still hates him.'

'How can she hate him, if she misses him so much?'

'God knows. Her story is she hated him because he was unfaithful to her.'

'Was he really unfaithful to her?'

'I don't know. All I know is that she says he was unfaithful with every last woman he came across.'

'But was he or wasn't he?'

I saw her shrug her shoulders with the expression of someone who's not entirely convinced, or in any event doesn't want to show they are. 'If you believe her, he was. But who knows what the real truth is? Either way, they used to make love, and it's that she can't forget, not his unfaithfulness. That's why she's transformed their bedroom into a kind of chapel, not because of his unfaithfulness. Hate you can forget in the end, but not love.'

'Perhaps she loved him and hated him at the same time?'

'What an idea! She loved him and that was that. The hate was nothing more than the need to be better loved herself. Father didn't love her enough, or rather, he didn't love her the way she wanted to be loved. That's all.' She was silent a moment, then went on, 'In any case, don't worry, her chapel has its days numbered. You're in her good books now. You think I didn't see you?'

'What did you see?'

'I saw you feeling her up. And her letting you.'

So she'd been spying on us, had seen us. But after the revelations about Jeanne's posthumous passion, I wasn't unhappy to find myself back in that atmosphere of childish, playful complicity that had surrounded our conspiracy from the beginning. It was almost with relief that I admitted, 'Yes, you're right, I felt her up. You've been telling me non-stop to do it and in the end I did it. Aren't you pleased?'

'She's the one who is really pleased. She invited you to dinner immediately, right? Unfortunately, I won't be able to sleep until next Wednesday because of your going and feeling her up.'

'What are you talking about?'

'I'm saying that until next Wednesday, Jeanne will do nothing but talk to me all night long.'

'She'll tell you I felt her up?'

'Never. But she'll talk round and round it for hours. I know my mother alright.' She was silent a moment, then went on, 'We must remember the bottle of champagne. We can go and get it together. She likes it dry, there's a particular brand.'

'And what do you think will happen?'

'This,' and she made her gesture for sexual penetration. 'Don't worry, I'll help you, even if I have to hold her down.'

I reflected that her innocent ignorance of all things sexual, which had so struck me at our first meeting, marched on undaunted, though it showed itself in this flaunting of an experienced cynicism she didn't really have. Embarrassed, I said, 'Enough, come on, don't talk like that. After all, she is your mother.'

'But if that's all she ever thinks about!'

A couple of days later, when I entered my father's office at the agency, I found him engrossed in an address-book. With his usual ham actor's exaggeration, he had his head hunched down and, as if to make it clear that he was doing something important, didn't look up as I came in. I stood, waiting. While I watched, my father made all the gestures of the person who, after a long search, finally finds the address he is after and writes it down on a separate piece of paper so as to be able to find it again. He ruled a line under the address, copied it onto a piece of notepaper, and only then raised his eyes to look at me. 'Ah, it's you at last, you've come! I've got something for you to do, look.'

He was silent for a moment, considering the note where he'd written the address, then said, 'A woman called Jodice – Esmeralda Jodice – she wants to buy or rent an apartment in the Parioli area. Now as it happens I've got an apartment myself in Via Ammannati which I was planning to sell or rent, sell rather than rent actually. It's a penthouse job, top floor. Go to Via Ammannati – it's number thirty-six, Signora Jodice will be at the front door at twelve – and show her the apartment. Here are the keys.'

Well, as it turned out I knew Via Ammannati very well since it was the same street that led to Villa Balestra, where as I said, I frequently went to take a walk and read the French papers. What's more, number 36 was in the very block where Jeanne and Alda lived. I started with surprise at this coincidence and exclaimed, 'I know that block already.'

My father's eyes widened, it was as though he were trying to hide surprise behind an exaggeration of surprise. 'How come?'

'Some people I know live there.'

'Oh, okay, good.'

'But how am I supposed to recognize Signora Jodice?'

'She says she'll have a rose in her hand.'

'But what's she like?'

'She's a good-looking woman, around fortyish, well-built, majestic even, statuesque, posture like a film star. She used to be a singer in fact, music-hall. You can't miss her.'

I said nothing, put the keys in my pocket and went out. I had plenty of time so I decided to go to Villa Balestra first, perhaps I might meet Jeanne or Alda, or both. But when I reached the park they weren't there. I sat on a bench and took a creased and badly battered pocket edition of Apollinaire from my jeans. I always carried it around with me and when I had nothing to do I would read through it again so as to convince myself once more that these were indeed the very poems I would have liked to write myself but that Apollinaire had written instead of me and for me. At the top of the page, in a poem entitled 'Across Europe', I read the line, in Italian in the original: 'Once I meant to say: what do you want?' and immediately plunged into a reverie as intense as it was obscure, as though concentrating hard on something while at the same time not knowing exactly what that something was. Apollinaire's question, 'what do you want?', somewhat impatient and fed up, clearly meant, at least for me in my present situation, 'For heaven's sake, what do you want: the mother or the daughter?' And when the question was understood in this sense, I couldn't help but reply, 'The daughter, obviously.'

But why the daughter? Was it because, as Jeanne had playfully insinuated, I liked little girls? No, I had never liked little girls; I liked Alda and only Alda. But why Alda of all people? It was with a sense of fear almost that I remembered how for some time now I couldn't look at Alda's eyes without immediately seeing, thanks to a striking and incredible similarity of expression, my mother's eyes that evening when she'd raised them towards me, full of still unsatisfied desire, at the very moment she'd straddled Terenzi's knees and helped him push into her. Yes, I 'wanted' Alda, but with that same expression my mother had had on that occasion, so important both for herself and for me; and for her part Alda was humouring me, sweetly and, it almost seemed, knowingly.

For a while I sat there stunned by this simple, direct observation: it's one thing to suspect something, quite another to be sure: and now I was sure that for some time I had been watching Alda mainly to catch in her eyes that mysterious evocative expression, the way someone in love will search, in the eyes of other women, for the expression that belongs to the woman he loves and only to her. Then I wondered if this likeness really existed, in which case it would be, however evocative, merely a coincidence; or whether on the contrary I had now reached a level of obsession where I couldn't help but see my mother in all the women I came across. I wasn't sure which of the two possibilities I would have preferred; both presupposed an incestuous attraction, but the second was more disturbing since it involved me and me alone and thus allowed me to glimpse in my own behaviour the ugly face of insanity. Rather crazily, I told myself that the only way to check whether the second alternative was true or not would be to arrange for my father to meet Alda and then to ask him if he could see any resemblance to my mother; two recognitions, rather than one, would make it almost true: if my father confirmed that there was a resemblance, it would mean I was not insane. But then I thought of another, better, in fact infallible method. In my wallet I had a photo of my mother: all I had to do was compare my mother's eyes in the photo with Alda's and all doubt relative to this resemblance would be at an end. I wondered why on earth I hadn't thought of this before, and once again I was obliged to see in this surprising omission the same sort of repression that for fifteen years had prevented me from thinking seriously about either my mother or my relationship with her.

I took my wallet from my jeans pocket, and found the

photograph. It was a photograph that had a whole history of its own. It used to be in my uncle's room, in a silver frame, standing on the chest of drawers. A few years ago I'd asked him if he'd give it to me, and he did. But the photo was too big for my wallet; it showed my mother from the waist up. So I cut off the bottom part of the photo, keeping just the face. Then, over the following years, every time I threw away an old wallet and switched its contents into a new one, I'd stop a moment to contemplate my mother's face. Then I'd slip the photo into its own compartment and think no more about it.

I had the photo in my hands now, so worn and streaked it had that imitation-marble look they use for the covers of children's exercise books. But as luck would have it, amongst all those creases and tears, the eyes had survived unscathed, whole and alive. I couldn't remember what my mother had been doing when the photograph was taken; it seemed as if a strong wind must have been blowing, since a lock of hair, apparently dislodged by a gust, fell slantwise across her face. But the eyes, as I said, were perfectly visible. And they had the same unforgettable expression they'd had when she'd looked up at me during her lovemaking with Terenzi. I studied the photograph carefully and found to my relief that there really was a likeness, and not a vague one either; it was obvious. So I wasn't insane then, just an attentive observer. At the same time, though, I realized that despite this resemblance there was a subtle difference between my feeling for Alda and that for my mother. My feeling for my mother was vengeful somehow, the kind of passion you have when a woman you love betrays you. Towards Alda, on the other hand, I felt the sort of mysterious, heart-rending affection I might perhaps have felt had I been confronted with my mother as a little girl, an impossible event, but all the same imaginable.

Confused and without having reached any kind of conclusion, I was just about to put the photo back in my wallet when I heard Alda's voice right behind me exclaim, 'There, caught you, who's the photograph of? Some girlfriend in Paris I bet.'

'No, my mother.'

'Ah, your mother, yes, she looks like you. You've got the same snub nose.'

'She looks like somebody else too.'

'Who?'

'You.'

She came to sit next to me on the bench, rudely snatched the photo and looked at it. 'I can't see any likeness.'

'Oh come on, it's the first thing that strikes you when you look at it: you've both got the same eyes.'

'No we haven't! Your mother, at least in this photo, has a – what – an animated, intense expression. Whereas everybody always says that I have an indirect, uncertain expression, because I'm short-sighted.'

She shook her head, and hurriedly handed back the photograph. Then suddenly excited, said, 'I've got some big news for you.'

'What?'

'You know what Jeanne said last night, after we'd been talking about you for an hour or two: "What would you say if we invited Mario to come and live with us? He came to Rome to see his father, but he doesn't like him and now he's in an embarrassing situation. He'd like to stay in Rome, but he realizes he can't go on living with a man who's a complete stranger to him. Why couldn't we put him up here?" You see? She wants to invite you to come and stay with us. What do you think?'

Moving as slowly as I could, I put the photograph back in my wallet and my wallet back in my pocket. And as I did so I thought it over, understanding only that as yet I understood nothing and would have to play for time. 'First of all I'd like to know what you think about it.'

'I think it would be fantastic.'

'Fantastic?'

'Just think, Mario; you, Jeanne and me – how happy we'd be together! I know what you're thinking, that you're too young to be a father to me. But it's not true, your age doesn't matter, the important thing is that you're a man; you would be the man of the family.'

'Great idea. There's just one small problem.'

'What's that?'

'That I don't feel anything in particular for Jeanne. While she, on the other hand, thinks I do.'

Suddenly getting excited, almost angry, she said, 'There, you promised, I made you swear, and now you're chickening out.'

'I'm not chickening out. But the truth is the truth. I don't feel even this much for her,' and I clicked a thumbnail against the edge of my teeth. 'How am I supposed to live with her?'

'It doesn't matter! What matters is that you'll be living in our house.'

'Without making love?'

'Okay, even without, just so long as Jeanne is happy and doesn't keep me up talking all night.' She reflected a moment, then resumed with fresh energy, 'Don't think about it, come and live with us, you'll be fine, you'll see. In fact, we ought to make a plan.'

'What plan?'

'When she invites you, you should accept only on condition that she lets you sleep in the chapel.'

'You mean the room where she used to sleep with your father?'

'Right. Otherwise there's no point in your coming. I've already told her that you've got to sleep there.'

'And what did she say?'

'First she said no, then yes, then no. In short, she doesn't know what she wants, as usual.'

'But where would she sleep?'

'Where she sleeps now. What she'd like to do though is to come and sleep in my room, put you in hers, and leave the chapel as it is. But I'm not standing for that. We've got to convince her to chuck all that junk out and give the room to you. Otherwise we'll be back where we started.'

'What junk is that?'

'My father's stuff. I told you that room was sacred for Jeanne, didn't I?'

'And so?'

'And so, can't you see? If she agrees to let you sleep there, it won't be sacred any more.'

I felt a sudden, indefinable repugnance and instinctively exclaimed, 'I'm not coming to live with you and I'm not staying with my father: I'll go back to Paris.'

Unexpectedly, she said, 'If you go back to Paris, I'm coming with you.'

'Are you mad, or what?'

She took my hand and began to say, all in a hurry, 'I can't go on living with Jeanne any more, the way she wants a man one minute and doesn't the next; one minute she wants to be faithful to my father's memory, the next minute she doesn't. I'll come to Paris with you. I'll get a job. I'm young, only fourteen, but I look eighteen. I could be an interpreter. I speak Italian and French and I'm taking lessons to improve my English.'

I tried to free my hand, but didn't succeed.

'Swear that if you go back to Paris you'll take me with you.'

'I'm not swearing anything.'

'Swear we'll go to Paris together.'

She squeezed my hand with mischievous, insolent strength.

'I'm not swearing anything, and let go of my hand.'

She suddenly looked so unhappy that I relented. 'Let's say, as soon as I get to Paris the first thing I'll do is look for a way for you to come too.'

'You'd find me a job?'

'I don't know about a job, but you could stay at my uncle's for a while, he has a very big house.'

She lifted my hand to her lips and kissed it excitedly. I withdrew my hand. 'I'll have to leave you now. I've got to go to an apartment here, in the same block you live in. My father asked me to show a penthouse apartment to one of his clients.'

'I bet it's the apartment opposite ours.'

'How do you know?'

'It's the only one empty. Nobody's lived there for ages. They've been doing it up just recently.' After a moment she added, 'I'll come with you.'

I don't know why, but I wanted to discourage her. Then I realized I didn't have a good excuse and let it go. Without another word we set off across the grass towards the gate.

SEVEN

The Helicopter

We walked out of the gate and then down the hill along Via Ammannati between small apartment blocks with cars parked along the pavements, oleanders in bloom, railings thick with ivies, until we arrived, on our left, at the block where Jeanne and Alda lived, plain and white, with rows of balconies from which geraniums hung in festoons.

I immediately spotted, standing by the front door, someone who corresponded pretty closely to the description my father had given of his client: a tall, big woman wearing a sort of long beige dress or tunic, straight and very loose. But she wasn't holding a rose as a sign of recognition; instead she had a box in her hands, the lid open, from which at that very moment she was taking something, a sweet perhaps. Having looked it over with anticipated gratification, she lifted it to her mouth.

Alda recognized her for me. 'There's your client,' and then speaking in a whisper, 'Introduce me to her.'

'Why?'

'Because I'm going up with you. Introduce me as a relative.'

'No, that's out.'

The client came to meet us, walking with a slow, somehow majestic gait, just as my father had described. I noticed two black boots sticking out beneath her light tunic, rather odd in this late spring weather. She was holding her box of sweets, still open, and as she came up to us she said, 'You're Mario, aren't you? I'm Esmeralda Jodice and you're here to show me the top apartment. You do realize I've been waiting a good ten minutes?'

I quickly apologized. She shook her head, 'Forget it, forget it,' and then, offering me the box, 'Want one?'

At which point I saw what was inside: lots of small yellow sugar-coated cubes of that oriental sweet known as *lukumo* – Turkish Delight. 'I was supposed to turn up holding a rose, but I saw these in the shop next to the florist's and couldn't resist. Go on, have one.' And without waiting for me to reply, she popped a *lukomo* straight into my mouth. I pointed to Alda, taking the sweet out of my mouth for a moment, 'This is Alda.'

'Hello dear, do you want one too?'

Signora Jodice made to pop a sweet into Alda's mouth as well, but Alda pushed her hand away quite firmly, 'I don't like sweets.'

'Oh, how rude,' said Signora Jodice, not at all put out. 'So let's go and see your daddy's apartment.' She didn't seem to be interested in Alda, but looked at me with open, even brazen curiosity. So I looked back at her.

She had a face which age had filled out, but which still bore the features of a not-entirely-faded beauty. Framed by two large waves of brown hair were a full forehead, large dark eyes, a tiny nose and a wide sensual mouth. A second glance would show that it was a childish face; but what was most striking at first were the signs of maturity: the eyes shipwrecked in a whirlpool of fine, concentric wrinkles, the nose puckered as if in anger, and a very visible down of hair forming a shadow around the red of the lips. Yet I felt that this maturity had something attractive about it precisely because it wasn't disguised, it offered itself for what it was. And all at once a simile came to mind: her face was like a fire that hasn't gone out yet, beneath the surface ash you could glimpse the intense red of a still-living flame.

Sensing my eyes on her, she said brashly, 'So, is the examination over? Come on, Master Mario, we've done quite enough looking at each other. Now let's go and look at the apartment.'

I felt myself blushing, and followed her as, grand and solemn, she walked ahead of Alda and myself towards the lift. Slap, slap, slap, at every step the massive shapes of her buttocks pressed, oblong, against the material of her dress. In the lift we took up the following positions: Alda to one side, Signora Jodice on the other and me in the middle. Then, as the lift was going up, I looked at the two women and had a bizarre sensation: Alda and Signora Jodice were really the same person, but at different ages, one at thirteen, one at forty. Or, if you like, Signora Jodice, her face filled out and body misshapen by maturity, was an enlargement of Alda, just as the spindly, slender Alda was a reduction of Signora Jodice. But what struck me most of all was the extraordinary likeness between these two women's eyes: large and dark, with that same look apparently of desire and torpor together, an expression created by the way the eyelids were constantly lowered to cut across the pupil. It was an unusual feature and one I couldn't remember having ever seen in anybody else. The fact that they both had it confirmed, in a quite disturbing way, the likeness between them.

The lift had just passed the first floor when Signora Jodice made an effort to be friendly to Alda, 'Do you live in this block?'

'Yes.'

'And you like it here?'

'Yes, partly because there's Villa Balestra right outside.'

'Of course, right, you've got the park just a minute or two away.'

Which allowed me to pick up another likeness, between their voices: Alda's coarse and shrill, Signora Jodice's coarse and hoarse. But oddly the difference between the shrillness of the one and the hoarseness of the other seemed only to confirm that this was indeed the same voice at two different ages.

The lift stopped, the doors opened, Alda said impatiently, 'Goodbye Signora Jodice, bye Mario,' and in a single bound was in front of her own door. She had the keys ready in her hand, opened up and disappeared.

'Well, what was eating her?' asked Signora Jodice, stepping out of the lift, with an air of criticism rather than enquiry. Then she said, 'You know, Master Mario, I know your father and you, physically, don't take after him at all.' I wondered why she insisted on calling me 'Master', and ironically into the bargain. I said curtly, 'I take after my mother.'

I fished the key from my pocket and made to open the door. And it was then that to my surprise I read on the nameplate, 'Dina Diotallevi', which was my mother's name. With the speed of a flame running along a short-circuiting wire, all the questions raised by the appearance of that name on the door raced through my mind. Why my mother's name? Perhaps because my father had bought her the apartment after their separation, hoping to persuade her to leave Paris, come back to Rome and live there alone, by herself? And if that was the case, why, after my mother must have turned him down, had he kept the apartment empty and ready all these years? And why now did he all of a sudden want to get rid of it?

Signora Jodice asked, 'Who is Dina Diotallevi?' I said: 'It was my mother's name,' and I stepped aside to let her go in. We stood in the hall. A highly polished floor with a pattern of black and red diamonds, two freshly painted white doors facing each other and some immaculate ivory-coloured wall panelling, all suggested recent renovation. Even Signora Jodice was impressed by how new everything looked. 'Oh, but how beautiful!' she exclaimed, swivelling round with the box of Turkish Delight still open on the palm of her hand. 'It's all new, there's that good smell of fresh paint, almost makes you feel you want to move in right away.'

Then something happened so complex in its dynamics as to make me think of those scenes you sometimes see in slow motion in films: Esmeralda (as I shall call her from now on) made to open one of the two doors that led off from the hall with the same hand in which, on her open palm, she held the box of sweets; I immediately saw that she wouldn't be able to open the door without spilling the sweets from the box and hurried to grab the handle for her; but our two hands collided and the box, which I had meant to save, fell to the ground, scattering the powdered cubes all over the floor.

Esmeralda cried, 'Oh, my poor *lukumi*! Do be a dear, Mario, and pick them up. Everything's so clean here, and then it would be a shame to throw them away.'

Perhaps I hesitated for a moment. At which she suddenly lost her patience, 'What are you looking at me for?' she exclaimed, stamping her foot on the floor. 'You don't expect *me* to pick them up, do you?'

I was taken aback by the rudeness of her sudden use of the familiar *tu* form, which seemed to imply the whole thing might have been planned in some way. 'I'm sorry,' I said in amazement, and without a word more got down on my hands and knees, took the box and began to gather the *lukumi*. But the little yellow cubes were spread all over the floor and Esmeralda began to point to those furthest away with her foot. At which I was again struck by the fact that she was wearing winter boots made from black leather. I don't know why, but without looking up I remarked, 'Why on earth are you wearing boots in this heat?'

Immediately, as if she'd been ready and waiting for this, the answer came straight back from above my head, 'Aren't we curious! Well, if you must know, these boots are very light, they're summer boots, and I wear them to hide a birthmark on my leg. Not that it's ugly, just slightly darker than the skin.' And after scarcely a moment's silence, 'You want to see it? I'll lift up my dress and show it you.'

What an absurd offer! To show the birthmark on your

leg to someone you don't know and who, what's more, is picking something up from the floor! And yet Esmeralda's voice carried such a peremptory authority that the proposal seemed entirely natural. I saw the dress slither up, waving from side to side, up and up, above the top of the boot, revealing the upper part of the birthmark, just a little darker than the rest of the leg, the colour of a summer suntan. The heavy, muscular leg lifted slightly, turning this way and that, as if showing itself off. 'What do you think, is it terribly ugly?'

'No, it's not ugly at all.'

'That's enough of that though, what do you think you're looking at?'

'I'm not looking at anything.'

'Nonsense, you're looking alright and heaven only knows what you're thinking. Go on, give it a kiss, a kiss on my birthmark, just so's I know you don't think it's horrible.'

Was it an order, or a plea? There'd been something of both in her voice. But again I sensed that some mysterious authority she exercised made my obedience natural and spontaneous. I bent forward, my hands on the floor, pushed forward my lips and planted my kiss. Immediately, from directly above my head, Esmeralda's voice commented, 'Well done, he finally made up his mind. And now another, higher up.'

The dress, like some wobbly theatre curtain, began to wave again and slither upwards, revealing the spectacle of two towering legs pressed tight together. And inexplicably I began to follow it up, planting kisses first on her knees, then on her thighs. She wasn't wearing stockings and beneath my lips I sensed the prickling of skin whose hair hasn't been properly removed. As I did so, her voice, no longer in the least flirtatious, but demanding and coarse, insisted, 'Higher, higher.'

To each of these 'highers' I responded with obedience and at the same time I kept asking myself, 'Why am I doing this?

Why does she think she has the right to make me do it?' Until, with her last, 'higher', I jerked angrily up, like a dog provoked by his master, and bit her pubic mound, filling my mouth with tough matted hair. She held me for a moment with my face pushed into her crotch, pressing a hand on the nape of my neck; then she pushed me away. 'You're really hungry for it; you'd never stop. Now come on, be a good boy and show me the apartment.' And a moment later, 'The *lukumi* though, you still have to pick them up.'

'I could push them into a corner.'

'No, put them in the box and I'll put them back in my bag. What would your father say if he found the place full of *lukumi*?'

I picked them up as fast as I could, then stood up, breathing hard. She held open an enormous bag she had on her arm and I poured them in, sweets and box, any old how. She watched me and remarked, 'You know you hurt me? Do you always bite women like that?'

I said nothing. I tried to recover my professional voice. 'In any event, this is the entrance hall.'

'In any event! I can see it's the entrance hall. Hurry up, come on, let's see the rest.'

I opened a door and she followed. Something prickly was bothering me in my mouth and I spat angrily. Then I announced, 'This is the sitting-room.'

'The sitting-room? Very nice, just what I was after, so long and narrow, it looks like a greenhouse with all these windows along the length of the wall; I'll put plants here, hundreds of plants!' And then, turning just slightly towards me, 'Why are you so angry? You spat out that poor hair of mine with real hatred. Come on, don't be angry, you did something very beautiful, that's all. And now, to show me you don't regret it, give me a kiss.'

Mechanically I offered my lips. She took the *lukumo* she was sucking from her mouth, then came to kiss me, lips open like some fleshy flower from the centre of which, like a single sharp pistil, her tongue darted out a moment as we kissed. Then she drew away and, stepping back to get a better view of me, said with satisfaction, 'You know you're a handsome boy? Who would ever have thought it, so timid, so well-behaved! How old are you?'

'Twenty.'

'You know you could perfectly well be my son?'

I said nothing. It was exactly the kind of thing I expected from a woman like her, at once mature and curiously proud of being so. She insisted, 'Would you like to have a mother like me? A mother who'd make love to you into the bargain, isn't that the dream of all you boys?'

Quite lucidly I thought that with this vaunting of incestuous maternity she was, without realizing, answering my question: Why am I doing this? Yes, the answer lay precisely in that remark, 'You know you could be my son?' I came to this conclusion with the amazed calm typical of those discoveries that are at once obvious and important. Immediately a logical consequence presented itself: if it was true, as it seemed to be, that Esmeralda had the same eyes as Alda and Alda had the same eyes as my mother, then it followed that my mother and Esmeralda were also alike and that this likeness might perhaps explain the mysterious authority Esmeralda had over me, and my equally mysterious attraction for Esmeralda.

But I didn't want to accept this idea which seemed clearly obsessive in nature, so that barely had I formulated it than I was trying to break it down, disprove it: Obviously I must be the victim of some kind of hallucination which is making me see my mother in almost all the women I run into. The 'almost' here, qualifying 'all', served to remind me of the significant exception of Jeanne, who didn't look like my mother at all and who, as a result, didn't arouse any desire in me, nor have any authority over me.

I thought all this looking dreamily down at a floor of narrow, light-coloured, wax-polished wooden boards. These boards stretched away as far as the distant french window at the other end of the sitting-room. And above them, as if by superimposition of two films, visible yet transparent, I seemed to glimpse those eyes with their strange expression at once sleepy and lustful, the eyes that linked Alda, my mother and Esmeralda, but not Jeanne. In a neutral voice I said, 'Yes, it's really nice. It looks like a gym, don't you think?'

'Don't you think! What kind of man are you! First you jump on top of me, then you remember your father's agency and start addressing me as *Lei*. Just call me *tu* and have done with it.'

'I'm sorry. I didn't know the apartment had been done up so recently.'

'Well, I knew. Your dad said he could hand it over tomorrow if I was interested, all amenities and everything.'

Once again now I wondered why my father had had the place done up and wanted to be rid of it. I had the impression of confronting a riddle, the solution to which was easy, very easy, and yet I couldn't get it. As if thinking aloud, I said, 'The name on the door is my mother's. My mother died years ago. My father has never mentioned this apartment, though in all likelihood he must have bought it for her long ago.'

'What's strange about that? Your mother died, he kept the apartment empty for years out of respect for her memory but then decided to sell it. And to get a better price he had it renovated. He told me himself: the work took two months.'

'I didn't know anything, he didn't tell me anything.'

'Whereas I knew everything. So then, is my little boy happy to have met his mummy in such a bright, new place?'

So she was still harping on with this mother business, even after being told that the apartment had my mother's name on the door. In fact, with unpleasant, vulgar gratification, she was emphasizing it even more now. I realized, however, that what was, or should have been, sacrilege for me, for her was no more than a fairly common sort of erotic game. And

I hadn't the heart to condemn her for it; on the contrary I had a feeling that there was something legitimate in her parody of maternal love. I suggested, 'Shall we look at the terrace?'

'Let's.'

She began to walk slowly along the wall with the windows. I stopped behind her to look through the big window at the pines of Villa Balestra. She gave me a sidelong look and said, 'Why are you following behind me? To look at my backside? Look then, please do, it was made to be looked at.' And then, almost comically, she made a wiggling movement inside her dress, first with one buttock, then the other.

At these words, and even more so this gesture, I again experienced a sense of vulgar sacrilege, doubtless due to her likeness to my mother. I thought with horror: If she hadn't died young, perhaps my mother would have turned out like this. With a single stride I was at her side and told her, 'Please, don't talk like that.'

She stopped and looked at me with an exaggerated, burlesque expression of amazement. 'Hark at him, the well-behaved little boy is back. He sneaks a look at my bottom but doesn't want me to notice! And are you or aren't you going to use *tu* with me? You don't call your mother *Lei*. Well, now let's see the terrace.'

I hurried to open the french window; she went through first and together we stepped out into the dazzling light of a sky dense with transparent white cirrus. Esmeralda went straight to the parapet where the terrace looked out across Rome. She stopped there, standing still, not so much, I realized, to contemplate the city, but for me to catch up with her.

Once again I obeyed her silent invitation and went to stand next to her, leaning on the parapet. For a moment we stood together without talking, then she raised an arm and pointed to something beyond the vast expanse of roofs and terraces: 'What's that hill called?'

I replied, confused, 'I don't know, I don't know Rome. I've always lived abroad.'

'I should have guessed; you've got a foreign accent. Where abroad?'

'In France.'

'Well, I'll tell you what it's called: the Gianicolo.'

For a moment I couldn't understand why she'd asked me the name of a detail in the panorama if she knew perfectly well what it was herself. But my puzzlement didn't last long. Because while pointing to the Gianicolo with one hand, her other arm had reached down between me and the parapet so that I could now feel her fingers blindly groping for something across the material of my trousers. She went on, 'You see that dome over there, on the horizon?'

'Yes.'

'That's St Peter's. And that white thing, you know what that is?'

'No.'

'That's the monument in Piazza Venezia.'

She'd found what she was looking for now; the tab of my zip. Suddenly her hand relaxed. I felt her lower the zip in gentle little tugs. Then with furtive dexterity the hand slipped in through the opening, between my pants and the bare skin, lingered, victorious and possessive in my pubic hair, slithered under my testicles, turned round and up, weighing them in her palm, then, with delicacy and determination, pulled the whole bunch of my genitals out into the open air. With conviction and no sign of a tremor in her voice, she said, 'I'd take the apartment just for this view.' She was twisting my erection from side to side now, as if to feel how hard it was; then, brusque and decisive, she turned and murmured in a whisper: 'You look at the view, don't worry about me.' And she crouched down purposefully beside me, her head at the level of my crotch.

But I didn't have time to follow her advice and look at the view. All at once, bursting straight out it seemed from the sky above us with a roar and suddenness I found threatening and punitive, came a big helicopter flying very low, almost skimming the trees of Villa Balestra. Deafening and violent, it raced toward us. I just had time to glimpse the pilot sitting at the controls, head in a crash helmet, then the helicopter was gone, a spectral dragonfly, grey and diaphanous, fading and melting away until finally it disappeared completely, and with it the noise. At the same time Esmeralda stood up abruptly, ran across the terrace and disappeared through the same french window we'd come out from.

My amazement at the inexplicable flight of the seemingly intrepid Esmeralda, apparently terrified now by the quite normal passing of a very normal helicopter, left me standing there so distracted that I didn't even realize the state my fly was in. Then the deep silence and absolute immobility that followed the din of the helicopter and Esmeralda's departure, brought me back to my senses and to an awareness of how strange, not to say ridiculous I must look: alone on a terrace,looking out over this solemn view of Rome, with my trousers open and my penis out. With a convulsive gesture I put back what Esmeralda had pulled out, and as I did so, took a worried look at the terrace around me.

The apartment had four French windows, three of which seemed to be closed, while the one Esmeralda had fled through was still open. My immediate thought was that it would have been impossible for anyone to have spied on us; the shutters were the traditional kind with the slats angled down, preventing one from seeing very far. And anyway, who was there to spy on us? The apartment was unlived in and the door closed. All the same, I couldn't shake off a feeling of shameful apprehension, as if seen doing something forbidden. But why forbidden? Once again I realized that Esmeralda's erotic game of playing mother had not been a game for me.

To strike an attitude, as it were, I felt in my pocket, found a pack of cigarettes and lit one. I realized that my hand as it held the light was trembling. Then, in the silence, a voice I knew only too well called mockingly, 'Peek-a-boo, peek-a-boo, I'm hiding, peek-a-boo, come and get me.'

So, I thought, recognizing Alda's voice, my feeling I was being spied on was right after all. Obviously I'd forgotten to lock the front door to the apartment and Alda, curious and perhaps jealous, had taken advantage of the opportunity to follow us. I felt disappointed. After the threatening and mysterious intervention of the helicopter plunging on Esmeralda and myself from the sky, this scornful childish peek-a-boo seemed to reduce the whole thing to a joke. In a bored voice I called, 'I know who you are, Alda as per usual. But I haven't got time to look for you. Come out and have done.'

I waited but no answer came. And now I was tormented by the question, had Alda been spying on us? And if she had, what had she seen? Me and Esmeralda looking at the view, behaving in a way that was, to say the least, suspicious? Or Esmeralda crouched at my feet with her head at the level of my crotch? Or again me alone with my fly open and my penis sticking out? These three possibilities sounded – and were – almost comic; but still I couldn't shake off an unjustified sense of shame.

Meanwhile I was looking carefully at the four french windows until finally I noticed that the shutters of the first window on the left weren't properly closed but just pulled to. So that was where the voice had come from; and, almost certainly, that was where she had been watching us from. Making an effort to sound relaxed, I said, 'Listen, Alda, you'd better come out. I've got to lock the apartment and I wouldn't like you to be left shut up in it.' To my relief she immediately replied with stubborn pertness, 'You won't go till you've found me.'

'But I've already found you. You're behind the first french window, on the left.'

'But you haven't really looked.'

So she wanted to play, just to play; and it was impossible to know if she had seen us. In a friendly voice I asked, 'You couldn't be so kind as to tell me why you're doing all this, could you?'

'Oh that's good! It's a game. I hide, you look for me and find me.'

'And then?'

'And then nothing: you go home. Listen, you look for me and I'll say, you're getting colder, you're getting warmer, depending on how far away you are. Come on, it's a game.'

'But I told you, I don't have time.'

'You had time for that woman. Do you think I didn't see you?'

'Really? And what did you see?'

I waited nervously for her answer and at the same time was annoyed with myself for being nervous.

'I saw what I saw.'

'You didn't see anything at all.'

'Oh yes I did!'

'So tell.'

'I'll tell you everything. But first you have to look for me.'

'I'm going, I'll leave the door open for you. Bye.'

'Wait, let's do this: you look for me, if you find me I'll tell you what I saw. If you don't look for me, I won't tell you anything.'

Abruptly I headed for the french window where the voice was coming from. As I opened the shutters, I thought I heard a rustle of footsteps. Then I saw the room was quite empty, just white walls and a light-coloured wood floor. But on the left-hand wall towards the far end of the room I noticed a small door left ajar, obviously the bathroom, and realized Alda was hiding there. In fact she immediately cried, 'Getting colder.'

'You mean warmer.'

'No, colder.'

I went and pushed open the door. It was dark, the bathroom window must be closed, but in the half-light filtering from the bedroom I caught sight of a washbasin with a mirror above it: the bathroom seemed to be long and narrow with all the porcelain fixtures lined up along the same wall. Looking in I shouted, 'Where are you? Come out. I've got you now.'

'Getting warmer.'

What playful instinct, and not just playful either, told me, at the very moment I found the lightswitch on the wall, not to turn it on, but on the contrary to close the door behind me, plunging the bathroom into total darkness? Arms stretched out in front of me, I moved a step towards the other end of the room and knocked my shin against something hard, probably the toilet bowl. Intensely annoyed, I said, 'Why don't you just tell me where you are?'

'Getting warmer, another step and you'll burn yourself.'

Thus, albeit unconsciously, the game had become ambiguous for her too. 'If I burn myself, it'll be your fault.'

At which my hand, in the dark, touched Alda's face. I found her hair under my fingers and gave it a little tug. I found her cheek, warm and smooth, and for a moment I caressed it. Then pretending to make a slip, I put a finger in a nostril and she sneezed. Until finally I found her lips and followed their wayward profile with a fingertip. Alda said cheerfully, 'So you've found me; now you've got to guess what I saw.'

'What do you mean, we agreed that you'd tell me if I found you!'

'Let's do it this way: you keep touching me and I'll tell you whether you touched that woman the same way or not.'

'But I didn't touch her.'

'Liar! Come on, let's play this last game and then we'll go.'

'No, this is one game I am not playing.'

'Come on, what's bothering you?'

I said nothing. Again my fingers skimmed her lips, then her chin, and finally her neck. At which, through the dark came Alda's voice egging me on, 'Cold, cold, lower, lower.'

Who was it had said the same thing, or rather the opposite, just a short while ago? Esmeralda with her insistent, 'higher, higher'. But Esmeralda knew what she was after, whereas Alda was playing. 'No, I'm not going further down.'

'You did with that woman, go on.'

'No, that's enough, let's go.'

Then, in the dark, a voice which sounded more like a woman's than a girl's mocked sarcastically, 'You're just scared, you're just scared.'

'What are you on about?'

'I'm telling you you're scared of touching me the way you touched that woman.'

'Oh, I'm scared am I?' In a fit of anger I reached out my hand, and went decidedly down this time. My fingers brushed across her right breast, no more than an unripe bump under her loose sweater; I had a confused idea of demonstrating my courage by grabbing her at random in some lower part of her body, her crotch even. But my hand was intercepted by her own; with unexpected strength she grabbed my wrist and held it tight, begging, 'No, don't. I'm afraid.'

This time I really lost my temper, more with myself perhaps than with her. I shouted, 'The game's over, all our games are over.' At which cry the light on the ceiling went on. Obviously while my fingers had been moving over her body, Alda had had her hand on the switch, ready to turn it on. Thus I now saw the long narrow room, the fixtures all in a line down one side, and Alda in the corner between the toilet and the wall under the cylinder of the gas boiler. She was looking at me with those ambiguous eyes of hers, their mixture of sleepiness and desire that made her look so like my mother and Esmeralda. Then, without a word, she stepped forward, I moved aside, she went out of the room and I followed her.

On the terrace, heading toward the french window, she asked me bluntly, 'What was that woman's name?'

'Jodice. Esmeralda Jodice.'

'And are you going to see her again?'

'Why should I see her again? She's one of my father's clients. I don't know her.'

'She ran off, but she'll be back, you'll see.'

EIGHT

The Family Album

I was late for lunch, but I found my father still at table. I was getting nervous now about the work side of the affair; I was afraid Esmeralda, whose flight I still found inexplicable, might have telephoned my father to complain about me. It would have been strange and absurd; but then hadn't everything Signora Jodice had done been strange and absurd from the start? However, a glance was enough to tell me there was no need to worry. My father, calm and deep in thought, was sitting with his plate in front of him and didn't even raise his head when I came in. He merely asked, 'Why so late?' I replied brusquely, 'I had to hang about nearly half an hour. Signora Jodice made me late.'

I sat down and unfolded my napkin. Oringia came in right away, bringing the first course. I began to eat in silence. My father chose an apple from the fruit bowl, put it on his plate, cut it in half, then into quarters and began to peel a slice. Then without raising his eyes, he said, 'And what did you think of her?'

'Who?'

'Our client, Signora Jodice.'

To my relief I realized I felt no sense of guilt, then was immediately annoyed with myself for feeling relief. Even if I had made love to Signora Jodice, why on earth should I have felt guilty? I said at random, 'She must have been a beautiful woman in her day.'

'She still is. She has lovely eyes, a magnificent head of hair, she holds herself like a real lady. Perhaps you didn't look at her very closely.'

So he was trying to get me to talk about Esmeralda. I hesitated before replying. Should I tell him that the lovely eyes were shipwrecked in a sea of wrinkles? That the magnificent head of hair was dry and dull? That her lady-like bearing was burlesque, typical of a third-rate music-hall warbler? I was about to answer with these criticisms when I caught, in my father's eyes, an expression not so much of interest but of ingenuous, deeply-felt anxiety. Without thinking why he might be anxious, I changed course. 'Yes, you're right, she is beautiful, in her way.' And then, I don't know why, out slipped the remark, 'But it's a middle-aged beauty; she could be my mother.'

Oddly, he fell silent. He seemed to reflect and at last decided. 'You mean she didn't make any, how can I put it, special impression?'

'Despite being middle-aged, she's a good-looking woman, that's all.'

'Obviously you didn't look very closely.'

There was something almost reproachful in his voice. I defended myself by sounding bored. 'Actually I looked very closely. I had all the time in the world to look at her.' I fell silent for a moment, then changed my mind. No, I wouldn't be reticent as I had planned: on the contrary I would satisfy my father and talk round my adventure with the instinctive ability of the sleepwalker who negotiates a cornice with his eyes closed. 'I looked so closely I even saw she had a birthmark on her leg. I saw it when I bent down to pick up some *lukumi* that had fallen on the floor.'

'*Lukumi*? What *lukumi*?'

Briefly I told my father about the accident with the Turkish Delight. I got as close as possible to the truth by winding up, 'She pointed to the *lukumi* with her foot. I had the impression she was using them as an excuse to show me her legs, she'd pulled up her dress.' And I was amazed to see that my father didn't seem to attribute any importance to an incident that for me had plenty. He said brusquely, 'Is that all, you didn't notice anything else?'

'No, what was I supposed to notice?'

'I thought you were observant,' my father said in a disappointed voice. 'I was sure you'd immediately be struck by something much more important than the birthmark on her leg.'

This time I said nothing, for I suddenly remembered that, yes, I had noticed something unusual, and something I knew was important not just for him but for me too: the likeness of our client's eyes to those of my mother, an indirect likeness, seen first, that is, as a likeness to Alda's eyes and then to my mother's. But now that my father was asking me, I didn't want to admit to these likenesses, though when I'd first noticed them they'd given me the impression I was suffering from some kind of hallucination. No, I didn't want to share anything with him, not even this apparently innocuous observation. My father insisted, 'Try and remember: didn't Esmeralda make you think of somebody else?'

I experienced a shock of recognition; but this time the reason was not the likeness between my mother and Signora Jodice. That morning, when he had given me the keys to the penthouse apartment, my father had spoken of Esmeralda as just another client whose name he couldn't remember. But now he was referring to her as Esmeralda. In short, everything fell into place, at least as far as his relationship with Signora Jodice was concerned: Esmeralda was the mysterious woman my father spent his evenings with. It thus seemed that, exactly as was happening with me, he couldn't help but rediscover my mother's features in all the women he took a fancy to.

But why, when giving me the keys to the apartment, hadn't he told me that the client was the so-called girlfriend he went out to dinner with in the evenings? Hardly had I formulated this question than it was smothered and as it were cancelled out by an obvious fact: Esmeralda's erotic playing mother with me was due not just to our ages but above all to the almost man-and-wife relationship she had with my father. And he in turn, with the trick of the apartment, showed how he wanted Esmeralda to seem like a mother-figure to me. So, slowly but surely, the visit to the apartment in Via Ammannati was revealing itself as a sort of play in which everybody had lied and taken on roles which weren't really theirs.

I didn't let out any of these thoughts, but insisted, 'No, she didn't remind me of anyone at all.'

At the same time, however, I vaguely sensed the unpleasant implications of my adventure: I now found myself my father's rival, with his mistress becoming or about to become my own.

All at once my father got up from the table and said with sudden decision, 'Hang on a moment. I'll show you something.'

He went to the other end of the sitting-room to an old writing-desk near the door. He opened it, looked and found a spring: inside the desk was a secret cabinet in which I caught a glimpse, albeit from far away, of the backs of some albums bound in leather. My father chose one of the albums, came back and laid it open in front of me on the table. Standing beside me he leafed through the album. It was full of photographs of my mother, with him, alone, with me, with others. But I realized that he was looking for one photograph in particular. All at once he said, 'Look, tell me if they aren't the same person.'

I looked: two photographs were glued to this page of the album, one of my mother and the other, I immediately realized, of Esmeralda as a young woman. As chance would have it, the photograph of my mother was the same, though with the lower part still intact, as the one I kept in my wallet. She was wearing a blouse and miniskirt and leaning back against a railing with sea behind and the wind blowing a lock of hair across her face. Esmeralda on the other hand had been photographed from the waist up wearing an evening dress with plunging neckline, leaving her arms and the tops of her breasts bare. I felt quite nauseated. The shape of the face, the main features and above all the eyes betrayed an undeniable likeness. I said curtly, 'Okay, I see, there are two photographs, one of my mother and the other of Signora Jodice. But where does Signora Jodice come in? And why have you stuck her photograph in this album?'

'What?' my father exclaimed. 'Can't you see they're identical?'

Irritated by an uncertainty that had been dragged out for too long, I would have liked to have demanded: Okay, out with it, what and who is Signora Jodice to you? But he got there before me. 'In this photo Signora Jodice is the same age as your mother and looks, to put it mildly, like her twin. I do realize, though, that by now you'll be wanting to know why I brought these photos together. Well, Mario, the moment has come to explain. But before I do there's something else I still have to tell you.'

With these somehow solemn words, he left me studying the open album, went back round the table and sat down opposite me. 'You see, Mario,' he resumed in a voice at once confidential yet theatrical, leaning towards me, 'you're a man now and I don't doubt you know the world better than I do. But when it comes to your mother, you are first and foremost a son, and as a son you simply can't begin to understand how I felt about her. Mario, I loved her, truly loved her, did crazy things for her. I told you how she forced me to be both Othello and Iago at the same time. Well, you can add a third immortal figure to those two characters of Shakespeare's: Romeo. Yes, Mario, your mother was my Juliet and I am her Romeo, still weeping over her untimely death.'

I didn't know what to say nor even where to look. I would have liked to have taken my eyes away from the two photographs, but the idea of turning from them to my excited and probably sincere ham of a father was too awful. 'Why am I telling you all this, Mario?' he resumed after a moment's silence. 'Because, as you will already have appreciated, Esmeralda is my girlfriend, the woman I have loved for two years now. But, and this is strictly between us, Mario, as man to man, I would never have made her my companion, never have loved her with a real impassioned love, had she not looked so amazingly like your mother.'

Without raising my eyes, I replied, 'Okay, but why didn't you tell me right away that Esmeralda was your girlfriend? Why did you put me through that charade of the visit to the apartment?'

'She wanted it that way, Mario. She said she wanted to get to know you without you knowing who she was.'

'But why?'

'Mario, the moment has come to tell you. Esmeralda and I have decided to get married within the month. But she wasn't sure you'd like her or that she'd like you. So she wanted to meet you as though you were an estate agent and she just a regular client.'

'I hope she didn't find me unfriendly?'

'On the contrary, she just phoned to tell me how wonderful you were.'

'But the name on the door to the apartment was Mother's.'

'Of course it was. For years and years I wanted your mother to live in that apartment. Now we'll all go and live there, you, me and the woman I love and am going to marry, mainly because she looks so like your mother. Yes, Mario, after a fifteen-year break, it'll be as if my life were picking up again at the precise point where it broke off: on the one hand a new wife, a son – likewise new, in a manner of speaking – and a new home, and then on the other, everything just as it was before, better than before.'

Was my father sincere? Did he believe it? In any event he was sticking extremely close to the part he'd chosen to play.

He broke off for a moment as if overcome by emotion, then resumed in the tone of one coming to a conclusion, 'The family, Mario, that's the goal I've set myself for so many years, and now I can claim to have achieved it!'

The family! There was, I reflected, in this exclamation, the same kind of nostalgia Alda had shown when speaking of domestic happiness. Except, I thought without too much irony, that in both cases the families concerned were very unusual ones: in Alda's the daughter was attracted by a father-figure and jealous of the mother; in my father's the mother was playing at incest with the son.

My father looked at me, waiting for me to recover from my surprise. For once I really did want to speak to him, 'man to man', as he would have put it. 'I think the love you felt for my mother makes you see something of her in all the women you meet. But it doesn't matter: if you love Esmeralda, you're doing the right thing to marry her.'

I was thinking of myself, as well as of him: I also saw my mother in other women, in Alda, in Esmeralda. But unlike him, I couldn't resolve my obsession through marriage. Meanwhile my father let himself be carried away on a tide of sentiment: 'You'll see, you and Esmeralda will soon get on, not exactly like mother and son maybe, but almost. I already told you, she phoned me to talk about you. You know what struck her most of all?'

'What?'

'That you're a poet.'

'I'm not a poet. I'd like to be one. But how did she know? We didn't talk about poetry.'

'I told her, and you know why? Because she's written some poems too.'

'Poems?'

'Yes, the lyrics to her songs.'

'We'll be a family of poets,' I remarked ironically, 'sonny poet, step-mummy poet, even daddy poet; I bet you've written some poems too.'

My father sighed, with an abysmal actor's falseness that made me cringe. 'Alas, Mario, I'm no poet. But I do have poetry here in my heart,' and he beat his hand on his breast. 'Let's say I'm a poet in the way I live. For me poetry has a single name, your mother's: Dina.'

He sighed again, then said, 'By the way, perhaps it would be a good idea if you phoned Esmeralda to tell her that you know about our marriage and feel happy about it. No other reason: so as not to give her the impression you're upset about our little trick. I'll give you her number if you want.'

This was exactly what I wanted from him. Yet with an inexplicable and mysterious reluctance I answered hurriedly, 'No, not just now. You can introduce me officially as it were in the next couple of days. Right now, straight off on the phone I wouldn't know what to say.'

He approved with warmth, 'Right, perfectly right, I understand, I understand your embarrassment. Esmeralda's so like your mother and soon she'll be taking her place too. You'll have to get used to the idea. So, just give me a few words at least that I can pass on to her.'

'Tell her I'm pleased to have met her. Tell her that from now on she must forget the estate agent and think of me only as a son.'

NINE

The Football Match

As soon as he'd gone I wanted to dash after him to ask for Esmeralda's phone number which only a moment earlier a strange fit of shame had made me refuse. But this was always the way with me: my awareness of my innate, reprehensible openness meant that as life offered me opportunities I tended to content myself with an initial, symbolic success, then withdraw, even though later I might, as was in fact the case now, find myself plunged in the most bitter regret. It was obvious that in phoning my father Esmeralda had meant to send me a reassuring message; but I hadn't immediately wanted to take advantage of it: for the moment I was happy just to know that what had happened this morning in the penthouse apartment could happen again in the future any time I wanted it to.

Except that now a new idea occurred to tip the balance in favour of my openness; this was the thought, or rather the sudden and brilliant brainwave, that, looking as she did so like my mother and being so ready to act the part, Esmeralda offered me a unique opportunity to put into practice what I hadn't been able to put into practice with the maid, Oringia: the re-enactment for therapeutic ends of the traumatic love scene between my mother and Terenzi, putting myself in his place and Esmeralda in my mother's. As with Monique, I would cancel out Terenzi's lovemaking with my own, wash away his sperm with mine.

It was an abstract scheme whose main advantage in the end was that it justified the continuation of my relationship with Esmeralda. But what prompted me to formulate the plan was the real and inexplicable desire that my future stepmother aroused in me, a desire that went beyond the plan itself, which in the end perhaps I could have done without. In any event, plan or no plan, I ought to make a move with Esmeralda as soon as possible, not in some unspecified future, but now, at once. This urgency, dictated really by desire, though disguised as rational and useful, made me bitterly regret having refused my father's invitation to telephone Esmeralda. If only I'd made a note of her number at least, telling him I'd call her when I felt like it! But no, I'd refused! I was so frustrated I felt like hitting myself over the head.

I quickly got up from the table and almost ran to my father's bedroom. I was hoping he might keep an address book on his bedside table where the phone was. But there was no address book. Both windows were open; instinctively I went over and looked out and down: I had the crazy idea of calling after my father, who had just this minute set off to the agency, of catching him up in the street and, with the slightest pretext, or even without one, getting Esmeralda's number off him.

By a chance as uncanny as it was coincidental, the window presented me with the same spectacle of cars stopped on red at the traffic light that I seemed to see every time I looked out at the road along the river. Not once had I looked to find the traffic flowing freely by on green.

My father was crossing the road, stockier and smaller than ever when seen like this from above. As I knew, he crossed the road so as to walk by the parapet along the Tiber. He tended to walk to the agency to get, as he said, some exercise and he preferred the pleasanter view of the river to that of the apartment blocks that lined the near side of the road.

Withdrawing from myself for a moment, it was if I saw myself puffing and panting across the road in front of all those waiting, throbbing cars just to ask my amazed father for Esmeralda's telephone number. Then, all at once, behind me, calm, soft but impelling, the telephone began to ring.

I half turned from the windowsill and hesitated. I hadn't been calling anyone recently nor getting any calls myself. The only people in my life in Rome were Jeanne and Alda and I could see them whenever I wanted at Villa Balestra. So obviously the phone was ringing for my father, and right at the moment I didn't feel like playing secretary for him. But the ringing went on, patient and insistent, as if whoever it was knew for certain that it was me there hearing it, and not my father. So I moved away from the windowsill and went to pick up the receiver. I recognized Esmeralda's voice immediately. 'Is that you, Riccardo? Where were you? Why on earth didn't you answer?'

My heart racing, I said, 'My father's not at home.'

'Who am I talking to?'

'Mario.'

The voice at the other end of the line suddenly jerked into life, 'Oh what a nice surprise! Actually I was after your father. But maybe, deep down, it was you I wanted. How is my little boy?'

I was standing next to the bed, one hand pressing the receiver to my ear. The other moved to the sudden swelling of my penis, and I couldn't help thinking that Esmeralda's voice alone, alluding as she was to her incestuous game, was enough to excite me more that Jeanne's whole body. Answering question with question, I asked, 'Could you please tell me why you ran off like that when the helicopter flew over the terrace?'

'Upset you, did it, right when things were getting hot? Doesn't matter, we'll find another terrace.'

'Yes, but why did you run away?'

'Because there are moments when I don't like to be watched.'

'But who was watching?'

'That little friend of yours who lives opposite. She'd opened the shutters and she was watching us.'

'You think she saw us?'

'You bet she did! We must have looked pretty funny, you standing contemplating the view and me crouched down contemplating your thing!'

Aroused and angry, I asked, 'When can we see each other?'

'Does my little boy still love his mummy, even if at the last moment she didn't give him the sweetie she'd promised?'

I thought: How vulgar. But at the same time I stuttered, 'Yes, let's say he still loves her.'

'In that case, today, right away if you like.'

Suddenly, from the back of my mind where it was now indelibly recorded, I recalled my plan of doing with Esmeralda what I hadn't managed to do with Oringia. But then I remembered that today was Saturday and hence the regular league football match, indispensable for any re-enactment of my mother's lovemaking, would be tomorrow, Sunday. 'Not today,' I said regretfully. 'Tomorrow.'

Intrigued, she immediately asked, 'Why tomorrow, what have you got to do today that's so important?'

'I haven't got anything to do.'

'So?'

I hesitated. I realized that while she was merely playing at incest, for me the experience was serious and immediate. 'To tell the truth, I'd prefer tomorrow, because tomorrow there's the game.'

'The game?'

'Yes, the football game, tomorrow's Sunday, isn't it?'

'Ah hah, you're a football fan, fancy that. But what have I got to do with the game?'

'I'd like to see it with you.'

'Take me to the game, what an idea! Apart from anything else I can't stand crowds. I've seen too many in my time.'

The more I pressed on with my plan, the more embarrassed

I felt, as if embarking on a desperate enterprise of uncertain outcome. But in the end there was always the justification of desire, that desire which the mere sound of her voice in the receiver had been enough to arouse. 'I don't mean go to the ground, we can watch it at your place, on TV. I want to watch the game with you.'

'I didn't realize you were such a football fan, you don't look like one.'

'But I am.'

'You know, you're odd. Do you want to see the game, or me?'

'Both.'

'First the game and then me, or vice versa.'

'No, together.'

'Together? What do you mean, together?'

I felt at once the desperation and belligerence of someone who senses they've got their back to the wall. 'Together means we watch the game together and at the same time we make love.'

'Oh, is that it!'

'Yes, that's it.'

'You know, you're really odd! You're making me curious. And how do you see it, this lovemaking in front of the TV?'

A memory came to my aid: in Paris, in an antique shop run by the father of a university friend, I'd seen a book of Japanese etchings showing various positions for making love. My friend had explained that in the past parents used to give this kind of book to couples as a present the day before they got married. Encouraged by this memory, I said casually, 'I see it like this: I sit on the sofa watching the TV, you straddle my knees with your back to the screen. I watch the game, leaving you to get on with it. You don't watch the game, you just do it.'

'Do what?'

'Make love.'

'You really are odd. What else then? Light or dark?'

'Dark, of course.'

'And how shall we be, with clothes or without?'

'With: we were watching TV together, all of a sudden we felt like making love and we did. Dressed, of course.'

'I don't really like making love with my clothes on. You don't feel free and you sweat. Especially a day like today with this heat. What else? Since you have the script, I may as well hear it all.'

'I don't want you to call me my little boy, my son, or things like that.'

This last request, I immediately sensed, meant the exact opposite of what it appeared to mean. What I really meant was: I do want you to go on calling me my little boy, my son and things like that. With extraordinary intuition, she answered, 'How can I not call you my little boy? Didn't your father tell you?'

'What?'

'When I phoned him earlier on he said he'd tell you everything.'

'Everything?'

Her voice became impatient, as if forced to talk about trifles of no importance. 'Yes, everything: that your father and I are lovers, that we'll be getting married as soon as possible. Come on, don't pretend you don't know!'

Making an effort, I said, 'Yes, he told me everything, and so?'

'So, how can you ask me not to call you my little boy, my son and so on. Don't you realize? In a month at most we'll be mother and son.'

'Stepmother and stepson.'

'Alright, alright, stepmother and stepson, as you like. Now I've got it: you don't want me to say you could be my son because it would give you the impression you were making love to your mother!'

So she went round and round the truth like a hound

round a bush where the prey is hiding. 'Not so much that I was making love to my mother, as that I was betraying my father.'

At this point there was an inexplicable and somehow solemn silence, then from the receiver, as if from the cave of an oracle, came this pronouncement: 'But don't you realize that nothing can stand in the way of love: neither family nor friendship, nor father nor mother?'

Was it Esmeralda's voice speaking, or that of an inspired and cruel Sibyl? I muttered, 'I know.'

The usual, throaty, coarse voice resumed. 'In any event, we'll do it the way you want, although to tell the truth a football match is the last thing that would occur to me when making love. I don't know quite why, but I really feel that this is odd, very odd. Tell me the truth: there's something behind this you haven't told me about. Making love watching TV is hardly something natural, or romantic maybe, like making love in a wood or on a beach by the sea. I feel there's something behind it.'

'No, there's nothing behind it.'

'Tell me the truth, it's something that happened to someone, maybe a little friend of yours; he told you about it and that made you want to try it too.'

She was very close to the truth now: the little friend was myself as a child, the child who had watched, terrified, his mother's lovemaking. For a moment I felt that same impulse to confide that Jeanne had inspired in me on the plane. Except that, as with Jeanne, I felt I could confide, or rather reveal everything save this one experience which I considered the secret part of my life. And this despite being aware that by refusing to give this confidence to Esmeralda I was in fact refusing myself.

Again I lied, 'I don't want to repeat anything, I don't want to imitate anybody. I invented it myself, I like the idea, that's all.'

[illegible] of a sudden she seemed convinced. 'Watch the match and make love at the same time!' she exclaimed, suddenly bursting into raucous laughter. 'Not a bad idea in the end. The woman is like the goalmouth in the match and the players fight to get in there and score! Not bad at all! You want us to go the whole hog, you want me to yell goal, when you sneak it in? Want me to be like the goalkeeper, make you really hungry for your goal, ha, ha, ha!'

At the other end of the line I could hear her having a good laugh. And I felt a strange gratitude for her vulgarity, so sensual and so natural.

Then she abruptly broke off laughing and unexpectedly confided, 'In any event, better the football with you than the charade with your father.'

'What charade?'

'The charade of pretending I'm not me but someone else. The resemblance game.'

I started in horror at the idea of being, albeit unconsciously, compared to my father. Pretending surprise I said, 'What are you talking about?'

'I'm saying that he's got it into his head that I look like your mother. Anyone could see that we've never at any age had anything in common. But he's got it on the brain, he thinks of me as a certified copy, in body and mind. Tell me though, do you have the same impression?'

'Not at all.'

'Whereas he thinks we're identical. And he'd like me to be even more identical, if one can put it like that. For example, in our more intimate moments he calls me Dina, like your mother. Then I'm not dark but red-haired, not just on top either but down below too. In fact my hair is my main beauty, red as a flame. In Viareggio, where I come from, they called me *vampa*, flash, punning on the English word "vamp". Get it? But no sir, to look like your mother he wants me to be dark, dark as dark.'

I tried to remember, and then, yes, my memory fished up the thick black fleece of her pubic hair, as if made blacker still by the polished whiteness of her redhead's complexion. Why I don't know but I insisted, 'He wants you dark there too?'

'He certainly does, and under my armpits. He'd want the same for the hairs in my nose if I had them. Oh yes, he's a perfectionist, your father! And then the clothes.'

'The clothes?'

'Right, he'd like me to wear a miniskirt, like she did. Here, however, I draw the line. I don't look good in a miniskirt. I'm a bit big. So we came to a compromise: I wear it in the house, but outside I dress how I want. And then he doesn't want me to wear anything underneath. It seems your mother didn't wear anything under her dress and was in the habit of sitting with her legs crossed so that he could sneak his dirty little eyes right up between her thighs. That's how she got him to lose his head for her and now he wants me to make him lose it again. I've got nothing against him losing his head, anyway it would hardly be a great loss. But I want him to lose it for me and not for an imitation of his deceased spouse.'

She chattered happily away with the confidence and freedom she drew from our complicity. But I was suffering: what was a harmless mania in my father was my whole reason for living. I said abruptly, 'Okay, we'll see each other tomorrow.'

'Till tomorrow then, we'll play football supporters together. Bye bye little boy. I beg your pardon, goodbye Master Mario De Sio.'

TEN

The Rubber Pear

I went out right away and, with that automatic naturalness one has when acting without thinking, got in the car and set off in the direction of Villa Balestra.

As I drove I reflected that, albeit with my own lucid and conscious justifications, I was planning to become the lover of my father's mistress, or rather, of my stepmother, given the imminence of their marriage. I didn't like the idea at all, but nevertheless it was the truth.

Of course there was the let-out of poetry: a poet, and what's more a poet whose poems have already been written by another poet, can allow himself any liberty. Looking for confirmation of this, I silently recited these lines of my beloved Apollinaire:

> Oh, my lost youth,
> Like a stripped garland
> Now here comes the season
> Of scorn and suspicion.

As a game I tried to translate the original French into Italian, complete with rhymes and lines; but at once I realized that in the Italian just as in the French, Apollinaire didn't work this time; and that awkward word 'suspicion' with which, out of love for rhyme, I had translated *soupçon*, gave me the disconcerting impression of those flowers which, strange and beautiful as they may be, have a fetid nauseating smell when brought to the nose.

Yes, I thought, by now my youth was a 'stripped garland', and the season of scorn and suspicion really was upon me. In less poetic terms, I was setting out on an ugly adventure, and the idea that this was a therapeutic project aimed at freeing myself from obsession by re-enacting with another woman my mother's lovemaking with Terenzi hardly made it any less ugly. In short, maybe my youth really was turning into a garland of withered, fetid flowers on my forehead. And I couldn't escape the suspicion that I was not a poet at all, but a small, vulgar philanderer involved in a lurid family intrigue.

But immediately afterwards I thought: What are you talking about with your stripped garland! I'm only twenty. And I felt better.

I parked my car carefully directly opposite Alda and Jeanne's building. As I got out I looked at their balcony above and caught sight of Jeanne standing doing something behind the windowboxes. With joy and relief, I shouted, 'Jeanne, Jeanne, why don't you come down?' I saw her lean out to look at me and shouted to her again, and she waved to say she'd heard and that I should go and wait for her at Villa Balestra. All of a sudden I realized what she was doing: she was cutting the roses that were already in flower from the bushes in the boxes; she had a bunch in her arms. Obediently I set off towards the gate to Villa Balestra.

I didn't wait long. About ten minutes later I saw her walking across the grass towards the bench where I was sitting. With her grey linen pleated skirt swaying at every step from rather broad thighs over slim, elegant ankles, she made a graceful and reassuring picture. All the same, I couldn't help thinking she was still the inconsolable maniacal widow who cut the roses from the balcony to put them in vases in the marriage bedroom now transformed, according to Alda, into a funeral chapel.

She sat next to me, smoothed the pleats of her skirt with

her hand and asked in her usual shrill Parisian sing-song, 'How are you, how are you?'

'Terrible,' I said with conviction.

She looked at me sidelong with a critical curiosity unusual in her and new to me. 'Yes, you look it.'

I was alarmed. 'What do you mean I look it? How?'

'You look tired and you're pale.'

'Very pale?'

'You're not the suntanned type, but today you're really pale, you've got lines under your eyes.'

In a low voice I said, 'I've got to talk to you.'

As if prompted by an irresistible impulse, she stretched out a hand and caressed my cheek. 'Talk to me? We've done so much talking, and for quite a while, no?'

'I don't want to talk just for talking's sake, I want to tell you something in particular.'

'Something in particular?'

'Yes, I've got to talk to you about something that's happening to me.'

She made a face of exaggerated surprise. 'But what have I got to do with it?'

'You're the only person who can give me any advice.'

She gave me a haughty look, sizing me up. 'I'm afraid you're taking me for someone I'm not.'

'Why?'

'I'm not capable of advising myself, let alone anybody else.'

All at once I asked myself the question: didn't this disdainful tone of hers maybe suggest that she'd been expecting us to pick up our relationship at its point of greatest intimacy, that is when I'd put my hand on her breast? Or on the contrary, did it mean that I absolutely mustn't repeat that caress which she hadn't known how to follow up, or perhaps hadn't wanted to? In any event, I thought rather cynically, a caress is just a caress and I may as well try. My hand, almost independently of my will, moved across the space, the palm coming to rest on her breast, visible as on the previous occasion thanks to the pinkish colour that seeped through the thin white material of her blouse. But she immediately and forcefully pushed me away, drew back and said, 'My breast isn't one of those rubber pear-shaped things they used to have in old cars. You can squeeze it as much as you like, it won't honk.'

Ashamed of myself, I said, 'I'm sorry,' and without hesitating got to my feet and made to leave.

At once, as if regretting what she'd said, she stretched out, grabbed my hand, and guided it to make the very caress she'd just a moment ago refused. 'No, don't go, sit down, now tell me, I'm listening, tell me what's happening to you.'

An elderly man walking by right at that moment looked at us in amazement and quickened his pace. We must have made a strange sight in a public park, her stretching up from the bench and pressing my hand to her breast, and me standing there letting her. I sat down again and said, 'I'm getting involved in something pretty ugly.'

'Who with? Your father?'

'Him as well, though indirectly. It's his woman.'

In the end, I told myself, these words of mine would confirm for her, if she needed confirmation, my invincible coldness in her regard. But strangely she hid her disappointment this time behind an entirely new kind of attention towards me, the way someone will pretend to renounce an impossible relationship, but only because they have in fact found another way of arriving at the same goal. 'Your father's woman? You never told me he had one.'

'I didn't know, he never told me himself.'

'But who is she?'

'An ex-music-hall singer. He was seeing her every evening, but he never arranged for us to meet. But what's the point? I don't want to bore you with my problems.'

She said bravely, 'You're talking to a woman who never managed to make herself loved by the man she loved. To make up for it though, I was his confidante and he told me everything, everything he did with the endless women he betrayed me with. It seems this must be my vocation. So, tell me, what's been going on between you and your father's mistress?'

Did she really want to know? Or was she resigned to the role which, as she explained it, life had imposed on her? At once reluctant and yet finding it impossible not to trust her, I said, 'My father asked me to take a certain Signora Jodice to visit an apartment. By coincidence it was that penthouse nobody lives in opposite your place.'

'Yes, the apartment that has your mother's name on it.'

I was brought up short. Despite all the secrets I'd shared with her, I'd never spoken about my mother to Jeanne. I had that same feeling – of horror almost – that an inhabitant of Tahiti or some other desert island might have on finding human footprints on the soil of his own territory despite the sign warning: 'Taboo.' I said excitedly, 'But how did you know?'

'Know what?'

'That the name on the door was my mother's?'

'Don't you remember that some time ago you told me that the uncle you were living with in Paris was called Diotallevi? As he's a maternal uncle it's logical he must have the same surname as your mother.'

For a moment I was confused: the horror over the broken taboo had gone, but now in its place came the disturbing sensation that Jeanne knew 'everything' about me, even my obsession with my mother. Trying to sound ironic I picked up my story. 'This Signora Jodice, though, never said anything about being my father's mistress; and for his part he didn't speak of her as being his girlfriend but just a regular client whose name he couldn't remember. In short, he set a kind of trap for me.'

'But why?'

'His story is they wanted to see if I would like her and if

she would like me, seeing they are about to get married. A kind of trial, or exam if you like.'

She said eagerly, 'And you did like each other, right?'

'Not exactly.'

'Why not exactly?'

I lied. 'She liked me, but I didn't like her.'

'Are you sure? You talked about a trap, so you must have fallen into it.'

Under her enquiring gaze I again found myself confused. 'I didn't like her, but at the same time I don't know what came over me. I really didn't like her; I saw her for what she was. Yet nevertheless somehow or other I liked her.'

'What's this Signora Jodice like?'

'Vulgar.'

'So you liked her precisely because she was vulgar. The trap was her vulgarity, isn't that how it was?'

I admitted, 'Yes, perhaps it is, but I don't understand why.'

'And what "really" happened between you and this vulgar woman?'

Could I tell her the story of the Turkish Delight? I decided I could, since Jeanne already knew that what had happened had been vulgar and the worst I could do now was confirm it. 'She had a box of those sweets called *lukumi*, you know, those oriental sweets. It got knocked over. I bent down to pick them up, they were all over the place. She pointed them out to me one by one with her foot, and to move her leg she pulled up this long, long dress she was wearing. All of a sudden she asked me to kiss her leg, first the calf and then higher up. I don't know why, I really don't, but I couldn't say no. She kept on saying, "higher, higher"; and I was asking myself: Why am I doing this, but I did it. In the end I found myself with my mouth on her crotch and I bit it, not hard though. And that's all.'

'That's all, eh? Are you sure?'

'Yes.'

'Didn't you go out on the terrace? For heaven's sake, the terrace is important in a penthouse apartment, one has to see it.'

'Yes, we went out. She showed me the view of Rome.'

'And that's all?'

'Yes, nothing else happened.'

'Oh come on, something else must have happened. You were alone on the terrace; a few moments ago you'd gone so far as to put your teeth into a very particular part of her body. You're not telling me that all you did was look at the view?'

It seemed she really did know everything. I admitted, 'Something else did happen, but it wasn't much. I'd rather not talk about it.'

'Why?'

This time there was a justifiable reason for my silence: the helicopter. To speak of the helicopter meant speaking about the incestuous significance of Esmeralda's erotic game; and speaking of the game meant speaking of my mother. 'Because, as I said, in the end nothing happened.'

There was a long silence, then she summed up, 'This ugly business of yours is something quite normal, extremely normal: the stepson makes love with the stepmother.'

'But I didn't actually do it.'

She said calmly, 'You would have if she hadn't run off.'

I was dumbstruck. 'How did you know?'

'Alda was on the terrace and she saw you. Alda always tells me everything, didn't you know?'

So, I thought, despite her promise, Alda had spoken to her mother. I said nothing, irritated and ashamed, my head down. Jeanne stretched out a hand and again caressed my cheek. 'Come on, come on, it's nothing, nothing at all; a rather vulgar adventure, broken off, what's more, just when things were getting hot, as they say. Nothing ugly about it.'

I rebelled against this, clinging for once to my secret

truth. 'It's ugly because she never stops telling me I could be her son.'

'Of course she does, it turns her on.'

I was struck by Jeanne's cynicism: not only did she know everything, but it seemed that nothing surprised her.

'And then because I can't stand the idea that, through this relationship with her, I'm putting myself in a position of inferiority to someone I consider inferior to me.'

'And who is it you think is inferior?'

'My father.'

'There's always a price to pay for pleasure, that's normal, right?'

I couldn't help exclaiming, 'You don't give a damn, that's the truth of the matter!'

'On the contrary, I'm interested, if only because when you talk about certain things, your expression changes and I like to look at you.'

'How does it change?'

It was a question dictated by vanity. But Jeanne took it seriously. She looked at me for a long time. 'I told you before, I think. Your eyes usually have a sad look. But when you talk about poetry or love they are more alive, more attractive.'

'But where's the love here?'

'Oh that's for you to say; how should I know?'

All the same, I seemed to be feeling better now: unexpectedly cynical, Jeanne had, if nothing else, dispelled that feeling of shame that the memory of my meeting with Esmeralda had aroused. 'So, you really don't think it's so ugly?'

I was expecting some expert maternal indulgence again. But I was amazed to see her shaking her head. 'Slowly does it, I never said that. On the terrace, looking out over Rome, it's an adventure like any other. In your father's house though, it becomes ugly, very ugly indeed.'

I felt myself blushing. 'But you just told me yourself that I had no reason to feel inferior to him.'

'Right, but outside his house.'

'And why outside his house no and in it yes?'

'Because there are things one doesn't do, that's all.'

'Why? Because she's my future stepmother?'

'Oh, no, I don't think that's important at all. A woman is a woman before anything else, after that she's your father's mistress, then your stepmother, then whatever you like.'

'So now you're saying that it's just any old adventure again.'

'Well, let's see, think: what matters is not going to bed with a woman who's your father's mistress and your future stepmother; no, it's going on living with him, being kept by him despite that relationship. You know what you should have done right after your meeting in the apartment?'

I chose to anticipate the answer implicit in her question. 'Yes, I know, packed my bags and left.'

'You see, you realize that yourself. So why didn't you?'

I said nothing. She went on, 'I'll tell you why: because of what you call your openness. You're attracted precisely by the ugliness of the affair, and that undoubtedly is openness of the highest degree. If not, you tell me what it is?'

I still didn't say anything. She insisted, 'It's absolutely vital that you leave. You can't stay a moment longer. You know how you'll look if you stay? Like a pimp, a gigolo.' And then a moment later, urgent, practical and once again maternal, 'Listen, what about this? On Wednesday, when you come to dinner, instead of bringing me a bunch of flowers, bring your suitcase with your stuff. We've got an extra bedroom. You can stay with us at least until the end of August when we're going on holiday. But if you want, you could stay here on your own right through the summer. Then we'll see. Okay?'

How wise and affectionate Jeanne was! But at the same time how very obvious it was that, as Alda had put it, 'she thought of nothing else'! I looked at her, trying, without succeeding, to separate the disinterested maternal part of her from the interested and sentimental. Then I took her hand

and brought it to my lips. 'Thanks, I really don't know how to thank you.'

She withdrew her hand and said with determined straightforwardness, 'Let's be clear about this. I'm inviting you to stay with us to solve your accommodation problem. As far as your amorous adventures are concerned, I don't come into it. You can perfectly well go on seeing your future stepmother, as long as it's neither at my house, nor at your father's.'

I would have liked to have told her in all sincerity that I didn't want to see Esmeralda again, either at my father's or elsewhere. But, at once moved and cautious, all I could do was repeat, 'Thank you, thank you, what matters most of all to me is that you've invited me like this.' Which didn't mean anything at all, because I hadn't said in the end what I would do. All the same there must have been a light of sincerity in my eyes because she stretched out her hand and for the third time caressed my cheek, saying, 'There, your eyes are beautiful again, and you know why?'

'No.'

'Because you don't know either how to lie or how to tell the truth.' Immediately afterwards she got to her feet and quickly walked away.

ELEVEN

The Mango

Returning home I reflected that I didn't have to hurry into anything, whether it be the re-enactment with Esmeralda of my mother's lovemaking, or the acceptance of Jeanne's invitation to go and live with her. It was Saturday, one day before the re-enactment and three before the invitation to Jeanne's, so I still had a lot of time to think it over and decide. But think over what, decide about what? The fact was, I realized, that so far the people doing the thinking and deciding had been Esmeralda and Jeanne. I had done some thinking perhaps, but without results; as yet I hadn't decided anything.

On reflection, there was no reason why I should put off the two decisions, none save the desire to demonstrate to myself that it would be me who took them and not the two women: everything had to be, or at least to seem, rational, both the decisions and the postponement of the decisions. Why this need for rationality, though? I didn't know myself. Perhaps because at moments of extreme indecision, reason, which is usually only a means, can become an end in itself.

Mulling this over, I arrived home feeling calmer and more relaxed, enjoying precisely that state of relief that comes from putting off an urgent decision. I would now lie down on my bed and pick up a novel I'd begun the day before; or stretched out in my favourite position, on my back with my head down and feet up, I would just daydream. But daydream about what? Maybe about the fact that life could wait.

Avoiding the lounge I went straight to my bedroom. But in the corridor I heard an excited babble coming from the lounge: the sound, I immediately appreciated, of the television.

At first I thought my father was in, not an impossible conjecture given that it was Saturday. But then I remembered that the evening before he had complained about having had to arrange an appointment with someone for this very afternoon, a client who was leaving for London. I even remembered what he'd said about the client: 'He's one of those eternally indecisive people who never know what they want. This time he's coming with his wife. Fingers crossed. I prefer the women to the men. They know what they want, the women do.' Suddenly, on remembering this, the babble of the television became inexplicable and unsettling. I thought of Oringia but immediately dismissed the idea: she had a small TV in the kitchen on the table, plus a larger one in her bedroom; she watched them all day; there was no reason for her to be turning on the one in the lounge.

I realized that my heart had begun to beat anxiously and that I was breathing hard. The fact was that I had heard the voice of the announcer in that same corridor before, a voice dampened and muffled by the closed door behind the couch in there. But when? No doubt about it: the night when, against my will, I had been forced to watch my mother. The babble of the announcer, so commonplace and normal, disturbed me now because it was linked in my memory to something abnormal and extraordinary that had disturbed me in the past.

Suddenly it occurred to me that I had somehow got myself into the incredible and vaguely terrifying situation of a person encountering a ghost. Where had I read about a piano that played on its own without anyone pressing the keys, in the silence of an abandoned house? Here it was the television babbling away on its own in the silence of an apartment, less romantic perhaps, but more frightening, as indeed the human voice is more frightening than any other sound that cannot be explained. Someone had turned on the television, someone was watching it. I reached out my hand, grasped the handle and pushed it down. The door opened and I looked in.

The first thing I saw was the screen filled by a football field and criss-crossed by the numerous tiny running figures of the players. It wasn't the big game, the Sunday game; it was one of the dozens of matches they were playing this week. Then, as if the game had suggested it, I realized that the TV's intense light wasn't flickering away on its own in the shadow of the lounge. Someone was sitting on the couch watching it.

It was Esmeralda, as I realized from the shape of her hairstyle, pinned down and flat on top, puffed out and flowing in a fan on her shoulders; Esmeralda, who our phone conversation of a short while ago had filled with impatient curiosity, so much so that she'd wanted to move our meeting forward a day; Esmeralda, ready to perform with me what she herself had intuitively and rightly referred to as a scripted re-enactment.

This realization dispelled my fear, but increased my confusion, plunging me into that familiar feeling of simultaneous repugnance and attraction which seemed to be inevitable in my relationship with my future stepmother. Now, however, I realized that the re-enactment of my mother's lovemaking had really begun the very moment I'd heard the babble of the TV commentator in the corridor. Carefully, I gave the door a slight push and slipped in behind the sofa without making a noise. The screen, so alive and vibrant with light and images, formed a strange and sinister contrast with the dark, still, and seemingly fake hair of the spectator. Then I made up my mind; I stretched out my arms, put my hands over Esmeralda's eyes and said very softly, 'Guess who?'

For a second Esmeralda didn't reply, which made me afraid somehow, as if it wasn't her but someone else. Then, without speaking, she raised her hands to take mine, lowered them to her mouth and kissed them, first on the backs and then on the palms. Then the all too familiar hoarse, harsh voice said, 'I know who it is. It's that little boy who plays at surprising his mummy.' Thus the reality of the past was being parodied in the present, at once the same yet different. Terribly agitated now, I went round the sofa and said in a subdued voice, 'Why did you come? We'd agreed we'd see each other on Sunday.'

'I said to myself: Why leave till Sunday what you can do today? So I came, and here I am, Master De Sio, ready to act out the part of lover and football fan.'

She looked me up and down with an expression of challenge. Impulsively, without thinking, I went over to the television, turned it off and said abruptly, 'No, we can't do it today, I said Sunday and I want it to be Sunday.'

She looked at me with curiosity, 'But there's a game today too.'

'Yes, right, but my father could come back any moment.'

'Well, I know he won't. He phoned me to say he was busy with a client today. In any event, as you will: the game will be going on a good while yet, let's go to my place, I've got a TV too. We can make it in time.'

'No, my father could turn up there too.'

'But I told you he's busy. I won't be seeing him till this evening, for dinner as usual.'

By now though I felt determined to put off the re-enactment. I said firmly, 'No, today's out, we can see each other on Sunday at your place. My father will definitely be going to the game. And I don't want anything to happen between us before Sunday.'

There was a long silence, then Esmeralda said slowly, as though underlining every word, 'Listen, Sunday's fine, if you're really going to insist, though I don't understand why. But first I want you to tell me something.'

'What?'

'I'm sure there's something behind this football business.

Are you such a fanatic that you want to watch the game even while you're making love? Who are you trying to kid?'

'But it's the truth.'

'No, it's not. Okay, fine, we'll put it off till tomorrow, but first of all you've got to promise me that this is nothing to do with your mother, understand?'

Profoundly disturbed by this completely unexpected intuition, I stuttered, 'What are you talking about?'

'I'm just saying that I've got quite enough on my hands with your father and his mania for likenesses. Now I don't want you to start having me play your mother's double as well. One is okay. Two would really be a bit much.'

I couldn't help but exclaim, 'But it's you always calling me my baby, my little boy and so on. It's you who wants to play the part of the double.'

Not bending an inch, she came back with surprising toughness, 'If anything I want to play the part of a woman who "could be" your mother. It's just a game. I don't mind the idea that you're a little boy who could perfectly well be my son: everybody knows older women like little boys. But the game stops there. What I absolutely don't want is to play the part of your mother, with whom, for reasons I don't want to hear, you would like to go to bed. We two are an older woman and a young boy, we are not mother and son. In short, incest makes my skin creep, get it?'

I couldn't quite see the subtle difference between pretending to be any mother and pretending to be a particular mother. All the same, the toughness of Esmeralda's tone made it clear that at least for her a difference there must be. I said, 'I know you're not my mother.'

'Nor her double either. Whereas you want me to play the part of the double, a blind man could see that. I wish you'd tell me why you care so much.'

'I don't care at all.'

'Oh come on, you're like your father, you have this need to delude yourself that your mother and I are the same person.

With him though it's understandable. He loved her a lot and sees something of her in every woman. But with you I just can't understand it.'

I realized that she was being sincere and telling the simple truth: she didn't understand it. But I didn't have the courage either to accept or reject this truth. I looked at her big curving fleshy mouth,veiled in a down of dark hair that seemed to throw across the red of her lips the same alluring shadow that sometimes shades the similar red of the female sex, hidden as it is by another, thicker mat of hair. I remembered how she had crouched at my feet on the penthouse terrace, bringing her face to the level of my crotch; and, at the thought that, had Alda not been there, that same mouth that was now talking to me so harshly and aggressively, would have taken me gently into her – at this thought,which was more a desire expressed in thought than thought prompted by desire, I felt utterly confused and ready to do just what she wanted, whatever that might be.

Still in the same tough tone, she went on, 'Now tell me the truth once and for all: this football match, making love during the match, your mother, my likeness to her, the fact that your father and I are lovers, the other fact that we're getting married and that I, as it were, am about to become your mother, they're all connected to each other, aren't they? It's like a jigsaw puzzle, fit the pieces together and they make a single picture. That picture exists, but I can't put the pieces together to make it; the one thing I know for certain is that it does exist. So then, here's what I think: if you want to play, even if it's the mother-and-son game, I'll do it. But if I have to be your mother's double, I'm not doing it, absolutely not. I want to have fun, that's for sure: but I want to be me and not someone else. Understand?'

I said nothing: I went on looking at her mouth, so similar to a female sex, and my excitement, evident from my uneasiness with my body, spoke for me. She must have already realized, because she suddenly threw me a sharp glance, not at my face but at the middle of my body, then she said suddenly, 'Come here.' She spoke with the same imperious authoritative tone she'd used in the entrance to the penthouse apartment when she'd repeatedly ordered me to move, 'higher'. And as in the apartment I obeyed. I moved toward her, first one step, then another, coming to stand up straight in front of her with my groin slightly pushed out. She stretched out a big knotty, bejewelled hand and grabbed hold of me with unexpected violence, speaking in a strange voice, not her own, but the voice, it seemed, of the maternal figure which, instinctively, she couldn't help but play the part of. 'Baby mine, why don't you relax? What on earth's wrong with you? Why are you standing there almost falling on top of me? You're not afraid I can't see you, are you? I can see you, don't worry; your mummy can see you and she's telling you to relax. Understand? Your mummy's telling you to relax. Get it?'

It was as if she were repeating this invitation to relax more to herself than to me. And meantime, as though giving way to an irresistible temptation, first she grabbed me, then let me go, then grabbed me again. At which, suddenly, with a powerful shove, she jumped up from the sofa: 'We're acting like two kids who can't wait and want to have everything right away. But it's dangerous here, he really might come back any moment. Let's go to my place.'

Impetuously she moved across the sitting-room and I followed her, docile and subdued. In the lift she added, 'Will you last till we get to my place?' and again she grabbed me, once more betraying her impatience. But as soon as we were in the street, she assumed her usual majestic slowness, walking towards a small blue car brightly sparkling with polished chrome parked by the river. We got in and she started to drive with almost excessive composure, stiffly upright, full of possessive tension, almost as if she had abducted me against my will and was taking me off to some kidnap hideout where violence could be done. Suddenly then, without turning round, she said in a low voice, 'Tell me about your mother.'

So, the jigsaw puzzle continued to bother her, the puzzle of the love scene she'd caught a glimpse of through the way I was behaving with her. I protested, 'I've got nothing to say about my mother. I was only seven when she died.'

'Come on, I'm sure you remember her very well. At seven a child sees everything, understands everything.'

'Obviously I was a stupid child, because I saw nothing and understood nothing.'

'In any event, in your opinion, in what way do I look like your mother?' Involuntarily, without thinking, I answered, 'The expression of the eyes is a bit the same, but mainly you have the same mouth.'

Now this wasn't true. The desire aroused a few moments ago by the shadow of that down of hair on the sex-red of her mouth, was making me forget that in reality the only real likeness lay in the particular expression of the eyes. I saw her lick her lips, as if checking on their shape. 'And what was her mouth like?'

'Like yours.'

'You wouldn't say so, if the photos your father has are anything to go by. She had a small mouth, a bit like a doll. I've got a big one, an oven.'

I looked at her mouth and acknowledged, 'Yes, you're right, but all the same there is something similar.'

'What?'

'I don't know. All I know is that you make me think of her.'

'Come on, are you or aren't you going to tell me what she was like, as you remember her?'

'She was very beautiful.'

'Dumb-ass beauty, you mean?'

What was Esmeralda after with me? In the end, precisely what I hadn't, even unconsciously, expected of her: she wanted to replace my mother's image with her own and at the same time to destroy my memory of her. With sudden emotion I said, 'Okay, dumb-ass beauty if that's how you want to put it, but in the sense of loving life, with complete illusion, in an innocent, ingenuous way, the way animals love it.'

She said nothing and drove on for a while intent on her thoughts. Then announced abruptly, 'I bet you've got a photo of her with you. Show me.'

'I haven't got any photos.'

'Come on, you're in love with her and you haven't got a photo! Come on, out with it.'

I hesitated, full of repugnance for what I felt was a sacrilege. Despite the fact that she was driving, Esmeralda stretched out a hand towards the bulge of my wallet in the pocket of my jeans and tried to pull it out, without succeeding. 'Come on, don't be an idiot, out with the photo and have done.'

How affectionate the insult sounded on her lips! I pulled the wallet from my pocket and then, delicately, the photo from my wallet, half faded away and trembling between my fingers. Esmeralda took it without turning and, still driving, looked at it. 'Can't make head nor tail of it. It's all faded. What do you keep this crap for? Why don't you make up your mind to chuck it?'

This time I didn't hesitate. The irresistible urge taking me toward a re-enactment with Esmeralda of the love scene with my mother, demanded the destruction of this miserable square of worn and streaky paper, and this despite the fact that the same eyes looked out at me from that photograph as had looked at me 'then'. I said quickly, 'You're right, chuck it!' Esmeralda immediately put her hand out of the window and opened the two fingers holding the photograph: 'That's that.' I saw the photo spin a moment in the wind of our passing, then disappear. Esmeralda said in a low voice, 'Now, give me a kiss.'

I leaned across and kissed the corner of her lips, whether

out of obscure gratitude or voluntary obedience I don't know. She returned the kiss by poking out her tongue sideways, then announced, 'Right, here we are.'

And in fact there we were. Esmeralda had turned the car away from the broad rising street we had been going up, into a small sidestreet lined on both sides by railings thick with climbing plants. The street seemed to be closed at the other end by a wall overflowing with ivy. Esmeralda explained, 'It's a private road. There are a lot of painters' studios.'

We stopped in front of a little iron gate half hidden by ivy. Esmeralda opened it and led the way, slow and solemn, along what looked like a country path between the trees and shrubs of a dense garden. Suddenly, without turning, she asked, 'Do you like tropical fruit?'

'It depends what kind.'

'Mangoes, papayas, kiwis and so on.'

'Yes, but why do you ask?'

'I like them a great deal. I bought a whole lot today.'

We walked a little further, then the path came out into a gravelled area; we were in front of a rustic-looking building, just one storey, with red walls and a sloping roof of rough tiles. Esmeralda opened the door and went on ahead, explaining with a satisfied wave, 'This is my studio. There are lots of plants, too many perhaps, but I wanted to create a private little paradise on earth. So I pot mostly tropical plants, they're the ones that make me think of Eden most with their big leaves and garish flowers.'

I looked. The studio was very big and designed like a loft with a slanting ceiling of great black beams; one wall, at the far end, was higher than the others, with a gallery running along it, while the opposite wall at the front was lower and almost entirely taken up by a big window. The tropical plants Esmeralda had spoken of were everywhere, the small ones in various pots on shelves one above the other, the large ones in big terracotta or cement tubs crowded together in the corners. There was a huge stone fireplace and, scattered all around it, chairs, an armchair, a sofa. Esmeralda pointed to the television whose screen looked out between two thrusting plants, 'As you see I have a TV too,' and then turning, 'Plus a sofa. Now I'll switch on and let's find the game.'

She picked up the remote control and pressed a button a few times. The screen lit up, and after a number of different scenes, the green of the football pitch appeared with the players chasing the ball. 'That okay?'

'Yes.'

'So, we've got the sofa, we've got the TV, we've got the game, what else does my little boy want?'

Very softly I answered, 'The dark.'

'Oh, of course, the dark. I need the dark too, much more than you do. In the dark you can't see the wrinkles, hey?'

Ritualistic and sardonic, she went to the window and drew some very heavy, lined curtains: the studio was plunged into a grey obscurity across which, here and there, the quivering light of the television screen picked out the bizarre shadows of tropical plants. Standing in the middle of the studio, she went on. 'Everything just so, I think. I'll go upstairs and get ready. Eat some fruit while you're waiting. I suggest the mango, it's exquisite. Here's a plate, knife and fork, and here's a mango.'

A bowl of fruit stood on a low table, vividly lit by the light from the screen. She chose a mango, put it on a plate for me, put a knife and a small fork next to the plate, bent down to dart her tongue quickly into my mouth, then went off towards the other end of the studio. I caught a glimpse of her calmly going up a wooden staircase that climbed diagonally towards the gallery. From a distance she called back with a sarcastic biblical allusion, 'Go ahead and eat the forbidden fruit without remorse; it's ripe and won't do you any harm.' I heard the sound of her footsteps on the gallery, followed by that of a door being softly closed. Then I looked at the screen.

The game was proceeding in regular fashion; one of the many, I thought, going on in Italy about now. And yet for me it was a special game, just as the one my mother had forced me to watch so many years ago had been special. And then, with the subterranean, explosive logic typical of unconscious preoccupations, a sudden precise thought sprang to my mind: What if the re-enactment didn't work? What if from now on I couldn't make love without watching a football match? It was a thought, or rather an image, that I immediately found comic. But the comedy was pathetic, unsavoury, and contained something very like fear.

I looked down at the low table dominated by the full bowl with its pyramid of tropical fruit. Then, as if awoken by the sight of those juicy fruits, I sensed in my mouth the dry thirst of unsatified desire to which Esmeralda's tongue, with that brief darting kiss, had somehow added a taste of ripeness. On the plate in front of me the mango, with its beautiful green and red colours blending into each other, was tempting. I picked up the knife and fork and started to cut it. I thought I'd cut off a thick slice and suck it. I knew that was how you ate mangoes.

But it was more than just ripe, this mango. Sinking my teeth into the slice, the pulp came apart in my mouth and the thick sourish juice dribbled over the corners of my lips and over my chin. I scraped the pulp down to the peel, then looked for a napkin to clean myself. There wasn't one. So I pulled my handkerchief out of my pocket, dried myself carefully, then hesitated: the handkerchief was soaked with juice. I couldn't put it back in my pocket, I thought, without staining my jacket, so I placed it just as it was, crumpled into a ball, beside the plate.

At the same moment a door opened above in the half dark shrouding the gallery, and Esmeralda's voice shouted, 'What's my little boy up to? Watching the game? Was the mango nice? One more second and I'll be right there.' I raised my eyes and saw, or thought I saw, up above, white in the shadow, her body, sturdy-limbed and completely naked, and, between one banister upright and the next, the dark triangle of the crotch my father had wanted black like my mother's. The image lasted no more than a second, but in that second I was horrified by the desire that Esmeralda's words and the sight of her body had immediately roused in me. This time words and vision had acted in an abrupt and impetuous fashion. I realized that from the absence of my normal sense of repugnance and from the sudden rearing up of desire. Yes, no doubt about it, this was what love had become for me, a ritualistic, mechanical make-believe without which I could feel nothing but impotent alienation, as had been the case in my relationship with Jeanne, despite her being more desirable than Esmeralda. This was love; and rather than liberation, all the future held for me was a debased and endless repetition of the incestuous act, now indissolubly linked to various ridiculous but indispensable details, like the football match on TV, the lovemaking on the couch with the woman straddled above, the expression 'little boy', and all the other finishing touches with which I would doubtless gradually adorn successive performances.

But in addition to this vision of my future enslavement, another feeling now prompted me to take an unexpected decision, one that took me away from this experience to which I felt so naturally led. It was a feeling of compassion for my father, something I'd never felt before now and inspired, I realized, precisely by his great love first for my mother and then for Esmeralda who was so much like her.

This histrionic, heart-rending love, so important for him, was a complicated and probably, in its own way, vital phenomenon. Yet I was cynically and quite consciously using the woman he loved to carry out an experiment that I sensed had failed even before it had started.

Spurred by an irresistible impulse, I jumped to my feet and headed for the door of the studio. Just as I was going out, I turned a last time and saw the TV screen. The game was over;

now there was some programme on ecology. Amid the thick tropical foliage, very similar to that of Esmeralda's plants, the flat triangular head of a big green and yellow speckled snake appeared, slithering cautiously along. I remembered Esmeralda's allusion to forbidden fruit and thought with relief and almost cheerfulness that at least this time the ancient and insidious tempter had not had his way.

TWELVE

Mango Juice

I'm in Paris, in my room at my uncle's, rue de Cherche-Midi. I'm reading a book, Apollinaire of course, the poet who before me and for me wrote all the poems I would like to have written myself. The book is lying open on the small desk where I'm sitting, my favourite reading position. To my right is a big window and, if I turn my head just a little, I can see the garden down in the courtyard and, around it, the regular white façade of the old Empire period building. This very moment I have just finished reading some lines that seem to have something to do with my life, my life which, for reasons I don't understand, seems static and futureless:

Let the night come: strike the hour
The days go past while I stand here.

I turn and look out across the courtyard. I have a definite reason for looking: every day at the same time an old man, very old, but upright and solid, respectably dressed in a dark suit like some provincial solicitor, comes out of a small door on the other side of the courtyard, walks down the three or four steps under the ancient glass and iron porch, goes to unhook a hose from the wall and, methodically, points its jet at the flowerbeds of the garden, moving in short steps along the magnificent bushes of hortensias and roses in bloom. When he has watered everything thoroughly, he rolls up the hose again, hangs it on the wall, picks up a rake and, taking his time, pulls it again and again across the gravel of the drive. Then he puts the rake back in its corner, arms himself with a pair of shears and spends a good while cutting and evening out the box hedge. The garden is clearly prospering thanks to this meticulous care. The grass around the flowerbeds is emerald green; the plants are laden with flowers; much of the courtyard wall is covered with the leaves of a huge American vine; a leafy tree rises in the middle of the garden, stretching its branches above the bald head of the old man who appears and disappears throughout these laborious comings and goings.

I often look at this old and somewhat obsessive gardener and every time I do so I can't help remembering another literary quotation, the line which closes Voltaire's *Candide*: 'We must cultivate our garden.'

Once again, as in the lines of Apollinaire, it's an exhortation to act! Apollinaire tells me to act in life, Voltaire in literature. Because of his passion for gardening I have nicknamed the old man, 'Monsieur Voltaire'. There's Monsieur Voltaire cultivating his garden, I think every time I see him. There he is picking some flowers to put together a bunch. There is irony in these thoughts; but perhaps, who knows, a little admiration too.

But now, in my dream (because I'm dreaming), Monsieur Voltaire is not to be seen. All the same I'm conscious of waiting for someone to appear, him or somebody else. So I read a moment, then look out of the window a moment. Perhaps I look out more than I read.

And now, instead of Monsieur Voltaire, three women appear, processing slowly along, their backs towards me. I immediately recognize Alda, my mother and Esmeralda, partly from the way they dress and partly from their bodies, typical, I immediately realize, of three successive ages: adolescence, youth, maturity. Alda, with her scanty tee-shirt and short tight jeans again reminds me of the uncertain capering of a colt or new-born calf; my mother, with her blouse open to reveal a bare shoulder and her miniskirt scarcely covering her backside, wiggles her hips provocatively; finally Esmeralda processes solemnly along, squashing, at every step, the oblong shapes of her buttocks against the material of her ankle-length dress.

Watching, I tell myself that they are manifestly the same person at three different ages, and I realize that this thought is dictated by the unconfessable desire that all three arouse in me as they walk along. Yes, I am equally attracted by Alda's knock-kneed capering, my mother's brazen arse-wiggling, Esmeralda's heavy sway.

The three women move slowly, as if out for a stroll, holding hands, although curiously they seem to be strangers to each other. This mutual feeling of being strangers is underlined by the fact that not only do they not talk to each other, but they don't even look at each other either: Esmeralda has her eyes on the ground, as if fearing she might stumble; Alda looks up, up, high above the courtyard to the sky; my mother, more surprisingly, suddenly turns round and shamelessly tips me a wink. At this point it occurs to me to open the window and call to them; I get up and try to open it, but the handle won't turn, I can't do it. Meanwhile, to my bitter disappointment, the three women slowly climb the steps under the porch and disappear inside the little door, though not before my mother, alone of the three, again turns to send me a look of complicity. At the same time, someone is pressing a hand on my shoulder and I'm trying to free myself from this insistent contact which I sense is connected in some obscure way to my inability to open the window. So I go on for a moment, trying to turn the handle and to shrug off that hand pressing on my shoulder. Finally, losing my temper, I turn round, and so wake up.

The first thing I was aware of was that the room was invaded by the dazzling light of the late morning sun. Yet I was quite sure that after fleeing from Esmeralda's studio I hadn't come home till late at night and that before going to bed I had taken care to close the shutters. I'm used to sleeping in the dark and so as to be certain I won't be woken I even tie a handkerchief tight round my eyes. Where had I been after my escape? Not really wanting to see my father, I'd first of all slipped into a cinema and seen the matinée film right through. Then I'd eaten something standing at a bar and finally I'd walked for a long time, so long that, street by street, I'd finally reached St Peter's Square and stood in front of the basilica which I'd never seen before, save from the belvedere in Villa Balestra. The square was packed with enormous tourist coaches and hundreds of people were walking round the colonnades, climbing the steps, milling round the fountains. Then all of a sudden I'd had a bizarre idea: I'd tag on to a group of tourists, blend in with them for their visit to the square and, when it was over, avoiding the attention of the drivers, climb onto one of those huge coaches and set off with all the others on the ritual 'around Rome by night' expedition. I avoided the first and largest group: they were Japanese and I would be far too obvious; then I heard someone speaking French and so I started speaking French too, to a middle-aged woman, bespectacled and benevolent. And all of a sudden there I was sitting at the back of a coach between the woman and her twelve-year-old daughter. I couldn't work out if they had realized that I shouldn't be on the bus. Certainly they made room for me very promptly and amicably; and so I set off to discover this famous city where I'd lived till now without ever leaving Parioli and the surrounding streets.

The coach was so tall that I found myself sitting almost on a level with the first floors of the apartment blocks. But being in the middle of the back seat, between the woman and her child, I saw very little, and that little somewhat confusedly, though this was partly because of my ignorance of the city's topography. Every now and then, however, after impetuous, horn-blaring charges through dark narrow twisting streets, the coach would stop and the whole party would get out and set off, obediently lined up behind the guide, to admire the steps to some large baroque church, or the overflowing basin of an ancient fountain, or some high, pointed obelisk. I got off with the rest; the two drivers, tired and distracted, didn't notice me. All the time I made an effort to keep talking to the lady and her daughter, who were from La Baule, a seaside resort which luckily I knew, having often been there in summer to go swimming. In my somnambulist zeal I even somehow managed to describe for them the sights we were visiting one after the other, sights I knew nothing about and which, like them, I was seeing for the first time.

Meanwhile, however, my mind never stopped going back and back to the shadows of Esmeralda's studio and to her white, naked body up in the gallery; at which I might even begin to regret having fled. But I immediately realized that my regret was superficial. An irresistible, inexplicable and dark force had prompted me to flee from the studio and even now, I was prolonging my flight from Esmeralda. All the same, I did try to keep a grip on things. I wanted to arrive home late enough not to risk bumping into my father; but not too late. Apart from anything else, I was extremely tired, I'd been up and about since the morning and all the events of that long and extraordinary day, beginning with the scene in the apartment in Via Ammannati, had got confused in my memory in the sort of befuddled, intoxicated stupor that generally leads to sleep. And in fact at a certain point I did doze off and sleep for a while, as if lulled by the powerful surges, abrupt braking and circumspect manoeuvring of the coach. Then a cry of joy from the La Baule woman's daughter – 'The Colosseum! The Colosseum!' – jerked me awake. Mechanically I got up from my seat, once again joined the line with the tourist party and got off the bus. In the pale summer night the famous monument made me think of a huge, empty skull weighing down on me with the blind shadowy eyesockets of its arches and vaults. The tourists had wandered off around the plaza. I guessed at the time and felt that I should be able to go home now without having to worry about meeting my father. So I broke off from the party, intent on listening to the guide's explanation, and with only instinct to show me the way, headed for the centre of town. Walking quickly I went from Piazza Venezia to the Tiber and then pressed on with my night-time walk along the parapets, under the plane trees, bridge after bridge, until I reached the familiar traffic light on the river road with the inevitable cars throbbing away as they waited for the green light that would let them go. I was so tired I could do no more than throw myself on my bed fully dressed; but towards dawn I woke up, undressed and had then slept deeply right through to the dream with the apparition of Esmeralda, my mother and Alda, all absurdly together in the courtyard of my uncle's house in Paris.

Now, as I said, I was sitting on my bed dazzled by a blazing, reddish sun, when I realized that the hand which had been shaking my shoulder to wake me was my father's. Impatient to talk to me he had obviously come into my room, thrown open the window and was now sitting opposite me on the edge of the bed. To talk to me about what, though? I immediately thought: 'Of course, he's somehow found out that I went to Esmeralda's yesterday. He knows everything and now I'd better be ready for an extremely nasty scene.' I was aware of feeling guilty, and at the same time extremely irritated with myself about this. In what way was I guilty really? I hadn't re-enacted the traumatic scene of fifteen years before. I had fled. In the end I had nothing to hide from him. To gain time I pretended amazement. 'Dad, what's up?'

As I said, he was sitting on the edge of the bed, turning to face me, an uncomfortable position, as if still stretching over to shake my shoulder. He stared at me as though with something important on his mind that he couldn't find the words to express. Finally he exploded, 'What's up is that I've got to talk to you.'

'Talk to me?'

'Yes, to you, Mario, not as father to son though, but –'

I don't know why, but I interrupted with sudden impatience: 'As man to man, right?'

Hearing me mimic his own cliché with aggressive irony unsettled him. 'Yes, Mario, in a certain sense I couldn't put it better myself. What I want to talk to you about is precisely one of those things that can only be spoken about man to man.'

His embarrassment told me I had nothing to fear. He knew nothing, so heaven knows what it was that had prompted him to make this very unusual and definitely man-to-man gesture of coming into my room and waking me up. Relieved, I looked at him with sudden curiosity. How did that mind, so different from my own, operate? What really lay behind that Molièresque Sganarelle-type mask with knitted brows, the staring eyes, the big twisted mouth? I don't know why but all at once I remembered my dream and in particular my mother, the way, moving together with Esmeralda towards the little door under the porch, she had turned and, cheekily provocative, winked at me. Almost without thinking, transported by I don't know what bitterness, I said, 'If you're planning to talk to me about Mother in your usual man-to-man style, that is, slandering her, then I'm warning you I won't put up with it, because precisely thanks to your stories I've managed to get an idea of her which is totally different from yours. You make her out to be a monster of duplicity, unfaithfulness and selfishness. But for me she was simply a charming girl, full of an unexpressed *joie de vivre*, whose main quality, whatever she did, was innocence. Okay, maybe it was an animal innocence that couldn't distinguish good from bad, but it was still innocence.'

I had spoken hastily and immediately regretted it. My father's face took on an expression of pain and amazement, as though being reproached harshly and unfairly for something he hadn't done and had no intention of doing. He stammered, 'But Mario, what's your mother got to do with it?'

Confused, I said, 'I'm sorry, some day I'd have had to tell you what I thought. But what on earth's wrong with you? What's happened? Is something up at the agency?'

He didn't answer. I saw him shake his head without speaking. Then, to my amazement, I saw that the expression in his big, pulpy black pupils seemed refracted as though through a veil of liquid. And finally I got there: my father was crying! The tears filled his eyes, brimmed on the edge of his lids, then he shook his head and they spilled over onto his cheeks. He stammered, 'No, Mario, nothing's happened at the agency. It's my life that's gone wrong.' Then, obeying some sudden dramatic impulse, he collapsed on the bed, his head on my knees.

Well, I had as usual gone to bed entirely naked. But the moment I'd woken up and discovered the surprising presence of my father, I'd quickly pulled the sheet up over my chest, leaving my legs uncovered. So that now I had my father's forehead pressing against my knees, a pretty unpleasant situation given the physical repugnance I had always felt for him. With a shudder I looked at his big head with its thick grey hair, carefully cut and combed, and said mechanically, 'Dad, what's wrong? Come on, try and pull yourself together,' an ambiguous remark by which perhaps more than 'pull yourself together' mentally, I was trying to tell him to get a hold of himself physically, that is to stop pressing his forehead down on my knees.

He shook his head in refusal and I heard him moan, 'No, I can't pull myself together,' or something like that. At which I again felt curious to know what he was thinking, or rather planning, and my curiosity led me to risk the gesture of compassion I hadn't until now felt like making. I stretched out a hand and gently shook his shoulder. 'Come on, don't talk like that, what's come over you?'

Immediately, at the lightest touch of my fingers, he jumped up to show me his red face all streaked with tears. 'Mario, you're my son, and precisely because you're my son I can't hide what's happened from you. At the same time though you're a man, you can understand these things, weigh them up. So, Mario, I told you that the client you showed the apartment in Via Ammannati to was my girlfriend, that she was soon to become my wife and hence your stepmother. Well Mario, I'm telling you that all that was just a dream, a wonderful dream. Mario, forget Esmeralda! Act as if you'd never met her! As if I'd never mentioned her!'

So it was true. It was, as I had feared, to do with Esmeralda, but not the Esmeralda who'd taken me to her studio yesterday, no, another Esmeralda who, or so it seemed, had nothing to do with me. I was really intrigued now, coldly and ironically so, like a complete stranger. I faked sympathetic amazement. 'But what's Esmeralda done that's so bad?'

He looked straight at me with his staring eyes. 'What she's done is she's a brazen slut.'

'But Dad –'

'Yes, a brazen slut.' Then, drying his eyes with the back of his hand, 'See this? I found it yesterday evening at her place, carefully hidden away in the drawer of the dresser in her bedroom.'

I looked down: between two fingers, just two, as if to underline his disgust, my father showed me something which I recognized as a handkerchief crumpled into a ball and spotted all over with yellowish stains. I knew it was mine at once because of the blue border; it was the handkerchief I'd had in my jacket pocket the day before and used to clean my mouth after eating the mango. Not wanting to risk staining my jacket by putting it back in my pocket, I'd put it down on the table next to the plate. Obviously Esmeralda had found it and hidden it in her bedroom, since, however innocent, it was still a trace of my presence in her house. I said curtly, 'Sure I see it, it's a handkerchief.'

'Right, a handkerchief; but not just any old handkerchief. First of all it's a man's handkerchief. Then she'd hidden it in the drawer of her dresser. What's more, this dresser is not in her studio but in her bedroom. And finally it's stained by some filthy yellow stuff. Now take a good look and tell me if that's just any old handkerchief?'

As if seized by frenzy, my father stretched out the handkerchief and showed me the stains. 'No, this handkerchief is not any old handkerchief, it's a handkerchief that speaks worlds.' He fell silent a moment, smoothing the handkerchief between his fingers. 'A day's gone by now, but yesterday, when I found it, it was still damp, sticky, soaked with the sperm of the man Esmeralda had made love to. Yes, sperm, Mario! This man wiped himself with his handkerchief. Or, more likely, it was Esmeralda pulled it out of his pocket and spat what she had in her mouth into it.' To interrupt this embarrassing flow of hypotheses, I asked quickly, 'But when do you think all this happened?'

'Yesterday, Mario, maybe ten minutes before I got there. I told you, the handkerchief was soaked. The man had only just left, Mario. She'd barely had time to rinse her mouth.'

Once again I tried to shift the conversation away from my father's pornographic vengefulness. 'But did you tell her you'd found the handkerchief?'

To my surprise he jumped up and said belligerently, 'No, why should I tell her? I'm not just Othello, Mario, I'm Riccardo De Sio, that is Othello plus Iago, remember that.'

'And so?'

'And so I don't want to give myself away, I want to pull the strings, to play the puppeteer who directs the show, to be the cat who toys with the mouse. I know, but she doesn't know that I know, and I know that she doesn't know I know.'

This conundrum was accompanied by a kind of satisfied sarcastic cackle which made me shiver. 'Anyway, the puppeteer's game has already begun. The discovery of the handkerchief is just the opening gambit; and it won't be a game for two, but for three.'

My heart took a dive. I didn't as yet know why, all I knew

was that whatever was going on I had reason to be nervous. 'Why for three? Isn't Esmeralda enough?'

He bent forward, staring at me dramatically. 'There are three of us: me, Esmeralda, and the other.'

'What other?'

'The handkerchief man. What do you take me for? You think I let myself get carried away and told her she was a slut? No, Mario, I've always known she was unfaithful. What makes me angry is the fact that she's being unfaithful now of all times.'

'What do you mean, now of all times?'

'I mean in this precise moment, Mario. You see, I chose the occasion of your coming down from Paris to ask her to marry me and she accepted eagerly. We both agreed, we decided to put the past behind us and begin a new life together, a family life! A life with you, me and her in the apartment in Via Ammannati. The life I had with your mother and hoped to have again with Esmeralda.'

Then, making a bitter and at the same time comic reflection, 'And instead I'm sorry to say that Esmeralda has acted exactly the way your mother did. Your mother betrayed me too, on the same occasion and in the same way. Yes, during our honeymoon in Paris. The man she betrayed me with was in the same sleeper, a couple of compartments down from ours. They resemble each other, morally as well as physically. The only difference is that your mother was honest and told me to my face. Whereas Esmeralda, when I catch her red-handed, immediately makes a scene as if it was me being unfaithful.'

I didn't know what to say. He had already told me all this the evening I arrived, and I still found it extremely offensive. 'Please, leave Mother out of it. What are you going to do now?'

'Simple, I told you, play the puppeteer who pulls the strings.'

'But you just told me to forget Esmeralda! I thought

you meant you were going to break it off with her, not marry her.'

He threw me a quick, enigmatic glance. 'The words of a jealous man, Mario, the words of a jealous man! The marriage will go ahead, must go ahead in fact, the puppeteer wants it to go ahead. But from now on Esmeralda is not my friend any more, not the woman I was going to marry, but a puppet like any other, a puppet who walks and waves her arms, or maybe when required spreads her legs, just as the puppeteer commands.'

I was staring at him now; his words echoed in my ears, but their meaning escaped me. Then a horrifying suspicion suddenly lit the darkness of my mind. 'But do you actually know who the man with the handkerchief is?'

For a moment an expression of regret crossed his eyes. Then he seemed to take heart, as if with a surge of pride, 'Of course I know, otherwise I wouldn't be Othello plus Iago, that is Riccardo De Sio, I'd just be Othello.'

So, he knew, or thought he knew? Another suspicion even more horrifying than the first again flashed out on the horizon. 'How do you know?'

He was silent a moment, as though trying to condense what he had to say in a single sentence, at once enigmatic and concise. 'Simple, I reconstructed what happened on the basis of an elementary equation.'

'Which is?'

'Which is, adultery equals a natural, innate disposition to betray plus a particular and perverse stimulus, the sum being multiplied by the square of the favourable location.'

I reflected. My father's burlesque equation could be interpreted as follows: natural disposition meant an innate tendency on Esmeralda's part not to keep her word; the particular and perverse stimulus meant our incest charade; the favourable location was the apartment in Via Ammannati. Yet the three parts of the equation could also be interpreted in a different way, a way which had nothing to do with me but with this so-called, mythical 'handkerchief man'. In this interpretation, while Esmeralda's tendency not to keep her word remained unchanged, the particular perverse stimulus might be a taste for adultery, and the favourable location Esmeralda's studio where, as it happened, the handkerchief had been found. But was this ambiguity conscious or casual? All at once I realized I didn't care and that the point of the matter lay elsewhere. The point was that for some long time my father had been perversely pursuing the same kind of repetition that I had just missed getting involved in with Esmeralda, escaped *in extremis*: just as in the past he had aided and abetted my mother's affair with Terenzi, so now he was aiding and abetting Esmeralda's affair with me, or, though it was all the same to him, with the mysterious man with the handkerchief. On arriving at this conclusion, I felt first a sense of horror, then relief: horror at the similarity in our behaviour, something I found unbearable, and relief because, in the end I had at the last moment acted differently from him. Yes, he, with his empty apartment and his illusion of being the puppeteer who pulls the strings, he was the real pervert, and had I made love with Esmeralda I might have become that pervert myself. He was a mirror I had run the risk of finding myself in.

But now that my obsession had apparently vanished, or was on the point of vanishing, what remained was the warped sense of pity I couldn't help feeling for him and which prompted me to analyse his behaviour, albeit in a different spirit now. For example, how could one reconcile the ruse he'd used to have himself betrayed by Esmeralda and myself in the apartment in Via Ammannati with the sincere though histrionic tears of a few minutes ago? True, he insisted on believing he was Othello plus Iago, but what did tears have to do with it? Iago doesn't cry after devising the trick that will destroy Desdemona. I asked brusquely, 'So why were you crying a few moments back? Esmeralda did exactly what you wanted her to: made love to the man with the handkerchief. You should be happy, shouldn't you?'

'Oh dear, Mario, it's all so complicated! I'm not a cattle breeder who says to himself: I've pushed the bull into the stall, he's mounted the cow, they've mated properly and that's that. Mario, I've good reason to cry. You won't believe it, but it's for your sake.'

Again I was struck by an irrational, unjustified sense of guilt. 'I'm sorry, but what have I got to do with it?'

'You see, Mario, I wasn't crying out of jealousy, I was crying out of sorrow, a sorrow that has nothing to do with jealousy.'

'But what sorrow?'

'The greatest sorrow of my life. Your arrival in Rome made me hope that my dream of rebuilding a family was about to come true. I was so happy the day you arrived! I could already see myself with you, my son, and Esmeralda, who would become my wife, sharing a happy, affectionate life in the apartment in Via Ammannati. It was a dream, I know, but isn't that what our lives are made of in the end? And now Esmeralda has destroyed it.'

I said coldly, 'How has she destroyed it? I don't understand. Or perhaps I understand all too well, I don't know. Let's see. Despite everything you've decided not to break it off with Esmeralda. So what's stopping you from marrying her and having a family like the one in your dream?'

He looked at me, undecided and for once sincere in his indecision. 'I will marry Esmeralda, but nothing can be as it was before.'

'Before what?'

He made up his mind. 'Before the pact Esmeralda made with me.'

'What pact?'

'It was like this. I told her: just this once I want to trust you, promise me you won't betray me right now. She solemnly promised to be faithful to me at least until we were married. I trusted her, in the sense that I fooled myself into believing that on the one hand I was still the puppeteer pulling the strings, and on the other hand that the puppet was a live thinking person capable of keeping a promise; in short, let's say the pact was that I asked Esmeralda to decide how to run her own life herself. That, Mario, is why nothing can be the same as before: Esmeralda didn't keep her word and there's nothing that can be done. It's for ever!'

I found this at once pathetic and sophisticated subtlety almost admirable. The dream Esmeralda had shattered was of a family made up of myself, himself and Esmeralda. But who had shattered it if not him, playing puppeteer and insisting on pulling strings not with a puppet at all but with a living person capable of choice? He had wanted Esmeralda and I to meet alone in the apartment, just as, years ago, he had wanted my mother and Terenzi to be alone after dinner in front of the television. But at the same time he had warned Esmeralda, 'You mustn't do anything with Mario, promise me that.' This request had allowed him, as I understood it, to be at once the lucid perverse puppeteer and the loving, trustful husband. All Esmeralda wanted instead was to amuse herself playing incest, and so she had, thus exploding the conventional dream of a traditional family. At random I said, 'You'll see, you'll forgive her.'

'No, Mario, I could forgive her still, but what would be the use, she won't forgive me.'

We looked at each other. Now I saw it all: Esmeralda had wanted to play at incest, but at the same time wanted him to forbid her, or at least she unconsciously expected him to forbid her. But he hadn't wanted to renounce the role of Othello plus Iago, that is Riccardo De Sio. And now, faced with this handkerchief stained with mango juice, he found himself for the first time confronting the bitterest and sharpest pain of all: that of the irretrievable. The irretrievable was the fact that I knew I had been lured into a trap; the fact that Esmeralda would never believe that he really wanted to have an affectionate, wholesome traditional family, free of perversity and voyeurism, without puppeteers or puppets. All he was left with, in short, was the pain – a pain, I thought, that for all it was expressed in the language and manner of a bourgeois Roman from Parioli, was nevertheless genuine.

So what had seemed an irreconcilable contradiction now turned out to be an indivisible whole: my father was simultaneously a perverse and jealous man and a traditional father without a family, eager to have one. So there was no contradiction between his crying from grief and his voyeuristic plan. As he had said of himself: he was first and foremost Riccardo De Sio, that is everything and its opposite.

But I felt oppressed by such sordid and in the end uninteresting complexity. I asked brusquely, 'Okay, or rather not okay: you know who the handkerchief man is. Now I'm asking you again: are you going to go on playing the puppeteer who pulls the strings?'

He sent me a look of almost fear, as if he'd realized that what I was saying was only the tip of an iceberg of knowledge I had, an iceberg which could easily have sunk the fragile vessel of his split personality. What's more, I saw that he didn't want us to get to the point of a full explanation. His face assumed a melancholy, bitter expression. 'No, Mario, enough of puppeteer and puppets. The puppeteer is packing up his little theatre, putting away his marionettes and leaving.'

'What's that supposed to mean?'

'It means, Mario, that everything in life repeats itself, and at the same time nothing does. Yes, Mario, Esmeralda betrayed me exactly as your mother did, and, as with your mother, I know who with: so everything repeats itself. But this time I don't feel I want to throw away a marriage as I did fifteen years ago, pulling the strings so hard I snapped them: so nothing repeats itself. This time I want the dream of having a family to become a reality, and so it will. Mario, I won't think about that handkerchief; I'll just remember that you've come back, you're here, and that Esmeralda and I are getting married. Perhaps I won't have a perfect, ideal family, as in my dream, Mario, but it will still be a family, with its dark sides, yes, but with its bright spots too.'

I felt a surge of impatience at this stubborn determination to keep his illusions alive. 'Yes, of course it will be a family. All the more so when you think that at least this time Esmeralda didn't betray you.'

I saw the incredulity on his face, he was almost annoyed. 'Didn't betray me? Don't talk rubbish! I've got the proof!'

'What proof?'

'The handkerchief. You're not telling me this isn't proof.'

'Give me the handkerchief.'

'But why? What's got into you?'

'I said give me the handkerchief.'

He took it out of his pocket and gave it to me, again showing his disgust by holding it with his fingertips. I informed him, 'It's not so gross as you think. These stains aren't sperm.'

'What are you talking about? What is this?'

'I'll tell you. Now if you don't mind, go and get a clean handkerchief from the first drawer of the dresser.'

'But what's that got to do with it?'

'I said go and get one.'

He got up and went to the dresser.

'Got the handkerchief? Now, compare it with this one: as you see, they are identical, white with a blue border.'

He looked and said nothing. 'I bought these two handkerchiefs in Paris before coming to Rome. Eight of them in all, white with blue borders. It was me who stained the dirty handkerchief, cleaning my mouth after eating a mango. Esmeralda offered me a mango while I was at her studio.'

'You went to Esmeralda's?'

'I thought I'd told you. Of course. She invited me and I went.'

'So the handkerchief I found in the dresser was yours?'

Suddenly I couldn't help feeling an annoying sense of *déjà vu*, of having already been through all this before. I realized that we were each explaining away the misunderstandings that had threatened to tear our lives apart, a little like the characters in classical comedies before the happy ending. But our lives were not transparent like those of the characters and as far as endings were concerned, this one seemed anything but happy. Then it came to me quite lucidly that in the script we were acting out he should now throw his arms round my neck to express his immense joy at having escaped this danger. Which in fact is exactly what happened. For a moment he seemed to hesitate between the truth of his life and the lie of the part he'd been playing until now. Then he made up his mind and lunged forward to embrace me. 'Terrific, Mario you're terrific! I see it all now; the road that leads to happiness is open in front of us, and we'll follow it right to the end. Come on, let's hug, hug your stupid dad who loves you and wants you to live with him and his future wife for ever. Come on, give your dad a nice kiss.'

We embraced, me still wrapped in my sheet, him in his blazer with the gold buttons. Then, as I felt his damp lips crush against my cheeks, I knew for certain that this was the last time I would see him. 'Yes, we'll be happy,' I said, 'you, Esmeralda and me.'

'A new life, a new house, a new son, a new wife! Now get dressed, it's late. I'm going out, I'll go and pick up Esmeralda and then we can all three go to a restaurant to celebrate our family. See you soon!'

He went out, I slipped out of the sheet, went to the bathroom and turned on the shower.

THIRTEEN

Return to Paris

After a quick wash and brush-up, I pulled down my suitcase from above the wardrobe and tossed in the few things I had any old how. Then I went into the passageway and dialled Jeanne's number. I heard Alda's at once reluctant and impatient voice and immediately said, 'You'd invited me to dinner on Wednesday. It's too long to explain over the phone but we'll have to switch it to lunch today. And as your mother offered to let me stay at your place, I'll be bringing my suitcase. Is that okay?'

She showed no sign of surprise. In a faintly conspiratorial tone, she replied, 'No problem. I'll tell Jeanne now. She'll be pleased. She'll make you a good lunch. In the meantime we can meet at Villa Balestra and sort things out.'

'What things?'

'Don't you remember? The champagne we've got to buy, plus everything else.'

I cut her short, 'Okay, I'll see you soon, towards midday, at Villa Balestra.'

'Great.'

I went back to my room, closed my suitcase and for the first time wondered how I should say goodbye to my father. Write him a note? Or just slip out quietly, as they say, leaving him with the job of explaining why? In the end I decided on a third solution: as a sort of goodbye note, I'd leave him four lines from Apollinaire which I felt were suitable for the occasion. I found a piece of paper and, translating as best I could, scribbled:

> I spin and veer in the wind,
> A crazed beacon
> My beautiful ship
> Has gone.

Taking the paper, I went to my father's room and, before placing it where it would be seen on the bed, read the lines again. I was perfectly aware that my father understood nothing about poetry; that it was childish, ridiculous even, leaving him that note on his pillow; yet now that I knew my adventure in Rome was over I felt an irresistible urge to reassert, as though with a business card, my dignity as a poet. But I realized that I was also re-reading the lines to find, as usual, some symbolic significance vis-à-vis my own life; and I told myself that in fact this short verse offered an exact explanation of why I was going. I thought: Yes, the beacon whose light is spinning madly like a belltower weather-cock in a thunderstorm, desperately, vainly scanning the empty sea for the beautiful ship in danger, that's me. With his poetic inversion of the terms of the situation, it's the beacon, i.e. me, which is attracted by the ship, and not the ship, i.e. my mother, by the beacon. Because until now, for better or worse, I, the beacon, have justified my enquiring beam with the existence of a ship in danger, and this ship had as its figurehead, my mother, her flowing hair, her hungry, torpid eyes. But now there's nothing to attract me in that empty sea; the beautiful ship has gone; the beacon has no purpose; its light no longer illuminates any shipwreck; it may as well go out. Which means what? That I'm saying goodbye to my mother for ever.

Another reason I was happy to leave the lines, as an explanation of my departure, was that poetry is of its very nature ambiguous and hence my father, as though confronted with the answer of some ancient oracle, would be able to think whatever he wanted. 'A poet!' he would finally decide. 'He came out of thin air and disappeared into thin air, a real poet!' I was almost smiling from affection, thinking of how my father would explain my disappearance from his life.

With these almost happy, or in any event light-hearted, thoughts in mind, I picked up my suitcase and washbag and pretty well danced out of the apartment. Not very much later I was parking the car in Via Ammannati and, still walking with a light step, I headed for Villa Balestra.

Alda was waiting for me on the usual bench. I sat down and said, 'Hi, I've got my suitcase in the car.'

'Jeanne's gone out shopping specially for you. She's going to make a fabulous lunch.'

'Is she pleased I brought the day forward?'

'Yes. She said you were rude and should have waited till Wednesday to argue with your father.'

'That's being pleased?'

'Oh come on! She complained to hide the fact that she was pleased.'

'But I haven't argued with my father. I just left.'

'Own up, he kicked you out because you'd made love to your future stepmother.'

So, as usual, during their pow-wows the two women had told each other everything I'd asked them not to tell each other. I protested, hurt by the idea that my father, who had wept over me, could have kicked me out. 'No, nothing like that. Right now my father will be looking for me and he'll do everything he can to get me back. I left without saying anything, I gave him the impression I was going to stay.'

'Does your stepmother know?'

'No, she doesn't know anything either. And I'll never see either of them again.' I was silent for a moment. Then, without knowing why, I added angrily, 'Maybe I'll get out of Rome for good and go back to Paris.'

'Now you're taking offence! It was Jeanne who told me that you were in love with your father's girlfriend.'

'Everything Jeanne knows, it's because I told her. And I told her I wanted to leave my father's place. That was when she invited me to come and stay with you.'

She took my hand, almost imploring, 'Come on, please, don't be angry. And don't say you're going back to Paris. Come and stay with us now and we'll all three of us be happy together.'

She squeezed my hand tight, as though to tell me I mustn't even think of leaving them. I asked, 'By the way, you said on the phone that we had to sort things out. What exactly?'

'What you're going to do today.'

'Eat lunch, that's all.'

'Yes, but after lunch . . . ' She didn't finish but looked down at where her hands were clasped together on her lap making the same old gesture for sexual penetration. I sighed, fed up: Alda seemed to me pointlessly crude and repetitive. 'What's that got to do with it? There's time enough, isn't there?'

'No, there isn't time enough. She's expecting everything to happen as soon as possible.'

'How do you know?'

'Last night we went on talking till three o'clock, and you know what she said?'

'How am I supposed to know?'

'She said lots of things. In the end she thinks you don't need physical love, but affection.'

'Maybe she's right.'

'Yes, but if she's right there's no point in your coming to stay with us.'

'And why's that?'

'Oh come on, you know, don't make me say everything ten times over. She thinks of nothing else. And if she's right that all you need is affection then we'll be back at square one. You'll be living in our house, well, like a big brother; she'll go on mourning my dad and at the same time looking for a man; I'll have to start staying up late again to hear her talk about it. I mean, nothing will have changed. Thanks a lot, but I'm not putting up with that.'

'Come on though, I can't just come to lunch, unpack my bag and then jump on her right away!'

'But that's exactly what you must do. That's exactly what she wants you to do. She's a slut, Jeanne, if you can't see that you're blind. She's an out-and-out slut.'

I was unsettled by this offensive, urgent language, as though she were some pimp offering a prostitute to a timid client. I objected, 'Okay, but there's no need to prepare this kind of thing. It happens naturally.'

'Not with you.'

'What's that supposed to mean?'

'It means that one never knows with you. Did you or didn't you say you felt no desire for Jeanne? So why should it happen naturally? It won't happen naturally and you won't do anything.'

Finally I had it: in her candid, inexperienced ignorance, Alda had taken my description of the physiological and wholly masculine phenomenon of the erection seriously. I burst out laughing, 'You're a kid, you don't know anything about these things.'

'Maybe I don't know anything, okay, but did you or didn't you say that when you're with Jeanne you don't feel anything?'

'What I meant to say was that I didn't feel I loved her.'

'No, you said it to explain that you didn't get hard. And you also said that you did get hard with me. You did say it, you can't deny it!'

She sounded hurt, as though I'd called her a liar. I tried to tone down the crudeness of our conversation. 'Let's suppose you're right. But the difference between desire and the absence of desire is not as clear-cut as you think. There are lots of different levels. You can start by not feeling any desire at all and maybe finish with quite a violent desire.'

'How?'

'Well, I don't know. Something new or strange could happen, something you've never experienced before. Then you go, maybe, from impotence to the exact opposite.'

She looked at me with that expression of hers, at once sleepy yet dense with intrigue. 'That's exactly what I want us to sort out between us.'

'But what are you talking about? Sort out what?'

'You don't feel any desire for Jeanne, but you do feel it for me. So let's arrange things so that, as you put it, something new happens, something strange, something never experienced before.'

'What are you talking about?'

'You concentrate on flirting with her, joking with her, making her drink, maybe squeezing her hand, maybe asking her for a kiss. All things you can do without desire, right? And while you're doing that, I'll feel you up with my foot under the table. And seeing as you do desire me, you'll turn hard immediately. Then Jeanne will think you've gone hard because of her and she'll agree to make love and everything'll be okay.'

I was struck by the almost scientific objectivity of her tone: it was as if she wanted to reduce her complicity to being a mere instrument of mechanical arousal. Then suddenly it again occurred to me that with the excuse of encouraging my relationship with Jeanne, Alda was really unconsciously trying to form an even more real and deeply-felt relationship between herself and me. It wasn't easy though, I thought, to separate the conscious from the unconscious in that diabolic childishness of hers. But so be it; Alda wasn't ambiguous just because of her age, but by nature too, and there was nothing one could do about it.

I protested, 'You're just an ignorant kid, and the way you talk about love shows it. It's true I said I didn't feel any desire for Jeanne, then, at that moment. But it could perfectly well happen that a word or glance from her could arouse my desire today, without any need of any help from you.'

'But you can't be sure, and I want to be sure.'

'But why?'

'Groan, because I can't go on like this.'

'So, let's suppose that it's at least ninety per cent sure. You don't know anything about this kind of thing. I'm twenty. When you're my age it happens all the time. I get on the bus, look at a woman, tell myself she's plain, ugly, gross even, then a jerk of the bus pushes us together and there, I'm getting turned on.'

'But why does it bother you? I play footsie under the table, then as soon as I realize you're going hard, I get up and off I go, leaving you two alone. That's all.'

Now, once again, thanks to my eternal, deplorable openness to things, I felt tempted. I was sure I wouldn't need any help from Alda to get turned on with Jeanne; but I couldn't help being intrigued by the daughter's behaviour. Did she or didn't she realize she was competing with her mother? Was she or wasn't she aware of the fact that she was trying to take her place? I pretended to think, then said, 'Now let me suggest something: if I realize I'm not getting turned on, I'll make a sign.'

She was immediately excited by the way our plot was turning into a kind of game. 'What sign?'

'Let's say that at a certain point, I'll invite Jeanne to drink German-style, what the Germans call *Brüderschaft*.'

'What is the German style?'

'You link arms and drink together.'

'That means I've got to play footsie?'

I hesitated. A signal is always affirmative: you make a signal to make something happen – that was how I'd seen it at first and how Alda had rightly interpreted it – not to cause something not to happen. But the demon tempter of my openness suggested the opposite, fielding this equivocation: if I felt up to drinking and maybe even kissing Jeanne after drinking, that would clearly mean I didn't need Alda's assistance. With a definite sense of tricking her, I said, 'No, that means I've got my hard-on and there's no need for you to play footsie.'

But what lay behind this ambiguity of mine? Obvious. I was creating a situation where Alda, impatient at my inertia and jealous of Jeanne's advances, would pay no attention to the signal and begin her footsie under the table in any event. She seconded this ruse of mine by saying impetuously, 'Agreed, okay, don't worry, I'll help you out.' Which was in its turn an ambiguous way of dealing with my own ambiguity. She got up. 'Now let's go and get the champagne, though. Today's Sunday, the shops are shut, we'll have to find a bar that has some.'

She began to walk hurriedly across the grass to the exit. Without looking at me she added, 'This is the last time I'm bothering with Jeanne. If she doesn't do it, I'm going.'

'Where will you go?'

'I'll go to France with you. I thought you'd promised me that as soon as you were back in Paris you'd invite me to your uncle's?'

'Yes, but –'

'I thought about it, France. You know what we could do in the end; look for a house in Paris and live together as man and wife. We'll stay at your uncle's just long enough to find a house.'

Apparently neither improvised nor casual, this new plan took my breath away. I objected, 'To tell the truth I was thinking of you coming to my uncle's just for a short holiday. And then, do excuse my asking, but why as man and wife?'

'Didn't you say you didn't desire Jeanne, but did desire me? And isn't a husband supposed to desire his wife?'

So, I found myself thinking again, on the basis of an insignificant piece of information about the male physiology, she'd gone so far as to construct a kind of novel. I didn't have time to show my surprise because she added hurriedly, 'I could be an excellent wife, just as good as Jeanne and even better. You'll say I'm too young still; but you'll be the only person who knows. Everybody thinks I'm at least fifteen. Another year and I'll look eighteen. So we'll look as if we were the same age.'

'But didn't you want me to be Jeanne's man, and therefore your father?'

We went through the gate. She replied briefly, 'Yes, I did, and I still do. But I don't *always* want that.'

'What do you mean you don't *always* want it?'

'Sometimes I see you as a father, sometimes as a husband, it depends how I'm feeling.'

'And how are you feeling now?'

'Today I see you rather as a father. Tomorrow, who knows?'

'Who knows?'

'Oh you and your repetitions! You sound like an echo in the mountains: someone maybe calls, "Alda", and the echo answers, "Alda, Alda, Alda!" Come on, drive quickly and we'll go and get this champagne.'

Driving, I was thinking about that 'who knows'. And I told myself that what I called my openness and reproached myself with, thinking it my major fault, was a congenital and unconscious trait in Alda, like the colour of her eyes or the shape of her nose. Open to being my daughter, she didn't reject the idea of being equally open to be my wife!

But then my own openness was now giving me the feeling of having arrived at the sort of crossroads bereft of signs where the lost traveller stops and stares. He hesitates, thinks that the bigger road he sees, wide and well tarred, well marked out, will maybe shrink into a path or even plunge into a ravine: while the little, narrow track may get wider and straighter, become a big comfortable road. In this situation openness meant not rejecting either the big road or the track, but accepting both of them to see where they led. 'In any event,' I suddenly wound up these reflections with a phrase I would often repeat to myself as a kind of consolation for my ambiguous decisions, 'one life is as good as another.'

Alda thumped my knee hard. 'Stop, stop, there's a bar where we can get champagne.'

I stopped; we were opposite a pastry shop. 'Give me the money. I know which brand she likes. Give me enough for two bottles.'

Impatiently she pulled my wallet out of the front pocket of my jeans, quickly took the money, left the wallet on the seat and jumped out of the car. I waited, smoking nervously and looking, through the glass of the windscreen, at a florist's display under a big green sunshade. When Alda got back in the car with the bag and the two bottles, I asked, 'Don't you think I should take Jeanne some flowers too?'

'Yes, terrific, so she can go and put them in Father's room, to decorate the chapel.'

I said nothing. I began to drive again. She went on, 'The champagne's enough. She really likes it. You'll see how much she drinks. When she's drunk, she always plays the same trick.'

'Which is?'

'Which is, she makes as if to whisper a secret in your ear and then surprises you with a kiss, one of those that makes your ear sing for ages.'

'But whose ear?'

'The man who's chasing her at the time.'

'Then what happens with the man?'

'Nothing, nothing at all. She talks about him to me for a few days, at night, then she doesn't want to see him again.'

Amid these intriguing aspersions, delivered in her coarse, monotonous voice, we arrived in Via Ammannati. Alda took the bag with the two bottles of champagne and I carried my own bag and suitcase. In the lift, like a pimp anxious to clinch a tricky piece of seduction, she told me, 'When she comes and opens the door for us, you give her a hug, she'll like that. She'll see you mean business. And take the bottles. You've got to give them to her yourself.'

One floor, two floors, three floors. The lift climbed and I was telling myself that it really was true: I was going to live with Jeanne and Alda, for ever maybe, or in any event for a long time. How easy it was to live, even if, '*la vie est lente et l'espérance violente*'! The lift stopped, the doors opened, Alda took my bag and suitcase and gave me a last piece of advice. 'As soon as she comes, hug her, give her a kiss. If she returns it, it means she's on for it and we're more or less home and dry.'

She threw me a last oblique wink of complicity, then put the key in the lock and went in. 'Jeanne, it's us, yoo-hoo, it's us!'

Jeanne came straight out of the door from the kitchen in her cook's apron, a ladle in one hand and saucepan lid in the other. She seemed genuinely pleased. She laughed, displaying sharp white canines, a sign in her, as I knew, of intense happiness. 'Well done, Mario, well done, Mario, very well done. You decided to come sooner and you did well. The only problem is that today is Sunday and the shops are closed. It'll be a bit of a makeshift lunch.' So saying she let herself be embraced in good grace, holding her arms wide apart with the ladle on one side and the saucepan lid on the other. But she evaded a direct kiss, determinedly offering her cheek. She went on, 'I'll go and cook, you two lay the table.'

So here was the sitting-room. I couldn't help looking round the big rectangular room with the eye of the guest who's getting his first sight of the place he's going to be staying in and is imagining what kind of life he'll be living there. There was a generous, plump, low sofa piled with cushions of various colours and upholstered in a patchwork material; no doubt I would sit, or rather sprawl there together with Jeanne and Alda to watch the television, which in fact stood opposite. Or maybe I'd read the magazines and newspapers

I could see stacked on the coffee-table between ashtrays, packs of cigarettes and a big vase full of flowers. From the bookcase, the modular kind in natural wood, full of books big and small, French and Italian, I would choose something to read for afternoons on my own when Jeanne would be off doing her research for the university and Alda would be going over her schoolwork at a friend's house. And at that big round glass and steel table in one corner, surrounded by six wicker chairs, I'd sit and eat with the two women three times a day. Looking at the room I experienced a sense of incredulity and unreality of the sort that makes you think: This is all a dream. But I was reassured by the affectionate, domestic, feminine feel of the room, that most comforting of feelings you get in homes which have so to speak, shaped themselves, without a planned style, simply in line with personal tastes and everyday needs.

Alda was already moving to and fro between sideboard and table, laying out the plates. She realized I was looking around and asked, 'Do you like our house?'

'Yes, really a lot, mostly because it's a normal house where nothing out of the ordinary could happen. A house for every day where people live an everyday life and that's the end of it.'

She threw me a curious glance of ambiguous appreciation. 'You haven't seen it all yet. You've only been in the sitting-room.'

She was silent a moment, as if consciously choosing her words before coming out with them. Then she said very plainly, 'It's not a normal house. Lunch isn't ready yet: come with me, I'll show you something.'

'What?'

'Oh enough! Come and you'll see!'

Intrigued by her somehow solemn voice, I followed her out of the living-room. She went to the end of a hallway which a big cupboard with three doors reduced to a bare narrow passage. She opened a door and stepped aside to let me go through. 'Tell me if this is a bedroom or something else not quite normal.'

Actually, at first glance, what struck me was how normal the place was. The two windows, one next to the other, were open, but with the blinds down; the healthy, dry, June sun didn't penetrate the room, but you could sense its warmth and silence even in the cool half-light. I noticed a big double bed, over which hung a print of Raphaël's Madonna; there was a dresser with three mirrors against the wall between the windows, an antique chest of drawers with an Empire clock under glass, plus a fitted cupboard running the length of one wall. Then, looking more carefully, I began to notice the abnormalities. First of all, the flowers; there was a vase of them on the dresser, another on the chest of drawers, a third and fourth on the two bedside tables. And then the way everything had been prepared for bedtime, although it was barely midday: a woman's nightdress, made from delicate blue voile, was stretched out on one side of the bed, the arms open, on the other side were a man's blue pyjamas, the arms, again, open. On the two bedside tables were two silver-framed photos, one of a bald man with round face and dark moustache – this on the side with the woman's nightdress – the other, on the pyjama side, of Jeanne. Beyond, in a shadowy corner, a dark blue military-style jacket and peaked cap hung on a coatstand; the husband had been a chief pilot on the Atlantic air route. Alda looked at the room as if to make sure that everything was in its usual place, then turned to me. 'You still think it's a normal room?'

Still incredulous, I asked, 'But who actually sleeps here?'

'You mean, who slept here? Jeanne and my father. Since Father died, no one.'

'But this nightdress, these pyjamas –'

'Are here because Jeanne, who sleeps in another room, wants this room left exactly as it was the night Father died. Like I said, it's not a room for living in, it's a chapel. Jeanne gets angry when I call it that, but she shouldn't. True, Father's in the cemetery, but his clothes, his uniform, his shoes, his pyjamas, are all here. How could it be more like a chapel?'

She went to the coatstand in the corner in the shadow, took down the dark blue cap with its gold stripes and peak and put it on her head in phlegmatic parody. 'This is father's cap, he was a pilot; after flying over the ocean thousands of times he died in a car accident near Casalpalocco.' She hung up the cap again, lifted a sleeve of the jacket to show me how many stripes there were, pointed at a pair of black shoes on the floor. 'Then if you open the cupboard you'll find all his jackets too, and his shirts, and his ties, and his socks. Everything all in order; carefully ironed, carefully preserved in mothballs.'

I said nothing. She went on, 'Now she wants to keep the chapel just as it is and have you sleep in my room. I'm supposed to go into her room, since it has two beds. But I'm not putting up with it. Either she chucks all this stuff away and has you sleep in here, with her of course, or I'd rather you went back to your father.'

'I can't go back to my father.'

'All I want is for you to do with Jeanne what you did with your father's woman on the terrace of that apartment. Do that and all this stuff of my father's will wind up in the bin, you'll see.'

'But why are you talking like this?'

'Like what?'

'Violent, scornful. After all, he was your father.'

'You know where he was going when his car came off the motorway and smashed into a tree? Not home, oh no, he was going to one of his women! And you know what he'd told Jeanne on the telephone from Rio? That the plane was late and he wouldn't be arriving till the following day.'

The door suddenly opened and Jeanne's head poked round. 'Hey, what are you up to in here? The food's ready, come and eat.'

She sounded jokey, or in any event indulgent and maternal.

'I wanted to show him where he'll be sleeping,' Alda said, with cool, sly provocation.

'Good idea. But we can talk about that later. It's ready, come on, let's eat.'

Lunch was indeed ready. In the middle of the table, rising magnificently above a tray, a white pyramid was speckled with green, red, yellow and black: a rice salad with tiny chunks of peppers, tomatoes, carrots and olives. Next to the tray a bottle of champagne had been plunged into an icebucket. Beside each plate was a rose, and rose-petals floated in the fingerbowls. Jeanne had taken off her cook's apron and was wearing red zouave-style trousers and a green oriental-style bodice with gold braiding and a neckline that dived almost to her waist, leaving her breasts half naked. I also noticed that she'd put some lipstick on, something she didn't normally do. She exclaimed merrily, 'First of all, let's drink to Mario's health now that he's coming to live with us.' She took the bottle out of the icebucket, stripped the foil from the neck and began to push up the cork. Alda, infected by the general fun, put her hands over her ears. But the cork slipped out of the neck and immediately fell to the table, making hardly any noise at all. Still, the wine frothed out just the same, foamy and generous. Jeanne shouted, 'Quick, give me your glasses.'

She laughed nervously, with a kind of harsh, cruel hilarity. She filled her glass to the brim and even before proposing her toast, drank the lot at a single gulp. Then she filled it again, filled ours and, raising her own in my direction, said, 'To your health, Mario. Here's hoping you stay with us a lifetime. Don't get used to the champagne though, we won't be having that every day.'

Alda confirmed sarcastically, 'Only on the big occasions: baptisms, weddings, funerals. What would today be, a marriage?'

'No,' Jeanne corrected seriously, 'if anything, a baptism. We're baptizing something like the beginning of a new life, our life together, you, Mario and myself.' She was on her feet, seemed to hesitate, then at last decided. 'Mario, now let's drink to us two: by accepting my invitation I know you've done something that maybe you didn't want to do, and it makes me happy to think you did it for me. Sorry, Alda, but this really is something between me and him.'

'Why say sorry, Jeanne? Obviously he hasn't come here for me.'

'He came first and foremost for himself.'

'I've come for both of you.'

So Jeanne and I toasted ourselves, under Alda's sleepy, impatient gaze. Then we drank to Alda's health, though she didn't get up, just raised her glass listlessly, then shouted, 'Come on, give each other a kiss and don't make such a fuss about it!'

Jeanne and I looked at each other, then Jeanne offered me, not her mouth, but her cheek, and beneath my lips I felt her extraordinarily smooth, sweet skin, already glowing it seemed from the wine she'd drunk. She immediately withdrew, I sat down, and she began to serve lunch standing up. 'Kisses are another thing you'd better not get used to though, Mario.'

'But Jeanne, all you did was let yourself be kissed on the cheek.'

'Come on, eat up, I've spent the whole morning making you this rice salad, now tell me if you like it.'

We began to eat. Jeanne hardly touched anything, did little more than carefully separate the rice from the greens with her fork. Alda, on the other hand, pretended to be hungry and ate with her head down. I ate slowly, looking alternately at mother and daughter; I was worried that Alda, obsessed as she was with her plot, might do something rash to stir things up. And in fact all of a sudden she exclaimed restively, 'I'm hot, I'm going to change. I'll be right back.'

Her voice was full of allusions. I followed her with my eyes and, as expected, going out of the door she turned to make me a kissing gesture, two fingers on her lips, but the kiss wasn't for me, but to be given to Jeanne. She went out and I realized that despite their crudeness, these hints, or rather commands, were doing their job. I looked at Jeanne and had the very definite feeling that I must do something. But what? I risked, 'So, are you happy I've come here to stay with you?'

Eyes down, at once cool and coy, she answered, 'Yes, as it was me who invited you. But there's one condition.'

'What's that?'

'I had the impression you were very taken by your father's girlfriend. You've come to stay with us and I'm happy about that. But I'm warning you that if she comes to see you here, or if you, more likely, go and see her elsewhere, then I'd rather you went back to your father.'

I exclaimed, 'Why should I see the woman again? What happened on the terrace of that apartment will never happen again.'

'I don't know what it is, it's just I have a feeling that there's something, I don't know, special, between you and her. In the past people would have said it was destiny pushing you two together.'

'What do you mean, destiny?'

'Maybe I didn't express myself very well. Alda described the woman to me: it seems incredible to me that you should have done what you did with her. And yet it's true.'

'I didn't do anything.'

She was quiet a moment, as if she found what she was about to say repugnant, and yet couldn't avoid saying it. 'Alda told me that when this woman realized she was there she ran for it. Then you lit a cigarette, but you were so excited you hadn't realized you still had your fly open and your penis out.'

No doubt about it: precisely because of the crudity of this description, my intimacy with Jeanne was heading in the direction Alda had pointed out for me. And yet I couldn't decide what I should do: get up from the table and go and kiss her, or answer crudity with crudity? With extraordinary intuition, she went on, 'I mean, one gets the impression that the woman attracts you not because you like her, but because you don't like her. That is for some reason that has nothing to do with her, but with you and only you: perhaps because she's your father's woman and you like the idea of her betraying him with you; perhaps because your father is going to marry her and you feel attracted to her the way a little boy may sometimes feel attracted to his mother.'

So, she'd come out with almost the exact truth. And yet it wasn't quite the truth: I was attracted to Esmeralda not so much because she was about to become my stepmother, but because of her likeness to my real mother. Then, perhaps for the first time, looking at Jeanne, I felt the desire to feel desire. All at once I jumped up from my place, came round behind her back, put my hands on her arms and leant down to kiss her, saying in a whisper, 'I swear I'll never see the woman again.'

My hands went down as far as her breasts; but she didn't let me kiss her. She pulled to one side, took her glass and said, looking up at me with a strangely gentle, indulgent expression, 'Oh, come on, don't go swearing troopers' oaths that maybe you won't be able to keep. Now drink from my glass and just promise me that from now on you'll behave well, like an affectionate friend and considerate guest.' She took a sip from her glass and then handed it to me. Moved to tears, I too drank from it.

At which moment back came Alda. She saw Jeanne sitting down and me on my feet behind her drinking from her glass and immediately came out with one of her typically envying, sarcastic laughs. 'Very nice, can't leave you alone for a minute without you taking advantage. Terrific, but don't you think you're hurrying it a bit? We're still at the rice salad. Why don't you wait for the sweet?'

She had hardly changed at all, just replaced her blouse with a sleeveless tee-shirt showing her thin, pale arms. Jeanne got up from the table. 'I think I'd better go to the kitchen a minute. I've got a soufflé in the oven and I wouldn't want it to burn.'

'It's already burning. There's a smell of something sticking to the pan.'

'Oh no! I'll be right back.'

As soon as Jeanne had disappeared, Alda sat down, took her glass, emptied it in a gulp and then came at me with, 'Why on earth didn't you kiss her? Don't tell me you did, I was behind the door. I heard you, I saw you: words, words and more words, but no action, or almost none. So listen carefully: now, when the moment is right, I'll bring up the subject of the bedroom and then either she lets you sleep there or you might as well get your bag and go.'

'If she wants to keep the room as it is, what business is that of mine?'

Obscenely, her voice drawling and scornful, she mimicked me, 'What can I do about it? What you can do is make up your mind to try even the tiniest fraction of what you did with your father's woman. Now listen some more: I'll suggest we go and look at the room. Then I'll make up an excuse for going off and leaving you two on your own. Then if you don't make her make love to you right there on that damned bed laid out for the night, you're a coward!'

'I'm not a coward!'

Her voice trembled, as if with some impatient pimp's professional anger, 'I'm telling you, it's all she thinks about! She's drunk, all you have to do is ask her how she made love to father for the first time.'

'And how did she?'

'On her feet in an aeroplane toilet. If you ask her she'll tell you herself. You know what she says about her first meeting with father? That now she can't hear the sound of a toilet flushing without seeing herself with him squeezing her tight while her hand pushed the button flushing that blue water they use in planes. She'd gone there to use the bathroom and couldn't fight him off because she'd only just got up from the toilet and had her panties round her ankles. Think,' she wound up with a childish laugh, 'she didn't want it and then all of a sudden an air pocket threw them into each other's arms, as they say. What is an air pocket anyway?'

I didn't have time to answer. Coming back just at that moment, Jeanne's voice answered for me, 'An air pocket is a terrible thing. Once, over the Alps, with a blue sky, not a cloud in sight, we fell almost a thousand metres.' In excellent humour, Jeanne placed the soufflé pan on the table. 'Change your plates so I can give you your soufflé. It's scalding hot, not a summer dish, but nice all the same.'

She served us the soufflé, then sat down and started to talk about air pockets again. All of a sudden Alda got up with her glass in her hand. 'While the soufflé's cooling, let's drink to Mario's health. Tell me, Jeanne, don't you get the impression Mario's been here with us for years and years?'

'Well, I hope he'll stay at least until we go on holiday.'

'He'll come on holiday with us, won't he? Otherwise what will he do in Rome, alone, in an empty house?'

'Take the opportunity to do some sightseeing, go round Rome.'

'Perhaps he'll see that woman he showed the apartment to.'

'Alda, stop drinking. One glass of champagne and you're drunk. No toasting, eat!'

Maybe Jeanne was right; although she herself had drunk a lot she seemed sober and completely in control, whereas Alda, still on her second glass, seemed quite drunk. Deliberately provocative, Alda emptied her glass in a gulp and then, separating the words out carefully as if to show she wasn't drunk, said, 'Anyhow, it feels odd seeing Mario sitting opposite me, in Father's place. I might almost imagine he was Father and ask, "Daddy, can I get down from table and go to Emilia's?" In any case I don't want my soufflé, the rice salad was more than enough for me.' And with actions to match her words, she moved to get up. Jeanne asked sharply, 'What's got into you? Where are you going?'

'In the other room, to read a book I started yesterday.'

'Sit down, don't be silly and keep your father out of it. Mario is Mario and Father is Father.'

Surprisingly docile, Alda immediately sat down, or rather slumped back on her chair so that her chest was level with the edge of the table. At the same time I felt her bare foot searching for mine and, having found it, pressing it hard. 'Anyway, you're right to tell Mario he can only stay a month here. That way he knows what to expect.'

'If he wants to come on holiday with us, to Capri, I'd be the first to say yes.'

'And if he stayed through autumn as well? And winter too?'

'I've got nothing against it.'

'But how can you expect Mario to stay with us if you're determined not to give him anything, to treat him like any old lodger paying by the day?'

'But what am I supposed to give him? Come on, eat up, don't talk rubbish.'

'You should give him yourself.'

To my surprise, not only did Jeanne not reject this provocative announcement, she indirectly accepted it, almost making herself a third accomplice in our plot. 'Don't take offence, Mario, when she's drunk Alda says the first thing that comes into her head. At the moment she's got the idea we should be lovers, so she says so.'

Alda's bare foot, soft, warm and clinging, began to rub against my ankle; and while Jeanne was looking down at her plate for a moment I saw the daughter throw me an urgent look, as if to spur me to action. But whether out of mere forgetfulness or because I was beginning to feel drunk myself, I realized to my consternation that I couldn't now remember the exact terms of our plot: had we agreed that I was to invite Jeanne to toast *Brüderschaft*, German-style, as a sign that Alda should feel me up under the table? Or as a sign that she shouldn't? In other words, was Alda supposed to intervene at the *Brüderschaft* signal, or not to intervene? Meanwhile the daughter was piling it on with her mother. 'It's no idea of mine. It was you who made me think of it last night when you said you liked Mario.'

'Yes, that's what I said. What's wrong with that?'

'You said something else too: two women shouldn't be living on their own. They need a man.'

'Maybe I said that too. But what's Mario got to do with it? I meant, in general.'

'We were talking about him, though.'

Jeanne picked up her glass, took a long drink, then, suddenly giving way to her daughter's insistence, admitted, 'We two, you and I, for our different reasons, would like Mario to become the man of the house here, but my feeling is that Mario doesn't want to be the man of any house.'

At these words, Alda's foot shifted sharply up my leg, pressing hard against my calf. 'And what do you say, Mario? Is it true you don't want to become the man of anybody's house?'

Caught between two lines of fire, not wanting to upset Jeanne, nor let Alda down, I restricted myself to a cautious, reluctant, 'It depends,' and took a drink of my champagne.

Jeanne immediately protested with unexpected vehemence, 'Depends on what? The truth is, Mario, you're a man who runs away from things. As a boy you ran away from Rome with your mother, then you ran away from Paris to look for your father, now you're running away from your father to come here. But tomorrow you'll be running away from our house too to go God knows where. You're like Rimbaud, you've got wings on your shoes.'

With drunken seriousness, Alda pontificated, 'If he runs away from our house, it'll be your fault, Jeanne.'

'And why's that?'

'I already said. You want everything and you give nothing. Not even a decent bedroom to sleep in.'

Half stretched under the table, her foot now pushing in between my knees, Alda was apparently determined to provoke her mother. But what I couldn't believe was that Jeanne hadn't noticed the strangeness of her daughter's slumped position. Until it began to dawn on me that she might not be entirely unhappy with Alda's provocation. Because it gave her an alibi for rejecting me? Or out of an unconscious (but how unconscious?) complicity with Alda in view of an improbable *ménage à trois*? Or yet again, out of rivalry with her daughter? The hypotheses exploded one after the other in my now drink-clouded mind like so many round, rainbow-coloured soap bubbles. Jeanne answered with vivacity, 'It's not true, I'll give him a nice room, the one you sleep in now.'

'Oh, a very nice room! It looks out of the back of the block over a magnificent view of garage roofs. Why don't you give him Father's room?'

'Now it's getting like last night again. This is an obsession of yours. I've already told you no: you can come and sleep in my room, Mario can sleep in your room, and as for Father's room, well it'll have to remain Father's.'

'I'm not coming to sleep in your room. Apart from anything else you'd keep me up all night telling me how much you like Mario. But if you don't feel you want to give Mario Father's room, at least explain why not.'

She was rubbing her foot so hard against the inner part of my thigh that for once I couldn't help but obey her. 'Yes, Jeanne, why? You say that it's her father's room. Wouldn't it be more correct to say, it *was* her father's room?'

I looked at Jeanne. Clearly her normal calm, rational face now had a puzzled expression, the expression of someone who is used to using reason but suddenly realizes that they can't use it any more and that the fault is all their own. 'Oh, so now you've both ganged up on me!'

'Jeanne, what do you mean? We just want to know why, when you have a beautiful, empty, unused room in the house, you don't want Mario to sleep there.'

Alda's voice sounded mocking and angry. Jeanne looked at me, looked at her daughter slumped down on her seat, her chest against the edge of the table, and then I had the curious impression, fleeting and uncertain, that she closed her eyes for a moment, as if preparing to throw herself headlong into the void. Then she said in a trembling voice, 'You're right. You can help me take his things away today. Mario shall have his beautiful room.'

So in the end Jeanne had given way. And I suddenly realized that our three positions had unexpectedly changed: Jeanne, in giving way, had become stronger than her daughter, who up to this point had been the insistent one. And I, as victor, would have to drop the superfluous and negative alliance with Alda as quickly as possible.

I took Jeanne's hand and brought it to my lips, 'Thank you Jeanne, thank you from the bottom of my heart.' At the same time though, I shifted my legs a bit under the table to tell Alda that it was time to stop this accomplice's caress.

But Alda pretended not to understand; on the contrary, I felt her foot climb a little further along my leg. Meanwhile, with suspicious promptness, she let out a cry of jubilation, 'Now, Jeanne, seeing as you're giving Mario your room, give him a kiss too, a kiss as if you were on your own. A love kiss.'

Jeanne began to laugh with a tempted, flattered air to her, looking me in the eyes as though to see if I approved of the idea. But Alda's insistence that we kiss made me suspicious again. What if, rather than a plot between myself and Alda to seduce Jeanne, the real plot were between Alda and her mother to seduce me? Or if, as I had already thought, Jeanne were pretending not to notice Alda's playing footsie so as to have a good reason later for ducking out of the situation in time? Amid this confusion, I still couldn't remember if the German-style toast was supposed to be a negative or a positive sign; whether, that is, it would tell Alda that she should caress me more than ever with her foot under the table, or not touch me at all. At the same time though, I sensed that this dilemma was behind me now: Alda's caress had dissociated, as happens in drunkenness, my desire from my will to repress desire. There was no struggle. I said abruptly, 'Let's drink together, Jeanne, to our friendship, our *Brüderschaft*.'

'What does *Brüderschaft* mean?'

'Friendship, brotherhood. You cross over your arms and drink together.'

Alda cried, 'Why brotherhood? You're not friends, you're more than that. Kiss each other for once, like everybody else does. I'll empty my glass slowly for as long as the kiss lasts. Then as soon as it's over I'll drink another.'

Jeanne said carelessly, 'Alda, you really are drunk. Come on then, Mario, how do you drink *Brüderschaft*?'

'Like this.'

I got her to cross arms with me, then we drank, both looking at each other above our glasses. Alda cried again, 'And the kiss?'

This time Jeanne smiled at me, put her glass on the table, took my glass from my hand, put an arm around my shoulders and offered me her lips. It was the kiss, at last, rational, chaste and maternal as Jeanne herself.

But at the same moment something happened which, though fairly predictable, I had so far refused to consider: I saw Alda, who had now slid down so far that her chin was almost on the table, wink at me in exactly the way my mother had winked in my dream whilst provocatively wiggling her hips between Esmeralda and Alda in the courtyard of my home in Paris. Then immediately afterwards her foot climbed decisively up along my thigh till it reached and forcefully pushed down on my penis the way one pushes down the accelerator pedal to start a car. My lips just touched Jeanne's, and at the same moment I ejaculated. The semen gushed out, hot, thick and plentiful, flowing with heart-stopping ease and sweetness, as if rushing out not into my pants but into the womb of a woman I loved.

It gushed, stopped a moment then began again; and I couldn't help shuddering fiercely, right in Jeanne's arms. At which I experienced a strange feeling of being split in two, as if the kiss had nothing to do with the ejaculation, nor the ejaculation with the kiss, which was in fact the case; and for one second I childishly hoped that Jeanne might think the same. But for Jeanne, who had doubtless seen something of Alda's manoeuvrings through the glass table top, this violent tremor that had nothing to do with her was merely the confirmation of my irremediable coldness in her regard. She drew away from me, bent down a moment to look under the table, then jumped to her feet exclaiming, 'I'm not wanted here,' and rushed out of the living-room.

Alda immediately took her foot from my crotch, sat up on her seat and asked with her usual abrupt and ambiguous innocence, 'What on earth's come over her? Why did she go?'

Still convulsed in my orgasm, I made an effort to answer, 'You should know if anyone does.'

I could feel my groin soaked through, and what with my agitation and embarrassment I couldn't make up my mind if Alda realized what had happened. I said bitterly, 'The pact was that you were only going to play footsie if Jeanne refused to drink with me German-fashion.'

She returned with childish indignation, 'No, sweetheart, exactly the opposite. The pact was that I'd play footsie if she did accept. That way I'd feel you up while she was kissing you, you'd go hard and she'd think it was her kiss that had done it.'

I reflected that in the end she was perhaps less drunk than I was, given that she still remembered this subtle dissociation between kiss and desire. I suddenly felt quite furious. 'You're an idiot, you've ruined everything.'

'Idiot yourself,' she retorted impassively. 'And then what am I supposed to have ruined?'

'Everything! You don't imagine Jeanne didn't see you?'

'I don't know and I don't care. What's wrong with you anyway?'

'Nothing's wrong.'

'If nothing's wrong, what are you waiting for? Go after her.'

'I don't even know where she is.'

'Nor far, that's for sure. I bet she's in Father's bedroom. She pretended to be angry, whereas in fact she just wanted to get you in there to be alone with you. Go on, what are you waiting for?'

I finally couldn't stand this aggressive innocence of hers, whether true or false, any more. 'You've made me come in my pants. That's what's wrong.'

'What do you mean?'

'Oh you don't know, don't you! It means it's as if I'd made love with you. And Jeanne knows.'

'As if you'd made love with me! How nice, I can't believe it.' She began to laugh quietly to herself; then got up. 'I don't understand any of this at all. I really must be too young.'

'Like hell too young! Don't make me laugh!'

'Look, go and talk to her in my father's room. I'll go and lie on my bed for a bit. Then maybe you can come to my room and tell me how it went.'

Staggering, holding on to the furniture, she went out.

For a while I just sat looking across the abandoned, untidy table. And, to use the word in its literal sense, I reflected, that is I contemplated my inner feelings, my situation, the way one might contemplate the fragments of a precious, fragile object scattered across the floor. The damp stickiness of congealing semen between my skin and the cotton of my underwear reminded me that the irretrievable had already happened. I had made love with Alda and Alda had made love with me. What was worse: this love and the way it had been made prevented me from making amends, since the only way to make amends now would be to make love with Jeanne too; and this, I was aware, would be physiologically beyond me. Apparently comic, the truth was that my situation was so sad as to be desperate: the mirage of a chaste, affectionate family life, which for a short while had seemed to smile on me, was disappearing. And I experienced the same sensation of impossibility that had made me flee my father's house. Then the entirely physical discomfort of the damp semen in my groin alerted me to a more modest and immediate reality. I pushed back my chair and looked. A dark, wet and plainly visible stain was spreading across the faded blue of my jeans. Dismayed, I told myself I could hardly go and see Jeanne with such a telltale stain on my pants. But what could I do? All at once I remembered that I had a change of trousers in my suitcase which Alda had left in the hall. They weren't jeans, true, but at this point I felt that it was up to Jeanne, and her alone, to interpret my change of trousers as a desperate request for forgiveness.

With the cheerful alacrity that comes upon moving from doubt to action, I hurried out of the living-room and went to the hall. My suitcase was there, in the corner. I bent and opened it, found my light beige trousers, pulled them out and turned to look for the door to the bathroom. I wanted to undress in the bathroom. If Jeanne came I'd explain I was changing my trousers because I'd got soufflé on them.

But now I realized that Jeanne was already standing there watching me, her expression not at all cross, but patient and indulgent. I couldn't say anything, feeling absolutely ridiculous with my trousers in my hand and that damp stain on my groin. Softly and firmly Jeanne took the now useless garment from my hand, threw it across the suitcase, then set off towards the door of the marriage bedroom. 'Come in here with me. I've got to talk to you.'

She went on ahead of me and sat on the bed near the pillows. I was embarrassed and stayed on my feet in front of her. She looked me up and down for some time, an unusual expression on her face, then said, 'You're right, that stain really is a bit too obvious. Before you go it might be wise if you did change your trousers after all.' The words 'before you go' made my heart sink. But immediately afterwards she made a gesture that soothed my sense of dismay: in an eager, furtive way, she quickly stretched her hand out to my groin, rubbed her fingers for a moment against the wet material, then brought them to her nostrils, greedily sniffing the smell of the semen smeared on her fingertips. If it's true, as I believe it is, that the sense of smell is the most animal of the senses, then this was a truly animal gesture. And it occurred to me that if, despite everything, the smell of sperm still intoxicated her, then I could still hope for forgiveness.

But I was wrong. Jeanne immediately recovered from this moment of sensuality, then said, calmly and reasonably, 'If it had been me had caused this stain and this smell, everything would be very simple, wouldn't it? Unfortunately though, that's not the case, and you know it, so there's no need to talk about it. Now sit down there and listen.'

She pointed toward the place on the bed where her nightdress was stretched out, the arms open. Seeing my embarrassment she took away the nightdress. 'Don't worry, it's just scenery.' Intrigued by this enigmatic expression, I sat on the edge of the bed, facing her.

She immediately went on, 'Perhaps you're thinking I'm going to talk to you about Alda. But you're wrong. The relationship between yourself and Alda is all too obvious and hardly important. Alda's just a child and you, as you said yourself, are open to any opportunity life offers. Isn't that right?'

Convinced I was telling the truth, I replied, 'There's nothing between Alda and me. I don't even think she realized what happened. She just wanted to make me a sign of complicity, with her foot.'

'A sign that all the same had an immediate effect on you.'

'Don't you believe me?'

She contemplated me with cold indulgence. 'Yes, I believe you. But that's not the point. If it really was just a sign of complicity, you wouldn't have . . . er, let's say, accepted it. You would have pushed her away, made her understand that she shouldn't do that to you just when I was kissing you.'

I lowered my head in confusion. After a moment's silence, she went on, 'But enough of Alda. Let's talk about me, or rather, about my husband.'

I was surprised: what connection was there between her husband and myself? Then I remembered that striking remark about the room we were in, 'This is just scenery,' and I told myself that probably that was exactly how it was. Her husband was connected to her, she to Alda, Alda to Esmeralda, Esmeralda to my father, my father to my mother, my mother to me, and I to everyone and to no one.

After a moment she went on, 'Despite the regrettable state you're in, I could maybe wait for you to recover a little to finish off that kiss that Alda interrupted. But unfortunately it's impossible. When you've heard the kind of relationship I had with my husband perhaps you'll see why, as far as we two are concerned, everything was over even before it started.'

My heart sank again, as it had a few moments ago when she'd said, 'before you go.' I managed to say, 'The way I see it, nothing is over.'

'The way you see it, perhaps not; the way I see it, it's over. And this is why. I loved my husband a great deal. He betrayed me with almost every halfway passable woman he ran into. I tried to stop loving him but couldn't. The truth was, I loved him because he didn't love me; and he didn't love me because I loved him. My obsession for him filled my whole life. I, on the other hand, simply didn't enter into his.'

'Perhaps you were mistaken.'

'No, I wasn't mistaken. That doesn't mean I was blind about him, though. On the contrary: I saw him with all his faults, which were many and ugly. But it seems when you love someone you love their faults too, most of all their faults in fact. I never stopped defining them and listing them in my head; my mind was a court forever trying him and forever finding him guilty. But there was nothing I could do. Just a whistle from him and I'd come running right away, wagging my tail like a dog who can't live without the master who beats him. He was a contemptible man; I knew it and I adored him.'

Embarrassed by this rational, frozen vehemence, I objected, 'He must have had some qualities.'

'No, none. As a man I despised him with all my heart. But, how I don't know, he managed to despise me a great deal more than I despised him. I say, I don't know how, but the truth is I do.'

'So?'

'He was very successful with women; perhaps after all this is a quality. He despised me because for him I was just a woman like all the others – worse, a wife. Naturally I tried to betray him, but couldn't. I'm faithful by nature. Other men didn't interest me.'

I gave rein to my curiosity; I pointed to the room. 'Just one thing I don't understand. If that's how your relationship was, his death should have come as a liberation. And instead you've gone on loving him. This room shows you have.'

'His death liberated me from him, but not from being conditioned by him.'

'What do you mean?'

'I'm conditioned by him in the sense that I'm afraid. I'm afraid of loving without being loved. I'm afraid that with someone else the horrible relationship I had with him would repeat itself. So when he died I swore to myself that I was through with love, that I would never love again all my life.

This room isn't so much an expression of grief, though I did go through that, but of a terror I continue to feel. And then, as I said a moment ago, above all it serves as scenery to convince the men who every now and then want me to love them, of the futility of their efforts and of the fact that I am a truly inconsolable widow.'

'But why inconsolable?'

'How could I be otherwise? If nothing else, he took away my youth. But hasn't it ever occurred to you that a dead husband can be just as much of a protection and an alibi as a live one?'

'So you don't want to love nor to be loved ever again?'

'No, absolutely not. I'm forty. Ten years pass quickly. In ten years I'll be fifty, I'll be an old woman, men won't want to know about me, I'll be safe.'

'If you hadn't realized that Alda was playing footsie with me, perhaps now . . . '

'I might have loved you. Maybe. You're the opposite of my husband: sweet, understanding, shy, intelligent, a poet even! Yes, maybe. But luckily I did notice that so-called sign of complicity between you and Alda. If I hadn't noticed I'd have found myself tomorrow back in my old situation of loving someone who doesn't love me and of not being loved by the person I love. And what's worse, with a man who all too soon would become my daughter's lover. No thanks very much.'

She spoke coldly and drily and made an unpleasant gesture of refusal that brought me back to the reality of my situation. I stopped thinking of her, began to think about myself; and a feeling of desolation swept across my spirit. I felt abandoned and, once again, perhaps for ever now, an orphan.

'And me? What shall I do?'

'What you'll do is go. You haven't unpacked your case yet. Take it and go to the airport. Go back to Paris. As soon as you're there, you'll be happy you're back, you'll see.'

Impetuously I threw myself at her feet and hugged her knees. 'Put me to the test. Let's pretend that nothing happened. Let's go back to the sitting-room now, eat dessert with Alda, then I'll put my things in the room you give me and we can begin the first day of our life together.'

She put a hand on my forehead and tried to force me away, 'Pull yourself together, don't be a baby.'

A baby! Yes, the truth was I was just a desperate child, my head still on her knees, my eyes wide open in the deep warm dark of her lap. She added, 'Alda is waiting for you in her room. Go and say goodbye, it will make her happy. There's no reason why you shouldn't.'

Perhaps I should have insisted, I don't know. But I was drunk, exhausted, and probably already tempted by the new opportunities her refusal offered me for the future. I got up again, dazed and confused, brushed my lips across her forehead and went out.

I went straight to Alda's room, found the door ajar and went in. Alda was stretched on her bed. The room was long and narrow with the bed against a wall and a desk at the far end facing an open window through which one could see the façade of another apartment block lined with balconies full of flowers. On a shelf above her bed stood a line of soft animals, dolls with wide open eyes, puppets with outstretched arms.

When I went in Alda didn't move. She had one arm over her eyes. She didn't seem to be sleeping so much as thinking. I sat on the edge of the bed next to her, took her wrist, lifted the arm from her eyes and saw they were the eyes of someone who's had too much to drink, at once fixed and incapable of looking. I said, 'Alda, it's Mario.'

She smiled vaguely. 'I can see it's Mario. You know what I was just thinking?'

'What?'

'Didn't you tell me your mother was called Dina?'

'Yes, short for Leopoldina.'

'I thought of this word puzzle. The woman your father's going to marry is called Esmeralda, isn't she? And I'm called Alda, right? And your mother was called Dina, wasn't she? So: Esmeraldina. The diminutive of Esmeralda includes all three of us: Esmeralda, Alda and Dina.'

'What are you getting at?'

'Nothing, it's a word puzzle. But leave me alone now, I want to sleep. By the way, how did it go with Jeanne?'

'Fine.'

Immediately she sat up and threw her arms round my neck. 'So, from now on you'll be my father. We'll be a family, we'll be happy.'

'Yes, we'll be happy.'

I left her room and went to the hall. My bag was there, the futile change of trousers thrown across it. I packed the trousers in the case and went out of the house.

A few minutes later I was driving the Mercedes to the airport. When I got there I'd phone my father and tell him he could pick up his car in the car park. Then I'd board the first plane for Paris. My journey to Rome was over.

EROTIC TALES

Alberto Moravia

'I was a good, conscientious nurse, with a vice,' says the virgin whose hands were always sliding under the patients' blankets. 'I became a sane, normal woman, and a murderess.'

'I am an old devil, very old, it's true, but I'm not a good devil and even less a poor devil,' boasts the man who has fallen hopelessly in love with the scientist he has lured into signing a Faustain pact. But for once the devil has met his match. No matter how alluring a form he assumes, the professor always sees through it.

Yet for the reader it is sometimes impossible to see exactly where reality takes over in these stories, and to what extent. A man's quest among the illusory images of Venice, another man's response to his wife's provocative urges to play at strangling her; dreamlike images, like the others in this collection, that linger to haunt and tease.

Erotic Tales portrays the provocative innocence of youth, the angry regret of the old, woman's frustration, man's frenzy for success, and reveals Moravia at the height of his powers – poignant, witty, scrupulously observant – presenting human passion at its most intense and elusive.

'Each tale carries a scorpion-sting of paradox in its tail'
Spectator

THE VOYEUR

Alberto Moravia

Edoardo, ex-left-wing militant turned professor of French, is a voyeur. He admits that he lives and loves mainly through his quizzical light-blue eyes, but somehow he misses what is going on beneath the surface. Why has his beautiful wife Sylvia walked out on him? And what lies behind his elderly father's bizarre exhibitionism?

Edoardo's problems go beyond his immediate family. There is the haunting thought that within each innocuous atom lies the possibility of nuclear holocaust. How can nature tolerate this? What other equally destructive forces seethe in secret within an outwardly serene household? More sinned against than sinning, Edoardo discovers that he has been unable to see for looking . . .

'Mesmeric clarity and persuasiveness . . . an old master working at the height of his powers'
Sunday Independent

'Microscopically observed and highly exhibitionist . . . a great read'
Sunday Telegraph

'Deadpan directness . . . dry intelligence'
TLS